NEVER BEFORE

IT HAD NEVER BEEN DONE TO A WOMAN

IT HAD NEVER BEEN DONE TO A WOMAN

NEVER BEFORE

A novel by
NANCY PRICE

A Malmarie Press Book
Malmarie, Inc.
Windermere, Florida

First Printing

Malmarie Press and colophon are registered trademarks of Malmarie, Inc.

ISBN-10: 0-9744818-5-8
ISBN-13: 978-0-9744818-5-2
Library of Congress Control Number: 2014958826
First Malmarie Press hardcover printing 2015
Illustrated by the author

For universities, colleges, schools and organizations: Quantity discounts are available on bulk purchases of this book for educational use, gift purchases, or as premiums for increasing magazine subscriptions and renewals. Please contact Malmarie, Inc., 11915 Cave Run Avenue, Windermere, Florida 34786.

E-mail: nancypricebooks@aol.com   Website: nancypricebooks.com

ACKNOWLEDGEMENTS

My children, Catherine and David Thompson, and also my good friends, Amy Lockard, Barbara Lounsberry and Michael James Carroll have read this novel in manuscript and offered many perceptive suggestions. Dr. Brent M. Hintz kindly read the book in manuscript, and supplied comments on the novel's medical aspects. My son John's widow, Charlotte Thompson, and her family: Derrick, Sugaree, Lauren and Andrew Gillikin, have helped me, and so have Julie and Richard Westin. I thank them all.

This book is dedicated to my son, David Malcolm Thompson.
who has enriched my life and my work, day by day and year by year.

NEVER BEFORE

1

They follow me, pesky as flies—chasing me with television trucks and big black lenses and questions, questions, questions: *What was it like? Why did they choose a girl like you? How did it feel to be the first one in the whole world? Where did you come from?*

Let them shout at my windows and pound on my door. I'll never tell them anything—never tell them that I ran away from home in Nebraska when I was seventeen.

I took a bus to Chicago with a few dollars in my pocket and everything I owned in a plastic sack.

Chicago was bigger than I had ever imagined: street after street of cars and hurrying crowds in a cold October wind.

I walked and walked until my feet hurt and I was half frozen. Finally I stopped to rest in the doorway of a place called "Dinty's Hamburger Heaven." A card in the window said: "Servers Wanted." I went in to ask a fat man behind the counter for the job. He hired me, and told me to be there at seven the next morning.

I bought a Dinty's hamburger, and stepped into the cold wind. Where could I go? Where could I sleep? Night was coming. I squeezed into a narrow space between two buildings and shivered in my old coat and jeans.

Brick walls hemmed me in, but I saw a small yard at the back, hedged away from the alley. Two lawn chairs with cushions stood on the grass.

1

No one was in sight. The window in a wall above me was dark. I grabbed the four chair cushions and shoved them under the bushes.

Now I had a bed under the dusty leaves. No one could see me, and I was out of the wind. I stretched out on the cushions to eat my hamburger, and fell asleep with the last bite.

Now I had a bed under the dusty leaves of the hedge.

Daylight woke me the next morning. I opened my eyes to find leaves of the hedge in my face and the steady roar of Chicago's motors and car horns in the air. Was I too late for work? I grabbed my sack, put the cushions on the lawn chairs, and ran to Dinty's Hamburger Heaven. The clock over the counter said six thirty.

"You the new server?" a woman asked me in a bathroom that was labeled "Staff Only Women." I said I was. A big sign told me to wash my hands, but there was no soap and no towels. I rubbed my hands together under cold water and cupped them to rinse my face. "Take a key from that hook and put your stuff over there in a locker," she told me as we went out together. "And put on a Dinty's shirt." The shirt she gave me smelled of cigarette smoke.

The manager called me over. "You'll be working with Becky," he said, and yelled for her through the kitchen door.

Becky came to smile at me. "You get the row of tables next to mine," she said. Her Dinty's shirt stretched to cover her broad bust; her jeaned legs were thick. "What's your name?"

"Mary Bryant." That new last name was my mother's name, and I put it on as easily as I'd put on the Dinty's shirt. I wasn't going to be "Mary Durfy" any more.

"I'm Becky Warren," she said. "We better do the fruit. It'll be busy here in a minute or two."

I followed her over a kitchen floor slopped with spills. She grabbed little dishes from a stack and scooped up canned peaches with her hands, and I helped her. The counter was sticky with

5

peach syrup.

"Can you finish up with the peaches?" Becky said. "I've got a table waiting."

I filled the rest of the dishes. When Becky came back, she said, "You've got an admirer!"

"What?"

"The handsome guy at table eight. He saw you come in. He said his name's 'Gunther Risling,' and he asked me what your name was, and I told him. Maybe that was dumb?"

I shrugged and didn't look his way.

Gunther Risling had asked my name. Becky had told him.

In a few minutes customers began to fill Dinty's—I was part of a wild rush of yells and clatter and trays sailing overhead. We used our hands for everything: scooping fries into baskets by the hot fist-full, dumping cornflakes into bowls, flinging pancakes on plates. After high school I'd worked at a Nebraska small-town joint, where business was slow and I knew the steady customers. It was never like this—plates toppled into sinks, trash dumped in corners, food scraped off the floor. The air was thick with the greasy smell of grills, and before long I carried it with me in my hair, on my skin, in my clothes.

We ran, hour after hour. How did Becky do it, heavy as she was? We had to run to use the toilet and run back. Becky said we'd get to eat lunch at one o'clock. I was so hungry that I sneaked some fries a customer left, and kept them in my mouth between my top teeth and my cheek to chew when no one was looking.

"Don't talk to customers except for orders," Becky told me as we filled water glasses. "Don't look at them. They'll want more of this, some of that—don't take any notice. They'll give up."

"I can't remember which order goes with which customer," I whispered. "I have to ask, 'Who ordered the fish? Chicken? Steak?'"

"Never mind," Becky whispered back. "They'll tell you, and you can smile and say 'Thank you.' They'll like to talk to somebody as pretty as you."

Becky kept her eye on me all morning. "Don't stand still, for God's sake," she said to me at a kitchen counter. "The manager will give you something to do, and it won't be nice. Fill the salt-shakers. Dump them out and fill them again." She had lined

6

up catsup bottles to wash their gooey sides. "Clean the syrup pitchers," she told me when I'd filled the saltshakers three times.

At last it was one o'clock, and we went off duty to go to the toilet, wash our sweaty faces, and try to get catsup and gravy spots off our shirts. We chose one of three lunches, and sat at a table in a kitchen corner. "My lord, girl, you're hungry," Becky said, watching me eat. She had double chins, very black eyes and a toothy smile. "Want my roll?"

"Thanks," I said. "The last food I had was in Nebraska three days ago, except for a hamburger here last night."

"Where're you living?"

"Under some bushes."

"In the park?"

"In somebody's back yard."

Becky watched me mop up beef juice with her roll. "It's October, kid. It's gonna rain, you know?" I nodded with my mouth full.

"I'm living with a girlfriend in a bread truck," Becky said. "It's not so bad, and it's cheap. When the truck's empty and the driver's through with his run, he parks it in this all-night lot that's guarded—he knows the guard." She got to her feet with a grunt, her tray in her hands. "See you tomorrow. I've got another job in the afternoons, but today I've got a half-day off. Don't forget your credit tips at the register."

"Thanks for all the help," I said. "I'd have been fired by now if you hadn't been here. Have I got enough break-time left for me to call my little sister—if you'll stay for a minute and let me use your phone? I'll pay you."

"Sure," Becky said, and we went in the staff rest room. "Let Rhody be there," I said to Becky while the phone rang and rang in my ear. "Please God, let Rhody answer."

I didn't give up. Finally I heard Rhody's five-year-old voice in my ear. Had she felt me wanting her across the miles? "Rhody!" I cried. "It's Mary. Is anybody else there?"

"No." That crisp word told me everything: Rhody hadn't forgiven me for leaving. She never would.

"Oh, Rhody," I said. "I miss you so."

"No. You don't. You went away."

"On the bus. And I can't even tell you where I am, or Dad might come after me."

7

"He says you took his money and he's going to get it back and skin you good."

"It's *my* money. I earned it this summer."

"He was sure mad," Rhody said. "He's off in his truck on a run."

"You're all right?"

"You didn't even say goodbye."

"Goodbye, Rhody—I have to say it now. I love you. I'll call any time I can, and I'll come for you when I've got enough money."

"You won't." Rhody's voice was sullen. "Never."

Becky could see I was crying when I said, "Goodbye...I love you, little sister... I love you," even though Rhody had hung up.

Gunther Risling had asked my name. I didn't have time to think about him. Other men watched me as I ran back and forth, but Gunther Risling had been the handsomest one. Becky had said he looked like a young professor—the University of Chicago was only a few blocks away, and the student and professors came to Dinty's. You could tell them from the rest of the customers, she said: they loaded the tables with papers and books, and they argued all the time they were eating.

At five o'clock my first day on the job was over. I used some of my tip money for supper, then found the university library. I looked like any student in my jeans and shirt, and it was warm there. I sat in a corner and lost myself in a book for hours.

At last my eyes wouldn't stay open, so I put the book on the shelf and went back to my dark yard, feeling lucky: I'd found a friend, and a job. The library was so close. I had some money. I wasn't hungry. But Rhody was alone in our bed, so far away in Nebraska. Was she crying?

I hadn't been able to fool her; she'd known I was going to leave home.

The day before I ran away, Rhody and I walked to a huge tree we called the Grandma Tree: our big cottonwood out in the Nebraska cornfields. The tree stood alone, day and night, talking to herself with her rustling leaves.

Rhody and I climbed high in the Grandma Tree. Rhody straddled her branch and licked a lemon sucker I'd bought her; it had grown so thin that she watched me through it with one lemon-yellow eye, then the other.

8

"You know I don't want to leave you," I said.

"Yes, you do!" Rhody wailed. "If you didn't want to, you'd take me with you!"

"I can't."

"You can! You know you can!" The breeze blew a strand of Rhody's dark hair over her sticky sucker and her angry eyes.

She yelled, "I hate you! I hate you!" and scrambled down the cottonwood's branches so fast I was afraid she'd fall. I remembered how she ran sobbing through the cornfield, stumbling against the brown-edged, razor-sharp leaves.

"Somebody's watching you again." Becky grinned at me when I came to work the next morning. "He's obviously got a weakness for beautiful blondes with long hair—how long is it?" She looked at the bun on the back of my head.

"To my waist," I said.

"He's started coming early so he can sit at one of your tables," Becky said. "And he's got books and papers, and a nice shirt and pants. Professor, I bet."

I took Gunther's order while he smiled at me. His brown hair was wavy, and he was certainly nice to look at.

He knew my name. He said, "Thanks, Mary." If he sat at one of my tables and watched me every morning, what did it matter? I had a job and a free bed.

But my third day at Dinty's brought rain. By noon it was a steady downpour.

"Rain," I said to Becky as we put a bit of lettuce on salad plates and topped it off with three tomato quarters, two thin slices of cucumber and six croutons. "There goes my bed, unless I want to sleep in mud." Customers brought rain through the door on their coats and umbrellas and feet. A server carrying a loaded tray skidded in a puddle and smashed dishes.

"Hey," Becky said. "My girlfriend Carrie's left town for a few days. You could have her sleeping bag, and sleep in the truck with me. You pay the truck driver ten dollars a night. It's not the Waldorf, but it's dry."

"Tonight?" I said.

"Sure. The truck's yellow, with *Adams Bread, Fresh From Oven To You* painted on the sides, and it'll be at the Lakeway Motel parking lot two blocks north on Ashley Street from here. But I'll have to let you into the truck when you come, and I've got to work until ten tonight."

"What a friend you are!" I said. "I'll read at the library until ten and then come to the truck—I thought I'd have to hide all night under some library table."

"There's enough books in that library to put you to sleep, all right."

"I looked up how much the university tuition is," I said, filling a tray with salads. "Even if I save all my Dinty's money but supper once a day, and sleep on the ground, I can't take any classes for years."

"You want to go to college?" Becky said.

"I've got to," I said.

That night the rainstorm had turned to a drizzle when I left the library for the Lakeway Motel parking lot. I held my plastic sack over my head, and could hardly see the bread truck in a far corner.

I knocked on the back of the truck, and heard Becky call "Mary?" inside it. I called back: "It's me! Mary!"

The truck's big delivery door slid open. I climbed to the truck floor and pulled my legs in. Becky turned on a flashlight. When I pushed the door shut, we were closed in a metal box that made our voices tinny. The air was warm and stale. "You can take off your sneakers and dump your stuff up front here," Becky said, crawling in her sleeping bag. When I burrowed into the other one, she turned off the flashlight.

Pounding rain began, drumming on metal overhead. I was dry, and I wasn't hungry. I prayed my silent thanks in the dark, and told Becky she was a true friend.

"Winter's coming," Becky said. "It gets pretty cold in here, I bet. I slept in the park when I first came to town, but it was summer."

"Where are you from?"

"Detroit. My folks kind of threw me out when I was seventeen," Becky said. "I came here and stayed with a guy for a while. Now I'm on my own. But I figure there *are* angels. Bread truck angels, maybe."

"You're my angel," I said.

"Me?" Becky laughed, but I could tell she was pleased. "There's that handsome guy at Dinty's every morning. Maybe he's no angel, but he's certainly watching you."

"Let him watch," I said. "Watching's free. But the men who grab you and feel you all over—ugh!"

"Yeah," Becky said.

Rain hammered over our heads. Becky and I were packed close in our sleeping bags, and it seemed easy to talk in the dark. "I've had another angel beside you," I said.

"Your little sister?"

I laughed. "My little five-year-old angel? I call her my sister, but I don't think she is. My mother's dead, and my father says he isn't my father—he just took me in. I'm an orphan, I guess. Our family has four girls, but I'm the oldest, so I had to raise Rhody, and she's hard to take—so nosy! And stubborn." I sighed. "No. My real angel was the old lady who lived next door to us in Plattsburg, Nebraska. Sophy Saul. She was tall and fat, and her white hair was fuzzy, like dandelion seed."

Thunder cracked overhead. "Sophy Saul," I said. "Sometimes Sophy gave us cocoa and cookies. One hot day after school started, she put out a wading pool and scrubbed the three of us in it while she ran our clothes through her washer and dryer."

"You liked it?"

"I did, but the others didn't. I hadn't cared so much about being dirty when I was younger—I just hit anybody who mentioned it."

"I had trouble like that," Becky said. "Everybody in our apartment house used the same bathtub, and we washed clothes in our sink. I was lucky if I had something to wear, clean or not."

The rain was only a gentle patter above us now. "I got dirty again soon enough," I said. "The kids at school called us 'The Dirty Kids.' One day when school was over, I ran home and sneaked to the far side of Sophy's house where my stepmother couldn't see me. I sat on a stump there until I had to go home and get supper."

"You just sat there? Why?"

"I guess I hoped Sophy might clean me up again, so people wouldn't say I smelled."

"Did she?"

"I sat by her house several days after school. Finally Sophy opened her window and said, 'Would you like to come in, Mary?' so I went in and stood on her kitchen rug, not touching anything.

11

The kitchen looked like the ones on television, I thought. And she asked me if I was enjoying school. I said I wasn't."

Becky chuckled under the soft rhythm of the rain.

"She gave me some cookies. 'Take all you want,' she said. 'Help me out. If you don't, I'll eat them myself, and get fatter than I already am.' So I helped her out as much as I thought I should. I hoped she wouldn't ask more questions. She didn't. She made me cocoa, and said it was nice having company, because her husband was too sick to get out of bed, and slept most of the time."

"She was lonely," Becky said.

"I loved her," I said. "Did you ever know anybody who could help you so kindly that you hardly noticed they were doing it? The next day Sophy called me in again and said, 'I'm sorry, Mary, but it didn't occur to me yesterday that you'd come from school and were so tired—and dusty, too, from the playground, you know. Would you like to freshen up before you go home? A shower would be nice, wouldn't it? After a hard day?' She showed me how her shower worked, and gave me soap and a washcloth and towel, and shampoo, and a nightgown of hers to wear while she washed my clothes."

"An angel," Becky said. "Definitely. An angel."

"And when I was all clean, she asked, 'Do you like books?' I nodded, and she said, "Just make yourself comfortable in my old recliner." That old chair! She'd used it for so many years that it kept her fat shape exactly, and I sank into it wearing the clean nightgown and flowery smells, and she gave me some books. 'You probably can't read yet, but you'll learn fast," she told me. 'Just look at the pictures now, and imagine the story."

"I got a book one Christmas when I was little," Becky said.

The rain turned to a downpour again. I sat up in my sleeping bag and said, "Sophy made me love books. When I was little, I couldn't believe there were as many books in the world as Sophy had in her bookcase. As I grew up, I read them over and over, snuggled in her big chair in company with her cat. They were the classics, and she had a lot of explaining to do about sex and childbirth and murder and such.

"And Sophy fed me. She taught me to cook and wash and iron and mend. I learned how to brown meat, mend jeans, make a bed, enjoy vegetables..." There were tears in my eyes. "She had a windowsill of beautiful African violets I loved..."

Sophy made me love books. I read them in her old chair in company with her cat.

"What happened to her?" Becky asked after a while.

"Her husband died when I was thirteen, and she went to live with her daughter in Massachusetts. We wrote letters for years, but last fall her letters stopped coming, and mine were returned. I've never heard from her again. I'm afraid she's gone."

I heard Becky turn over in her sleeping bag with a sigh.

"You're so tired, and I've been keeping you awake," I said. "Guess it's because you're the first grownup I've been able to talk to since I lost Sophy Saul." I lay down again in the dark. "Goodnight. Thanks for my bed out of the rain."

"Goodnight," Becky said. "You're welcome."

3

Becky's alarm went off at six. Half asleep, we crawled out of the truck to another day of rain. We had breakfast at a little coffee shop, and washed up in the restroom there for the long hours at Dinty's.

Day after day it rained. Every morning Gunther Risling was at one of my tables. He said hello and smiled, and left a big tip. Becky teased me about him, her black eyes sparkling.

After three days the rain ended. Before the morning rush started, Becky said, "I just found out my friend Carrie's coming back tomorrow, and she'll sleep in the truck again. The driver doesn't want three in there. Maybe you can find a second job so you can room with somebody, if you can find somebody." We were washing tables under the small, narrow eyes of Dinty's manager, and Gunther's blue eyes. "Most servers have two jobs so they can pay rent."

"Pay rent?" I said. "How can I save anything for college?"

"A friend of mine shares a room with two girls, and another one sleeps in her car at a friend's place," Becky said. "But what will she do when it gets cold?"

The morning rush had started. One of Becky's tables filled, and another one of mine, and we began to pass each other on the run.

"Where'll you sleep tonight?" Becky said as we ate lunch.

"The ground's dried out. I'll be all right in the back yard."

"Listen," Becky said. "I just heard there's a 'Help Wanted' sign in the window of Hal's Grille in the next block. You can ask. Maybe they've got a part-time job."

16

I knew where Hal's Grille was—I slept under the bushes in the Grille's back yard. When I went there after work, the 'Help Wanted' sign was still in the window. Customers filled the tables and sat at the Grille's counter that separated the tables from the kitchen. An old man and woman worked at the kitchen sink. Finally they noticed that I was waiting. "I saw your 'Help Wanted' sign," I told the old woman.

They both looked me over: two sour and suspicious old people. I braced myself to answer questions.

"We got to have somebody," the old man said to the woman, not me.

"I can be here afternoons from five o'clock on," I said.

"All right," the old woman said. "You can start now. Five-fifty an hour plus tips. Thursday you get the night off. We close at ten."

"Yes, ma'am," I said. "Thank you. I'll do my best."

"Wash," the old man said.

When I came back from the bathroom, the old woman handed me a small apron, a pencil and an order tablet. "What's your name?" she asked.

"Mary Bryant," I said, putting on the apron.

"Hilda and Hal Schatzle," she said. "Write the orders and bring them here."

A man had just settled at a table. "May I help you, sir?" I said to him.

"You certainly *can*," he said, looking me over.

I wrote his order on the tablet and went to Hilda. "Give him silverware and a napkin," she said. "Pour his drink. The order goes here." She pushed the order down on a nail beside her grill. When she handed me the man's lunch, she put the order on another nail by Hal's cash register, and he made a copy.

Hour by hour the tables and counter chairs filled and emptied. The students dumped their bags on the floor. I slid through narrow spaces carrying dishes, glasses, cups, a cloth to wipe tables, or a dustpan and brush. The place was full of chattering and clattering, but it was clean, and I didn't have to run.

Ten o'clock came at last and the place emptied. The Schatzles said nothing to me. Hal filled the dishwasher. Hilda scraped the grill. I shut myself in the bathroom and took a quick sponge bath with soap and paper towels. When I'd put on my other set of clothes, I washed the dirty ones as well as I could and hid them in my plastic bag.

I had washed my apron. I hung it on a hook by the counter and waited. Had I done a good job? Could I work there?

"Here," Hal said, handing me silverware and napkins. "Set this table."

He had begun to set three place settings. "For you?" I asked.

"And you. We eat when we close."

We ate in silence, but the dinner was very good, and so was dessert, while people and cars passed the Grille's front window.

I certainly wasn't hungry when we were through. I cleared the table, swept the floor, and set their two places for breakfast.

"Five o'clock tomorrow," Hal said to me at eleven o'clock. He gave me my money, and closed and locked the Grille door behind me.

Chicago stretched away for miles on every side. I took a deep breath of city air, turned my back on the noisy street, and ducked into the passageway that ran along one wall of the Grille. There were my lawn chairs and my hedge. The ground was almost dry under the bushes.

I spread my clean clothes over the top of the hedge to dry, crawled on my cushion bed and fell asleep. I dreamed of a black, spitting grill, catsup-smeared plates, Hal's ropy arms lifting racks of cups, Hilda's gray hair in a hair net...and then loud voices, close, indignant, with German accents...

I started up, looking through leaves to see Hal and Hilda.

"No cushions!" Hal said.

"Stolen!" Hilda said. "I tell you, ya?" They stood, glasses in their hands, scowling at chairs stripped to vinyl slats.

"Oh, please!" I cried and crawled from the hedge, dragging the cushions. "I'm so sorry!" The two backed up and stared at me. "They're not dirty!" I brushed the cushions with my hands and put them on the chairs. "I just borrowed them to lie on."

"She sleeps here?" Hilda said.

I grabbed my washing from the hedge and backed toward the passageway with my plastic bag. "I'm sorry! I'm in your way—"

"You got no home?"

"I just came to Chicago," I said. "But I'll find somewhere to sleep, once I have enough for the rent. It's not too cold yet, and I'm certainly not hungry."

"Dangerous out here," Hilda said. They looked at me in weary puzzlement, as if I were a mistake they'd found in the day's receipts.

"I'll come to work on time tomorrow," I said.

"The storeroom," Hilda said. "That old cot."

"Better than the ground," Hal said. "Come on."

I followed them through the Grille's back door. Hal locked it behind us and switched on a light in a small room. Shelves lined the walls, sagging under the weight of canned food and cases of cold drinks. Hal dragged a folding cot from one corner and set it on its four legs. "You'll be safe," he said.

"Thanks so much," I said.

"Don't touch the shelves," Hilda said.

"Don't give food to your friends out the window," Hal said.

They shut the door behind them.

The ceiling above me was bare rafters. The floor was bare concrete. I took a bundle of string from my bag, tied a line from nails in the walls, and hung up my wet clothes. When I turned off the light and crawled on the cot, a shelter lined with food surrounded me.

"I can't believe it," Becky said the next morning. "Are those Schatzles going to make you pay rent?"

"I'm going to work as hard as I can for them, and maybe they won't ask much," I said.

"There he is again," Becky said, tipping her head toward my row of tables. "Your admirer."

I went to Gunther. "May I take your order?" I said, keeping my eyes on the glass of water in my hand.

"Do you live around here?" Gunther asked.

"Not far away," I said in the kind of voice that warns you: *no more questions*. So he didn't ask any, but watched me with every bite he took.

"You going to sleep in that storeroom tonight?" Becky said as the morning rush began. "What if they won't let you?"

"I'll have to hide all night in the library," I said.

"If those two don't let you sleep there, you sure don't want that job for what they're paying!"

"But I get a big dinner, and I don't have to run for hours. And it's clean."

19

"That guy sure watches you," Becky said. "It's a wonder he stops looking long enough to put his fork in his mouth, not his ear."

I was too busy and too worried to think about Gunther. Rain was beginning to fall. I ate my Dinty's lunch, worked until almost five, and then ran through the wet to Hal's Grille. Until ten o'clock I served and swept and scoured without being told, one eye on the rainy street. I took my sponge bath. The three of us ate in silence. I worked afterward, getting the Grille ready for morning.

At eleven Hal stood by the front door, jingling his keys. He gave me my wages, then looked out at the wet streets. "The storeroom?" he said. "You want to sleep there?"

"Oh, yes!" I said. "Please! If you don't mind."

He looked again through the Grille's streaming window. "All right," he said.

I thanked him and hurried down the narrow hall to the storeroom, closed the door, and listened for a moment to rain pounding on the one small window. When I dragged my cot from the corner and lay down in the dark, I was dry and warm under my coat.

How lucky I was: two jobs and a bed under a roof. Every afternoon and evening for a week I worked hard for the Schatzels: I loaded or unloaded dishes if Hal was ringing up a sale; I polished chrome, cleaned the big refrigerator, and washed windows when business was slow. I ate Hilda's good dinners without a word, except to thank the two of them when we finished eating.

When a week had gone by and Hal paid me at night, I looked at the money and said, "I could pay you. Could I possibly stay in your storeroom for a while? I haven't found any place yet that I can afford to rent."

"It's hot in there. Then it gets cold," Hal said.

"We got to store things," Hilda said, joining us.

"The heat and cold won't bother me," I said. "I'll stay out of the way. I don't need much room."

They looked at each other. "Stay for a while," Hal said. "We'll see."

They hadn't mentioned money. How happy I was when I went into my storeroom. I kept my clothes on a bottom shelf and my cot in the corner. I took a snapshot from my plastic sack and propped it against a row of soup cans. It was the only picture I had

20

of my mother: a smiling young woman in a sleeveless dress. She sat with both arms around her baby girl who had once been me. I wore a frilly dress and raised both of my hands as if I were waving. The sun shone on our blond heads.

Every night I put the snapshot there. It welcomed me every morning when I crawled from my cot to spend sixteen hours on my feet.

One Thursday, my afternoon off, I opened a savings account at a nearby bank, and celebrated with hot chocolate with cream at a snack bar next door. No one was there but me and the elderly woman behind the counter. "I'm working at Dinty's, and at Hal's Grille, too," I told her.

"Hal's!" she said. "Them Schatzles—they pay you almost nothing, I bet. That's how they stay in business—undercut us, keep wages lower than anybody, work all day themselves—have for years. They'll work you to death. You better find yourself a real job."

But I had looked at notices on bulletin boards in stores for blocks around, and I saw I had a bargain: the rent for a single room was more than I could pay if I wanted to save anything. As winter grew colder and colder, how lucky I was that I had a cot in a storeroom and a big dinner for nothing. The Schatzles never asked for rent.

B ecky teased me about Gunther Risling, but after a while he stopped coming to Dinty's. I didn't forget him, but I was almost too tired, day after exhausting day, to miss his blue eyes following me from table to table.

The storeroom was cold, and getting colder. I went to the Goodwill store and found an old comforter quilted with a layer of wool inside. When I wrapped myself in it to read or sleep, I was warm, while snow clotted my small window and gave the bare lawn chairs in the yard white cushions.

The Schatzles had put a roof over my head, but I hardly knew them, and they never asked a question about me. They worked together like two ancient machines. Were they brother and sister? Husband and wife? They wore no rings. Every night when I shut the storeroom door behind me, I heard their slow steps on the stairs to the rooms above. Every morning at six they ate at a table together, and watched me leave their Grille for breakfast with Becky and the long day at Dinty's.

I tried to imagine what the world must look like to Hilda and Hal. They worked me hard, but they were old—too old to be on their feet all day. They wore layers of clothes in the kitchen's heat and steam, and shuffled through their days as if life were as heavy as the thick leather shoes they wore. How still they were, and sharp-eyed. Not once had they said a kind word about my work, and they never smiled, but they heaped my plate with food every night. There was a thorny kindness in a blanket they brought for my cot, and an old lamp they gave me to read by, and, at last, a key to the back door.

The last day of November Gunther found me at Hal's Grille. I turned around and there he was at the counter, smiling at me. He ordered dinner. I poured his coffee at the coffee machine and saw his face reflected in it, pulled long in the curved surface like taffy, his eyes on me. When I gave him the coffee, he sat on a counter stool, his eyes still on me, while he stirred and stirred as if he wanted to make a hole in the cup.

"Your hair is so beautiful," he said. (I'd never cut my hair much; it hung down my back, a heavy braid.) "You're as lovely as a madonna."

I pretended I hadn't heard, but then he said in a low voice, "Will you have dinner with me when you have a night off here?"

"I'm sorry," I said. "I couldn't." Hilda was close behind me.

"Why not?" he asked, stirring his coffee. I didn't look at him, I looked at his hand. It was shaking.

How could I tell him I couldn't use the money I'd saved to buy decent clothes for a date? Hilda handed me a tray of dinners for one of my tables, and I left. When I came back he said "Please," in a low voice. "It's important." I shook my head.

"My name is Gunther Risling, he said. "I know yours is Mary Bryant. I found out you're working here, and I've been getting up courage for days to ask you."

I looked into his blue eyes and thought he was being truthful. I'd seen his hand tremble as he stirred his coffee.

"All right," I said. "Seven thirty on Thursday. My night off."

"Yes!" Gunther said with a big grin. "I've got a car. Where do you live?"

"Here," I said. "The back door. Go through the little outside passageway from the street."

I left him then to rush to the bathroom and stare in a mirror until I stopped whispering swear words to myself. Why had I said I'd go? And why had I told him to come through the passageway to my door—my own door that the Schatzels had finally given me the key to—the first door in my life I was able to lock?

The next noon I missed lunch at Dinty's and took money from the bank to go shopping. In an hour I had new boots, and a cheap, velvety shirt to wear with my jeans. I put enough money in my pocket for a cab home if Gunther tried anything. What did I know about him?

Snow was falling on Thursday when I left Dinty's, and it was almost dark as I shut myself in the Grille's bathroom. I shampooed my hair and took a sponge bath to scrub the kitchen smells off. Would my hair dry in time? At least it would be wavy and curl here and there, falling down my back. The storeroom was cold as I dressed and put on powder and lipstick and my old coat. I brushed and brushed and brushed my hair, until there was a knock on the door.

Gunther stood in the old doorway and seemed to fill it completely. "You have a room here?" he asked, and I said Yes. The room was dark, and I went out with him quickly, turning my key in the lock—he wasn't ever going to see my cot or my old comforter or my clothes hanging on a string.

His car was at the curb, an old car, but clean. He took me to a little restaurant where there were waiters and white tablecloths. When we'd ordered, he leaned toward me and said, "You're the most beautiful woman I've ever seen. That wonderful hair. It's like quicksilver."

He was so intent, single-minded, wound tight—he made me nervous. "I've never been in a real restaurant," I babbled, just to say something that was, at least, true.

"Never?" He looked blank, then smiled. "Good. Nothing's more boring than a woman who's bored."

I certainly wasn't bored. There I sat in candlelight, sipping wine with a handsome man in a nice suit who wanted to know all about me. No man had ever asked.

24

Questions and answers brought us closer and closer; I felt it. I'd never talked to a man like that, so how would I know that the dream-like dance of falling in love had begun? Most people would recognize it, I suppose, but it was as strange to me as the steps of a minuet. To begin, Gunther came forward with a fact about himself, and waited. I stepped forward with a fact about me.

Gunther was an instructor at the university. I'd finished high school in Nebraska, then worked in a restaurant. He'd had more graduate years because he had a teaching job, too. He wasn't Mexican, but he'd lived in Mexico most of his life. His father had been a doctor there.

I'd been adopted, I told him. I called the ones who adopted me my "stepmother" and "stepfather," and their three daughters my "stepsisters." The littlest sister, five-year-old Rhody, was the one I loved.

His parents were dead. He taught classes in the university zoology department. Microbiology.

I was saving my money to go to the university. "But I'll never get there," I said, trying to smile. "I'd never imagined it would cost so much."

What did we have to eat? I didn't notice and I don't remember. I was too astounded at the signals I had suddenly begun to give. Where did they come from? I was using them for the first time, because the boys in school called me "Mary Dirty " and would never have asked for a date. Those new signals fluttered my eye-lashes and turned my voice to velvet, like the gifts of some fairy godmother sending me to the ball.

And Gunther was sending signals, too: I picked them up with my newfound, astonishing antennae. He seemed to notice only me; he kept me in the light of those blue eyes of his. Everyone in the country must have seen those eyes by now on television, or in newspapers and magazines—those eyes with their short, thick lashes and heavy brows. When he complimented me, his words came in a rush, as if they'd escaped in spite of him.

"You were the oldest child?" he asked. "The adopted one?"

"And I had to take care of the others," I said. "Especially the baby. Nobody cared much about her but me, so I raised Rhody myself. She's smart and wild and dear to me. I miss her."

Gunther's dinner was growing cold. He leaned toward me over our small table. "So you have a 'stepfather' and 'stepmother,' as

25

you call them. No aunts, uncles…"

"A grandmother in Florida. Once in a while she sends me a card."

"I lost my parents," Gunther said. "I don't have any brothers or sisters. I rent an apartment here with another fellow who's a grad student, too."

I asked him what he hoped to do when he left the university. His blue eyes gleamed. "I want to amaze the world, that's all!" he said, and laughed. "Can you imagine anyone as ambitious as that?"

"Yes," I said. "I can."

"Can you? It doesn't sound weird to you? Egotistical? Even crazy?"

"No," I said. "I've got dreams like that. I want to go to college, and then write the best novel of the twentieth century. That's all." We smiled at each other as the waiter took away our plates.

"You've got to start classes," he said. "I'll think about getting you into college. Maybe a scholarship and a student loan? You say you had top high school grades. A job on campus?"

Other diners were leaving. We didn't notice. We ate our desserts, talking between spoonfuls of our chocolate sundaes, laughing at their long dribbles of delicious goo.

At last we looked around us. The candle on our table had burned out in a puddle of wax, and the room was empty except for one patient waiter. He smiled a little, showing us out to the snowy street, as if he too had once been amorously insane.

I told Becky about my date while we ate breakfast.

"Didn't I tell you he was interested?" Becky said. "Didn't I?"

"He wanted to know everything about me," I said. "Especially about my family, and how I raised my 'baby sister.' I told him she's not really any relative of mine."

"Rhody."

"I didn't tell him that my 'stepfather' never married my mother. He just took me to raise. My mother was living with him, but she had me with another man—I don't know who he was—so when my 'stepfather' found out, he killed her."

Becky's fork-full of sausage halted halfway to her mouth. "What?"

"My 'stepfather' killed my mother, so he went to prison," I said. "Maybe I wasn't his baby, but at least he left me with his wife. She made me a nursemaid for her two nasty little kids, and then Rhody. Nobody wanted Rhody. I certainly didn't. Her mother brought her home, gave her to me, and went to bed to get drunk."

"Some mother," Becky said.

"We three girls just stood there and looked at that baby. She was red and bald and wrinkled and spitting up. The ten-year-old said, 'Do we have to keep it?' and the eleven-year-old said, 'What am I going to tell my friends? It's disgusting!'"

"And how old were you?"

"Thirteen. My 'stepfather' said to me, 'Take care of that baby. You're old enough to be some use around here.' He was leaving for another run—he's a truck driver. I told him: 'I'll need money for diapers and bottles and shirts and blankets and milk...everything. You want her to die?' So he gave me money every time he came home."

"And you were her mother," Becky said. "At thirteen."

"I suppose at first I wished Rhody *would* die," I said. "She was skinny and cranky and yelled all the time. When I ran home from school at noon, she was screaming, and she was still at it when I came back at night. My 'stepmother' tuned her out like some television show. But Rhody was smart. Pretty soon she'd stop crying when she heard my voice." I had tears in my eyes. "Why am I telling you all this?"

Becky patted my hand on the table. "You graduated from high school?"

"In May. I got a job in a hamburger place, but my 'stepfather' made me give him most of the money. He said, 'You owe us plenty. You're not running off just because you got an education. I'll track you down. Don't even think about leaving.' But all I thought about was leaving...and Rhody. He came home from a run and got drunk, and I stole some of my money back from him, and here I am." There were tears in my eyes again. "When Rhody was little, I kept her night bottle under my pillow, so it would be warm. She got nice and plump after a while. She always slept with her head under my chin."

Becky and I finished breakfast and started the day at Dinty's. Gunther didn't come, and I missed his blue eyes and his smile. I

27

had to be careful at my work all that day, because if I thought about kissing Gunther, I might bring customers coffee when they said they wanted tea, or baked potatoes when they'd ordered fries.

Gunther didn't come to Hal's Grille that night. The next day I had the morning off, and went to the library to look for Gunther in the university directory. I found him, and the address of his apartment was there, and his phone number.

He didn't come to Dinty's or Hal's Grille all that week. "Maybe he's out of town," Becky said.

"Maybe he's out of interest in me," I said.

"You've got his number—call him. You can hang up if he answers."

So the next noon I called him. A strange man said, "Hello?"

"Is Gunther Risling there?" I asked.

"Neola?" he said.

"No."

"Gunther's not here," he said. "Want to leave a message?"

I didn't answer, hung up, and said to Becky: "*Neola*. His roommate asked if I was *Neola*. Well, of course! A girl's name! Gunther's got girlfriends—of course he has—and I've got absolutely no brain at all. I'm a hamburger-joint waitress just out of high school. What would a man like him want from a girl like me—except the usual thing?"

What did Gunther Risling want? Another date. He came for breakfast at Dinty's the next morning and said, "How about dinner Thursday night?"

I was a fool—I said Yes. I'd decided that I was going to have good times and good dinners, and be on guard.

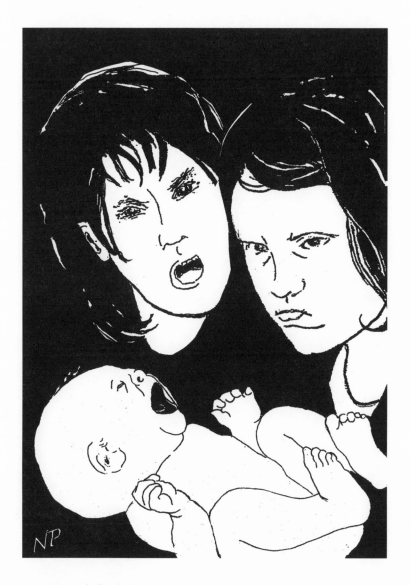

We girls looked at the baby. The ten-year-old said,
"Do we have to keep it?" The eleven-year-old said,
"It's disgusting!"

5

That was the evening Gunther kissed me. It was my first kiss, though I was sure it wasn't the first for him. I suppose my never being kissed seems unbelievable, but would you want to kiss boys who'd called you "Mary Dirty" for years, supposing they ever wanted to kiss dirt?

There I was in Gunther's warm car with his even warmer lips exploring mine, and a man's face and fragrance and breath too close for anything but panting and quivering. He was as breathless as I was, kissing and kissing, whispering "Mary...Mary" against my cheeks, my nose, my hair, my neck. My scalp seemed to lift off. I was trying to paste myself to him. It was scary.

That night I talked to myself in the storeroom before I went to bed. I pressed my forehead against a row of cold half-gallon juice cans and whispered, "Don't let him do that again. Even if he talks about getting you into the university. And he didn't talk about it tonight, did he? Live without him."

Without him. I kicked off my boots, hung my new shirt on a nail, yanked my cot out of the corner, and lay down in the dark. My "stepfather" had called me "a natural-born whore." I said, "Not me!" to the storeroom shelves of boxes, sacks and cans. "Not me!"

Gunther wanted to take me here, take me there. I knew I hurt his feelings when I told him: "You're a student and I'm a waitress. I love going places with you, but it costs money, and we both have plans, don't we? You've got to save money to get your degree, and if I'm ever going to college, I have to save mine."

I tried to keep my spirits up by calling Rhody. The first time my 'stepmother' answered the phone. I hung up and called again in a few days, and there was Rhody's voice, bringing her so close. "Rhody!" I said. "How are you? It's almost Christmas. Are you alone?"

"No," Rhody whispered. "Mary—"

My 'stepmother's' drunken voice broke in: "You're a whore, like your mother! You robbed us! After all we done for you! Just you wait. Your father's going to trace this call—"

I shut that mean voice off and gave Becky her phone. If my 'stepfather' tried to find "Mary Durfy," he wouldn't. I used my mother's name now, not his. "Rhody's there and she's all right," I told Becky.

Gunther kept coming to Dinty's, or the Grille. "Poor boy," Becky said. "He watches you like a faithful, kicked dog." Becky and I had Christmas Eve together, and I gave her a present: her favorite cupcakes. She hugged me and said she was a romantic, and would get me married to Gunther yet. I asked her what the Rislings would live on, and she said, "Love and kisses." I told her she could have her love and kisses—I'd take the Christmas cookies she'd brought me.

On Christmas Day, winter slush was up to my boot tops when I met Becky at our little coffee shop for breakfast. "Can I use your phone?" I asked Becky. "My family's never celebrated Christmas, except for my 'stepfather' and 'stepmother.' They get drunk. I think they'll be in some bar now, and my 'stepsisters' will be off somewhere, too, except for Rhody."

I was right. Rhody answered the phone and said, "Everybody's gone but me. Where are you? Why don't you come?"

"I have to work," I said. "I'm putting almost all my money in the bank. I told you I would. Are you all right? Are you warm? Do you get enough to eat?"

"No. I'm hungry. I want to come where you are."

I tried to cheer her up. "Do you know where I slept at first when I took the bus here?" I asked her. "On four lawn-chair cushions under a hedge!"

"I could sleep under a hedge," Rhody said.

"With old dry leaves in your face, and nothing but the sun to be your alarm clock? What if I hadn't waked up in time in the morning? I'd have lost my job!"

"You'd have come back home," Rhody said in a sulky voice.

"And where do you think I slept when it started to rain? In the mud?"

"I hope so! I hope you got good and muddy and cold and wet!"

"But I didn't," I said. "I had a friend. She worked with me at the hamburger joint, and she let me sleep with her in sleeping bags in a bread truck. The driver delivered his bread, and then we slept in the truck, nice and dry all night. I bet you've never slept in a bread truck that says 'Fresh From Oven To You' on the side."

"I've got our *whole bed* to sleep in now!"

"Is the Grandma Tree still there?" I asked. "Is it snowing?"

"It's snowing." Suddenly Rhody's voice sounded happy. "And guess what? Dad had an accident with his truck and almost got killed, and they made him pay a lot for driving drunk. And the girls didn't steal the clothes you sent me—they're so fat they couldn't squeeze into a single one!" She giggled.

"That's why I sent you clothes for Christmas," I said. "If I'd sent you toys or books, they'd have taken them. Did the coat fit, and the hat and mittens?"

"I can make snowballs now, and throw them at those boys when they chase me! I hit Tommy Frankel right in the eye, and it's black and blue, and his mother came and yelled at Mom, but Mom could yell more dirty names than his mother could."

"How about the pants and shirts? You've grown. I know you've grown!"

"They're so nice! Dad didn't like my presents from you, but he let me keep them so he didn't have to buy any. He said the ones you sent were con-tam-inated. He calls you names all the time." I could imagine her there, her long, dark hair straggling across her cheek.

"Names don't hurt us," I said. "We'll call each other loving names and wipe the bad ones out. Merry Christmas, my dearest Rhody. And a happy new year, too. I love you so much."

"I love you, too." Her voice sounded so small, so lonely. I could hardly bear to hang up and break the connection, for our line of words joined us for a little while across miles and miles of snow.

Gunther had warned me he'd be visiting some friends in Mexico during the holiday break, but soon he was back at the Grille, saying, "Please. Just let me take you to dinner," but I said No. He scared me: I melted like cheese on a hot hamburger when he kissed me, and he wanted a lot more than kisses.

But January was as cold as I'd been to Gunther, so why was I surprised that he stayed away? February was dreary, dreary, dreary without him. I was exhausted every night, and slept when I had my afternoon off, and saw nothing in my future but years and years of waiting tables.

And then, halfway through February, there was Gunther at the Grille counter when I turned around with a tray in my hands! I tried not to look as if I were glad to see him. I said very calmly, that yes, I'd have dinner with him.

Gunther's whole face glowed: he was delighted. I warned him I wouldn't date him often. He said he didn't care—he wanted as much time with me as he could get. It was very flattering. He was very handsome. I wasn't even eighteen.

The next night he took me to the same little restaurant. "Our place," he said when he came for me. "Where we can talk."

Everyone in the country has probably seen Gunther on television by now. Can you imagine what he could do when he had me alone in the light of those blue eyes? He made me feel that I was the only person in his world.

He told me more about himself. His parents had drowned off the shore of Mexico while he was studying in Chicago. Their bodies were never found.

"I'm sorry," was all I could say. "I'm so sorry."

"My father didn't think much of me," Gunther said, and ran his fingers through his wavy brown hair. "He was determined to make a doctor of me. When I refused to be one, he wouldn't give me a cent. I found jobs, got scholarships—it took me extra years. And when he and mother died, there were only debts. I had to sell their house in Hermosillo to pay all they owed, and there was nothing left."

"Why wasn't your father proud of you? You worked, paid your own way..."

34

"I wasn't the son he wanted, the doctor he wanted. But I have a good friend, and he was everything my father had hoped I'd be. His name is Benedicto Carlos, but everybody calls him 'Ben.' He's older than I am, but we grew up like brothers: he was always at my house, talking with my father. His father was dead—a Mexican. His mother was American, and she had money, but she wanted her only child to be a priest, not a doctor, so he worked at odd jobs. That was all he could do. My father wouldn't help *me*, and Ben's mother wouldn't help *him*."

Customers were filling the restaurant, but Gunther seemed to be alone in his thoughts. He hadn't even tasted his wine. He said, "So finally my father must have decided that since I refused to be a doctor, he could help my friend Ben be a doctor instead. He put Ben through medical school, and gave me nothing for my college work." Gunther stared at his wine glass, his eyes narrowed to blue slits. "Nothing."

Before I could think of anything I could say, Gunther gave a bitter laugh. "I've told you my life story," he said. "Now tell me yours. Everything."

It was my turn to laugh. "Certainly not," I said. "Selected bits. The ones I'm not ashamed of."

"Is Rhody a selected bit?"

"I called her on Christmas Day," I said. "She was alone. She made me cry, she was so lonely. She's never forgiven me for leaving."

"I can imagine," Gunther said. "I'd never forgive you either."

Those eyes of his! I rushed on to say whatever was in my head: "Just before I came to Chicago last October, Rhody found out where I kept my wages from my summer work—the little bit of money my 'stepfather' didn't take. I'd hid my money in the roots of a tree. And Rhody stole it. On the night when I planned to run away, I found my money was gone! I couldn't get away without money, couldn't go to college, couldn't do anything but work at a hamburger joint the rest of my life! I went to bed and cried."

"Rhody wanted you to stay."

"She heard me crying—we slept in the same bed. Finally she told me that nobody had stolen my money. She had it. She gave it to me and I took it and caught the bus for Chicago."

"Is she blonde like you?"

"She's dark-haired and skinny and smart and trouble," I said. "And I miss her."

"When I stay away, do you miss me?" Gunther said.

We talked and talked, and walked in the spring dark when the restaurant closed. It was after midnight when we crept into the little passageway and stood at my door.

"Don't," I said as Gunther held me tight, kissed me until I was dizzy, then tried to unbutton my shirt. Moonlight flooded the little back yard. The Schatzels' window above us was dark.

"Why?" Gunther murmured against my lips.

"You have your life all planned," I whispered. "I can't help you. You need a rich wife to pay for all you have to do to be famous... to get the Nobel..."

He pushed me away; for a second I saw a look almost like horror on his face. He ducked into the narrow passageway and was gone.

I'd told Gunther to find a rich wife–and driven him away. February went by, week by slow week, and he never came.

Becky had moved into a room with another girl when it was bitter cold, but when March came, she slept in the bread truck again to save money. She never asked me where Gunther was: she was my friend. If she saw me watching for him at Dinty's, week after March week, she said nothing.

But the first day of April—Gunther came! He sat at one of my tables and said Hello.

I said Hello and waited for his order. He didn't ask for food—he asked if I'd go with him to the Art Institute at five the next Thursday, my afternoon off at the Grille. We could have two hours there before the Institute closed. He hunched over the table and looked as if he'd jump up and run away if I said No.

"All right," I said. Neither of us smiled.

So there he was the next Thursday afternoon, waiting in his car for me when I left Dinty's. I'd tried to wash Dinty's smells off of me, and I'd changed to my best shirt.

The city was rain-soaked, but the Institute galleries were dry and cool and almost empty, as if the city had left its most beautiful things there, and gone home. We strolled from paintings to statues, and statues to exhibits. I pretended to look at them, but

I was really watching Gunther's intent face, and thought he was pretending, too. I couldn't ask him where he had been for such a long time. When we talked, it was only about art.

Gunther stopped before an ancient portrait of a Madonna and child. The Madonna was long-nosed and blue-skinned, and her child looked as if the spokes of his halo were nailed through his head, but their eyes gazed at me with human affection.

"My mother always believed in me," Gunther said, staring at the Madonna. "She told me I'd be famous someday."

"You will," I told him. "Of course you will."

"I will!" Gunther cried. He looked pale and drawn, and grabbed my hands. "You really think I will, don't you?" His words echoed through the big rooms. "You'd help me?"

Everything I felt must have showed in my face, for he kissed me over and over, and I kissed him back, and he said: "I love you! Marry me!"

Marry him?

I couldn't say a word.

"I stayed away so long because I didn't have anything to offer you, did I?" he said. "I could tell you how much I loved you, that's all. But now I've got a teaching assistantship for fall, and a grant, too! You can start your classes! We can rent an apartment! Do you love me? Will you marry me?"

"Oh, yes!" I said in a choked voice. "Yes!"

How happy we were! We went to dinner and he took me home. I tried to kiss him goodnight and shut my door, but he came into my storage room and turned on the light. "Is this where you *live*?" he said.

My newly washed underwear and socks hung from a string. Books lay on the sagging cot. "It's free," I said.

He gave a soft groan and took me in his arms. "Marry me *now*!"

I pulled away from him. "Now?"

"In May. Will that do? We'll plan it tomorrow night when I take you to your birthday dinner. Eighteen! You'll have a birthday cake. Have you ever had one?"

"No." I hated to say it. I hated the storeroom, the cot, my dripping clothes on a string.

"Tell the Schatzles that tomorrow's your birthday. Make them

37

let you go early at eight." He kissed me once more and left.

The Schatzels were as silent as usual the next morning when I stopped by their table on the way to Dinty's. I asked them for time off that night.

"Your birthday," Hal said at last.

"A friend has invited me to dinner," I said.

"Some boy, maybe?" Hal glared at me, and Hilda pulled her mouth tight and sour. "All right."

So after work I hurried to give myself a sponge bath and a shampoo, and let my clean hair ripple down my back over my one good shirt. I didn't creep out my back door of the Grille—wasn't it my birthday? The Schatzels stared at me as I went to the Grille's front door, and I pretended not to hear what college boys at a table said. There was Gunther in his car at the curb; he got out and opened the door for me and we drove away.

"Our special restaurant," Gunther said. "I asked for the same table, the same wine, and the same dinner we had on our first date."

A smiling waiter opened the door for us. Candlelight shone on the starched tablecloth. When our wine came, Gunther held up his glass. "To us!" he said. "To your freshman year next fall!"

How could I believe that? I lifted my wine glass and said a little prayer.

"I'll have enough for us to live on *and* pay your tuition. No more waiting tables for Mrs. Risling! It's homework for you."

I couldn't say a word, not even when Gunther slipped a small diamond ring on my finger. He said the diamond wasn't real, and he was sorry, but I just kissed him. No more Dinty's or Hal's Grille. No more years watching my bank account creep up from dollar to dollar.

"How would you like to be married in Mexico?" Gunther said.

"Fly all the way to Mexico and back?" I said. "All that money?"

"I've got enough for the tickets, and we can stay rent-free with my friend, Ben Carlos. Remember him—my childhood friend that my father put through medical school? Let's fly to Acapulco for our wedding after my classes are over. I've got research to do there with Ben." Gunther squeezed my hand with his diamond on it. "He'll be my best man. Would you like a Mexican honeymoon?"

"Oh, yes!" I said. My amazing future sparkled before me, as bright as his diamond.

"Then we'll get you registered for the fall semester before we go, and find a small apartment for us around here. We'll both be at the university next September!" Gunther kissed my hand, finger by finger, and then pressed his warm mouth to my palm, but I could only give him a worried smile. What was I thinking? *A honeymoon in Mexico? What would I wear?* I looked down at my only nice shirt and jeans. He couldn't afford to buy me clothes, and I couldn't ask him for money, either.

The waiter brought the first birthday cake I'd ever had, a small pink cake with eighteen pink candles to light our smiling faces. We made wishes, I blew out the candles and cut the cake. "I'm so happy!" I said.

We walked afterwards, strolling, hugged close together in the spring air. The dirty Chicago streets looked beautiful to me, like a new country—that country of love-and-marriage where you expect to live forever.

When we kissed and kissed and said goodnight, I undressed and crawled into my cot and felt Gunther's ring on my finger, hard and cool. I pressed it against my cheek until it grew warm. It was a promise and it was beautiful, but cumbersome and strange. I'd never imagined I'd wear an engagement ring.

The country of love and marriage. Half asleep, I asked myself: had I ever known anyone who was happily married? No. So maybe a loving marriage wasn't a country at all, but only a small town you drive through and—before you can turn off or stop—it's fading in your rear-view mirror.

6

The next morning at Dinty's I made the whole fairytale real—I showed Becky my ring and told her: "I'm getting married!"

"Married? You and Gunther?" Becky stopped cleaning tables and stared at me. "Well...congratulations...best wishes...hope you'll be happy...my lord, that was quick, girl!"

We hugged each other, and I said, "I wish you could come to the wedding, but it's going to be in Acapulco in Mexico next month, and we'll honeymoon there. And I'm going to the university in the fall! He'll pay my tuition. We're going to rent an apartment here. Can you believe how lucky I am?"

"Bet you have good-looking kids, you two."

"Not for a while." I was blushing a little. "I've got to get my degree, and Gunther's work takes so much time, so we're going to wait. Gunther asked me about all that, and he's ordered pills for me. It'll be a simple wedding. Gunther's best friend will be best man, and we'll stay in his apartment."

During our next date, Gunther told me that my high school transcripts had come from Plattsburg. "What do I do now?" I asked.

"Never mind," he said. "I'll get you accepted and registered— say you're out of town and can't do it yourself."

In a few days, Gunther gave me papers that showed I'd been accepted for my freshman year of college, and my fees were paid. I read the admission papers over and over, especially that wonderful word: PAID.

That week I gave my notice to the manager at Dinty's, and before I went to bed in my storeroom one night I told Hal and Hilda I would be leaving.

"Going away?" Hal said, his old face blank.

"In two weeks," I said. "I'm going to be married, and I'll start classes at the university in the fall."

I held out my ringed hand, and waited for them to say something: Congratulations? Best wishes? Finally I said, "Thank you for letting me sleep in your storeroom free, and giving me such good suppers. It was very kind of you."

They looked me over with the same scowls they had given lawn chairs with missing cushions. Then Hilda went back to scrubbing pans, and Hal locked the front door.

I couldn't sleep that night. I was dazed...excited...scared—I'd given up both my jobs, and my free home in the storeroom, too. I was barely eighteen. All I'd ever been was poor. I pulled my old comforter up to my chin. The sound of Chicago traffic echoed from shelf to shelf in the dark storeroom.

In a few days I said to Becky, "I'm scared. Sometimes I think that all this is just a dream, and I'll wake up. Do you think Gunther really means it?"

"You got a ring!" Becky said. "Didn't you rent an apartment? He paid your tuition for fall! What more do you want, his name signed in blood?"

"That wonderful apartment!" I cried. "Gunther carried me over the threshold. It's small, and it's cheap, because it's so far from the campus. But it has a real kitchen that works—stove, sink, refrigerator, everything. A real bathroom with a shower! A bedroom with furniture that matches! Rugs! I'll make curtains, and do some painting, too. Gunther laughed at me when I ran around touching everything and saying, 'Oh, look! Oh, look!'"

Day by day, April went by. I worked for the last time at Dinty's, and the Grille, and was paid for the last time. I looked at the many columns of small amounts in my bank deposit book. Autumn, winter, spring—I had been so proud of every dollar I'd saved.

But I had to go to the bank, withdraw my money, and close the account. For days I roamed Chicago, happily hunting for the first

41

nice clothes I'd ever had: my trousseau. At last I found a wedding dress on sale; it was beautiful, I thought: satiny white, with lace medallions like snowflakes drifted over it. By the time I paid for a flimsy suitcase, I had loaded shelves in the Schatzles' storeroom with a wedding gown, slippers and veil, a swimsuit, robe, sandals, summer dresses, pants, shirts, shoes, pretty underwear, a white nightgown and a negligee.

Every cent I'd earned in six months was gone. I had my diamond, I told myself. Hadn't I come to Chicago with everything I owned in a plastic bag? Now I had a whole trousseau in a suitcase!

But I felt as if I were walking on thin air.

The airplane Gunther and I boarded that last April morning was so huge that it seemed lethal to me, like a monster bullet, or a bomb. As we roared into the sky, most of the passengers looked bored, but the sight of the earth from cloud level struck me dumb. The world I had lived in all my life shrank to a tiny toyland, then vanished under the thick ceiling we rose through. Rain had been falling in Chicago, but we were lifted to sunshine over continents of clouds without end.

Gunther took my hand. "Hope you don't mind if we're not married right away," he said. "I've just found out that I can use Ben's new laboratory he's built. It has the equipment I need for what I'm doing, but Ben's got to finish his work with me before he can set up his new practice. He says he's afraid we'll be working too hard to have the wedding just yet. Will you wait?"

I squeezed his hand, and said I could wait if he could. He gave me one of his flashing blue looks and kissed me, though flight attendants and passengers were all around us. He said. "That's the hardest thing I'll ever have to do!"

It was a long, long trip, but I was with Gunther, and we landed at last in Acapulco. When I think of my first sight of Mexico, I see Ben Carlos. He stood at the gate watching us come: a tall, slender, black-haired man with a stunned look in his eyes. He and Gunther threw their arms around each other, brown head against black, and slapped each other on the back, shouting in Spanish.

"And this is my soon-to-be wife, Mary," Gunther told him.

"Such a beautiful woman," Ben said, bowing in an old-fashioned way. The shocked look I had seen in his eyes was a wary look now, almost angry.

42

We climbed in Ben's small car, and I sat in the back while the two men in the front seats talked with each other in Spanish. I hadn't slept the night before we left, and had been too excited to nap very much on the plane. I closed my eyes, half dozing in the warmth of Acapulco.

Gunther called, "Mary! Look! Punta Diamante!" I opened my eyes to see a long curve of beach shining below, edged with white flounces of surf. Hotels were shelved on tiers down slopes to the water. "We won't be staying anywhere in that scene," Gunther said, "but there are beaches enough for everybody in Acapulco."

Ben's apartment building was far from the hotels and glittering surf. The men carried our suitcases up to the third floor. "The bedroom's ready for you, Mary," Ben said. "Gunther and I can sleep in the living room."

Ben put my suitcase on the bed. When I opened it, my wedding dress was just under the lid. I shook out the white satin to hold it against me. "Do you like my wedding gown?" I asked Gunther, and felt myself blushing. I can imagine the shy, happy look I gave him. What did I know about weddings? I didn't know the dress was supposed to be a surprise.

Gunther and Ben said nothing for a moment. Were they embarrassed? Then Gunther said, "Very pretty. Very nice." I hung the dress in the closet and began to unpack my clothes.

"Sorry I can only give you rice and tortillas for supper," Ben said. "But maybe we won't notice—I've got some champagne."

For days I hadn't slept much, too excited to shut my eyes. When I drank a glass of champagne…and then another…the drinks added to my weariness. I ate Ben's rice and tortillas in a floating world. By the time we drank our coffee, I could hardly keep my eyes open. I settled among pillows on the couch and enjoyed the liquid sound of a Spanish conversation. Now and then the men turned to speak English to me, breaking their talk politely and listening to anything I managed to say.

I watched them through the lashes of my half-shut eyes. Two handsome young men—how had I managed that? Ben's black hair was glossy and thick, with blue glints where light fell. His cheekbones were high and his face was brown. I saw him smile once: a white flash of teeth against his tan.

Gunther threw himself back in his chair, then sat bolt upright to make a point. How wonderfully alive he was: his blue eyes gleamed with his earnestness, and Spanish words came fast from a mouth I wanted to kiss. In a few weeks Gunther and I would have our wedding day…

Dreaming of love and a wedding, I was hardly aware, for a while, of a change. The more Gunther talked, the more Ben was silent. Gunther's Spanish flowed over Ben like waves over a rock. Neither man spoke to me in English; they seemed to have forgotten me.

Their Spanish took on a hard, defiant edge. Ben scowled. Gunther pounded his fist on the arm of his chair. Words collided. Silences grew long.

Why were they angry? My eyes closed. I opened them. They shut. For only a minute, just a minute, I laid my cheek on a fat pillow beside me…

I woke in a bed in daylight. I tried to sit up, but I was too dizzy. "Gunther?" I called. "Gunther?"

"Darling, you've been sick." Gunther said, and came to sit beside me on the bed. "Don't try to talk yet. Drink this." He held a cup to my lips and I drank. He spread my hair on the pillow, and I sank back into darkness and frightening dreams.

Sometimes I opened my eyes to sunlight. Sometimes it was dark, and only a shaft of light fell through the living room door. "What's wrong with me?" I asked once, trying to focus my eyes on Gunther in the lamplight beside my bed.

"You've had food poisoning. It must have been something you ate on the plane." Gunther kissed me. "You'll be all right in a few days. Try to sleep."

How unromantic! How embarrassing—to fly to Acalpulco for a wedding and honeymoon and be sick! "I'm sorry," I whispered, and went back to sleep in a breath or two.

When I woke again, sunlight lit the bedroom. I sat up, and found I was wearing my new nightgown. "Gunther?" I called.

He came at once. "Awake?" he said.

I blinked at him stupidly. "I was sitting on the couch…"

"And you were pretty sick after that."

"Something I ate?" I asked. "How long have I been in bed?"

"It's Friday the thirteenth."

"I've been sick that long?" I cried, and thought of being undressed by two men…nursed by two men… I fell asleep again.

When I woke, Gunther was bending over me. "You're the prettiest thing when you're asleep, with your white-gold hair spread on a pillow," he said.

"I'm the *hungriest* thing, all right," I said.

Gunther brought me breakfast, and lunch and supper, too. I slept another long night and woke to Gunther's voice and sunlight again. "Ready for breakfast?" he said.

"I'm certainly rested," I said, "and I feel fine."

"Then how about a swim?" he said. "Can't wait to see you in that swimsuit. Ben said he'd meet us at the beach. I've seen his laboratory and clinic—it's the pride of his life. What a state-of-the-art place! He sank all his money into it. It's brand new."

"He's made money?"

"Plenty of it. He's a genius at 'in vitro fertilization.' Couples who want babies are beginning to come to him from abroad, he's so successful." Gunther looked around him. "He hasn't spent any money on a place to live, obviously. Says he doesn't have much money left."

"He's fond of you," I said. "I don't think he's so fond of me."

"He thinks you're the loveliest thing he's ever seen."

"But he's not very friendly."

"He doesn't…" Gunther hesitated. "He doesn't like what I'm doing."

"Marrying me?"

"Marrying anybody when I'm in graduate school and poor. He's not old enough to be my father, but he thinks he is. Never mind. You'll win him over."

Win Ben over? I couldn't imagine how, but I often saw him watching me. When the three of us dropped our robes in a palm-roofed "palapa" and waded into Puerto Marques Bay, I'll admit I looked nice in my swimsuit, a red bikini that covered the right places, but barely.

I'd never seen so much sky-blue water, or sand as fine and white as salt. When we walked at the tide's edge, waves wiped our footprints out patiently, tirelessly. When we lay on our blankets, the sun's heat seemed to soak into my bare skin like water.

"You're so fair—you'll burn," Gunther told me, and used that excuse to stroke sunblock on every inch of me not covered by my suit. Ben wore white trunks that showed off his tan, and he watched us with dark eyes as unreadable as the scribbles receding waves made on the shore.

The three of us lay half-dozing, drowsy in the sea-sound and sun. "Give us a poem," Gunther said to me. He turned to Ben. "She knows poem after poem," he told him. "Stores them in her head like we store scientific terms."

I rose on my elbow to kiss Gunther. "About the sea?" I said. "About the sand? I know one, but it's not very happy." We all turned to look at the beach where bathers trotted along the water's edge, writing their footprints there, for a moment. I said: "The poem ends:

Behind my back
seas pull the rug out, pull the past out, pull
my footprints out. I walk the crumbling floor
between dark waters and the darkening shore.

"The crumbling floor," Ben said. He wasn't looking at me or talking to me.

Gunther sat up with one angry shove. "I'll make my mark!"

Both men were sitting up now, sun gilding their shoulders and hairy chests. I sat up, too, and they seemed to remember me then. Ben came to his feet and walked away.

Gunther hugged me close, and smiled as he dropped a pinch of sand, grain by grain, in the cleft between my breasts. "You can't imagine how I depend on my Mary," he said. "I can't do what I want to do—not ever in this world—without you."

Behind my back
seas pull the rug out, pull the past out, pull
my footprints out. I walk the crumbling floor
between dark waters and the darkening shore.

7

Lazy, hot days. For more than a year I'd worked from dawn to almost midnight in Plattsburg, then Chicago, and tiredness seemed to have sunk into my bones. The next morning I lay beside Gunther on the sand, kissing him every now and then beside the hissing waves.

I yawned over lunch. "Take a siesta," Gunther told me. "An ancient Spanish custom." He didn't have to coax me. After lunch I slept the heat of the afternoon away, never waking, never dreaming.

When the men came home, I cried, "What's happened to you?" Ben had a cut on his forehead and bleeding knuckles; Gunther's face was bruised, and he had a black eye.

Neither of them looked at me. "A fight," Gunther said. "Some men down on the Zocalo jumped us. They got most of our money, but we messed them up quite a bit. With the cash gone, I'm afraid we can't eat out much, or go to clubs and shows."

"The money's not the important thing—neither of you were badly hurt," I said. "I can cook. We can eat here."

"*Mole poblano de Guajolote*," Gunther said. "How about making that?" He grinned.

"What is it?"

"The pride of our finest restaurants: wild turkey stew with a sauce of tomatoes and chocolate."

"You expect me to cook that?" I said.

"They served it in Montezuma's palace. Food for a king."

"But neither of you are Montezuma!" I said. "And I'm a

49

Nebraska cook who knows what to do with leftovers! That's all."

So I went to the stores with Gunther as my translator, and cooked our dinner that night in a kitchenette that seemed luxurious to me, though there wasn't a single mixing bowl and none of the pans had lids.

The men came to my first dinner with polite expressions on their faces.

"It's *good*," Ben said when he'd tasted everything.

"Wonderful!" Gunther said.

I didn't hold their surprise against them; I was too relieved. Day by day I cooked Sophy's best dinners, and the men cleaned their plates. "She's beautiful, and a good cook, too," Gunther said.

"How lucky can you get?" Ben's voice had the edge it often had when he spoke to Gunther.

The three of us walked in the Zocalo late that night. Gunther kept his arm around me, and my new summer dress fluttered in breeze from the water. I'd never strolled between two handsome men.

Sometimes we saw children begging. A small girl snatched at some pesos a man gave her, and the crowd of children went after her until she couldn't be seen under a pile of small brown bodies. Might I have been a beggar like that in some city, when my mother was dead and my father in prison? Admiring eyes followed me. Men whispered in Spanish to me, even though Gunther or Ben glared at them. Guarded by two men, wasn't I a woman of value, soon to be married, soon to have my own husband and my own home?

The two men worked long hours at Ben's new building, but we had long hours together, too. We couldn't afford to ride horseback along the sand. Scuba diving cost too much, and so did parasailing, or having drinks in a swim-up pool bar. But the Diego Rivera murals were free, and the Chapel at Las Brisas. Gunther and I kissed in the hot breeze at the San Diego Fort, or in the cool depths of the Cathedral. Ben showed me his new laboratory and clinic, and we drove along streets of large homes surrounded by gardens. "These houses are like the ones in Hermosillo—the town where Ben and I grew up," Gunther said. "Ben's mother still lives in hers."

Moonlight changed the beaches to silver water and silver sand. One evening the moon was rising as Gunther and I strolled on a shore of the Peninsula de Las Playas. I teased him about his black eye: "Are you planning to marry me looking like you won me in a fight?"

"It was a fair fight," Gunther said.

We spread a blanket and sat listening to waves rolling in on the dark sand. A ferryboat went by. It was bound for Roqueta Island, Gunther said. Reflections of its bright colors flickered on the waves with the moon's light.

"Ben's not happy, is he?" I asked. "Does he ever visit his mother?"

"I don't think he ever sees his mother, even though she's not well. She didn't help him," Gunther said. "But he had my dad's money—he didn't have to work to pay for his training." There was anger in Gunther's voice.

Ben had dropped us off at the beach. In a little while we saw him coming toward us in the moonlight, a lean, tall man who seldom smiled. He wasn't smiling now. Bad feeling between the two men had deepened, I thought. They talked to me, but hardly spoke to each other. Only Gunther explained the rules of jai alai to me, not Ben. Only Ben had taught me Spanish, not Gunther. I was beginning to feel like their no-fight zone.

Ben stopped beside us where we lay on the sand. "Do you mind if I take Gunther for a walk?" he said to me as moonlight cast his big shadow over us on our blanket. "I'll bring him right back."

I watched them drag their long shadows away, striding out of step as the moonlight brightened. I could see by the stiffness of their bodies that they were arguing. They stopped, waist deep in water, facing each other as if they meant to fight in the surging waves, their feet stabbed deep into crumbling sand. What could I do, caught between two angry men?

One morning Gunther woke me. Sunshine spilled over us as he kissed me and said: "Darling! I'm almost done with my research. Will you marry me next Saturday?"

Would I marry him? I laughed and kissed him and said, "Yes! Oh, yes!"

How happy I was as our day came! Gunther said, "No justice of the peace for us today! You'll be married in a very romantic place—you'll see." I remember how I sang as I made breakfast for the three of us that morning. My song was a Mexican lullaby that Gunther had taught me. "My Mary's so clever," Gunther whispered, hugging me at the kitchen sink. "She hears a song once, and she can sing it."

Afternoon came, and I dressed for my wedding in the small bedroom. I opened my window and looked at a small balcony below. A very pregnant woman sat there under lines of washing, her bare feet on the railing. I watched her as I braided a long string of pearls into my hair.

Pearl necklace, pearl earrings, sheer stockings, white slippers, the simple dress sprinkled with lace snowflakes…

I heard a tap on my door. There was Gunther in a dark suit with a carnation in his buttonhole, a bouquet in his hands, and such an adoring look in his eyes that I could hardly stand to look at him. "For me?" I said, taking the bouquet.

"For you? Yes: all of me," Gunther said. "The bouquet is from Ben. But no flowers can ever be as beautiful as you." He touched a snowflake on my dress, and the pearls in my hair, and kissed me.

I managed to get myself and my dress and veil in Ben's small car, and thanked Ben for my bouquet. He said I was welcome, and drove through city streets and out of town without saying another word.

After a while our road was surrounded by what seemed to be dense jungle, until we followed a road that looped upon itself and came to an end at a long, low house and a weedy flagstone courtyard.

Gunther helped me out of the car. "We'll be married here?" I said.

"This whole estate belonged to Ben's grandfather," Gunther said. "No one lives here now." The three of us followed a long path to the house, and peered through a window at tiled floors gleaming under oak beams. The rooms were huge and the ceilings were high. Far away through the house I could glimpse a row of arches framing a garden.

Ben said, "My mother has the lawns mowed here. That's about all. The roof's leaking. The jungle's moving in."

"Ben's grandfather owned a silver mine," Gunther said.

We followed another path into a ruined garden. The shapes of flowerbeds were buried in weeds, and a stone fountain held rainwater and green scum. Two marble ladies under its basin had lost not only their clothes but their heads.

The great garden stopped at a stone wall. Beyond it was nothing but the robin's-egg-blue haze of a far shore. "I've always said that Ben's grandfather had one of the finest views near Acapulco," Gunther said, as I stood at the wall with him. The long curve of Punta Diamante gleamed below the roofs of its rich hotels. "But you're wondering where we can have our wedding?" He smiled at me. "Ben's grandfather built a private chapel."

A weedy path turned a sharp corner away from the wall and led through trees to a small building with an arched doorway. Two weather-blackened, life-sized statues of angels guarded it. "Is this romantic enough?" Ben asked in a dry voice.

"It's like a fairy tale," I said. The battered faces of the angels watched us cross the old doorsill. The space beyond was so dim that I saw nothing but a glowing stained glass window at first, and the small, bright eyes of candles.

Empty pews. An altar. A figure at the altar waiting for us. We paced down the aisle, my ruffled petticoat rustling under my satin skirt. The dark figure was a young, solemn priest in black. He wore a stern look in the candlelight as we stopped before him. I stood between Gunther and Ben as Spanish sentences, coming low and fast, showered over us.

We knelt. We rose. Gunther put a wedding ring on my finger, and I put my diamond ring beside it and smiled at him. Ben stood close to us in the half-dark and damp scent of that place. I glanced at him once, and met his sullen brown eyes.

Gunther kissed me. We turned away from the altar, followed the aisle to the door, and walked into the sunshine between the blackened angels.

I took a deep breath of the hot Mexican afternoon. "Mrs. Gunther Risling!" my new husband said.

How beautifully sunlight fell on the ruined gardens. We walked back to sit on the wall between stone urns and drink champagne high above Punta Diamante's glistening surf. Gunther showed me our wedding license: lines and lines of Spanish. I wanted to give champagne to the priest, but Gunther said the priest had left.

"To the bride!" Ben said, lifting his glass. "May she have a loving husband and many healthy children!" That ironic voice of his…I blushed and laughed a little, but Ben wasn't smiling. He stood in his black suit before the pastel miles of beaches and sky.

We went back to his apartment to change our clothes and have our wedding supper in a restaurant. Then we drove to Ben's apartment, and he left us at his door: he would stay the night with friends.

How we hurried upstairs, bride and groom! How I loved Gunther! How fast we shed our hot fine clothes, hurrying to make love! We tied my wedding bouquet to the bed's head, like a blessing dangling above us.

How happy we were! I was only eighteen, so young, so yearning. Anything he wanted, I would do. Anywhere he went, I would go. A man loved me. A man had married me. I could slam the door forever on Mary Durfy, and the Slut's Child, and a "step-father" yelling, *You're a natural-born whore*. Goodbye to the grease of hamburger joints and a cot on cracked cement.

A different person, wrapped in love, I woke at dawn with my new name. There was my husband beside me in the morning light, his head on my shoulder, his arms as tight around me as if he had dreamed I would run away.

I remember sailboats docked on turquoise above their sunken shadows. I've never forgotten long hours in soft sand…kisses on a twilight beach…the noise and music of Mercado Municipale crowds. Gunther bought me a necklace there, and I have it yet, with the memory of his warm fingers pushing my long hair aside and fastening the silver links.

"Do you like it?" he asked when we lay in bed that night.

"I've never worn anything as beautiful as this," I said.

Gunther smiled. "It's only a trinket. You should have seen the jewelry my mother wore."

"You're from a different world," I said.

"Tell me about yours," Gunther said, holding me tight against him. "You've seen the kind of town I grew up in. What was your home like?"

I sighed. "A two-room house with a privy in the yard."

Gunther raised himself on an elbow and looked at me. "You've never told me your family was so…"

"Poor," I said.

"Why didn't you tell me?"

"I…was so ashamed," I said. "I thought you'd never love me."

Gunther was quiet for a while, holding me close. Then he said, "You told me you had a friend. Sophy somebody-or-other."

"Sophy Saul. She was my angel," I said. "She lived next door, and we had good neighbors on the other side, too: the Andersons. They helped us with food."

"Food!" Gunther said. "You were hungry?"

"Most of the time. Sophy and the Andersons fed my 'sisters' and me when they dared. They knew when my "stepfather' and 'stepmother' went off in their truck and left us—sometimes for days. Mr. Anderson came over and fixed our front door once when our folks were gone. After a while I think they got hooked on the pleasure of kindness, the way my father and stepmother got hooked on whiskey. Our family *was* a constant temptation to do good."

Gunther chuckled, his mouth under my chin.

"One day Mrs. Anderson knocked on our new front door," I said. "She'd seen our folks drive away. We finally heard her over the ruckus of the television—we could watch any shows we wanted when we were alone. So there we sat in the middle of dogs and litter and garbage, entertained by adults getting hot and excited without any clothes on. Mrs. Anderson's place was a small house, like Sophy's. It was small, and she had five children, but being clean was one of her necessities, along with being charitable and Christian."

I could feel Gunther chuckling. I guess it *was* funny, if you looked at it that way. I said, "Mrs. Anderson came in, I remember, stepping over some clothes my father had left in a pile after his 'late nights,' (that was what he called getting drunk.) His clothes smelled too strong to be put anywhere but by the door. Mrs. Anderson gave the room and the television such an outraged look that I might have thought she despised everything she saw, but I knew she was fond of us. 'Children!' she said—she had to yell over the loud, sex-scene music that was just building up to the usual heights. I turned off the tv. She said, 'Now girls, can't we get this

55

house all nice and clean, and surprise your folks when they come home?'

"We stood around not thinking we could. Every dish we had was in some dirty pile or other. Daddy left his beer cans in a corner, but the dogs rolled them around the floor among plastic spoons and straws and our puppy's messes and my stepmother's romance magazines.

"'Let's start with the cans,' Mrs. Anderson said, so we did. When they were all in the trash bags she'd brought, she clucked over the beds, and took whatever bedding we had away to be washed, along with my father's clothes from the floor, and other clothes lying roundabout, and our one towel by the kitchen sink.

"When she came back, she brought soap and dish towels and we started on the dishes. She set us up in a line: I washed, the next biggest girl rinsed, and the littlest girl wiped. While we did that, Mrs. Anderson washed cupboard shelves, talking to herself under her breath.

The oldest of my stepmother's children was a whiner. She was worse than any of our dogs, even the puppies. She hadn't rinsed half the dishes when she started in: 'Mama don't make us do dishes...Mama let's us-all watch television'...whine, whine, whine. I wanted to kick her. I was looking forward to what the house looked like when it was cleaned up, and Mrs. Anderson was working so hard that her shirt was soaked. She just let the whiner whine.

"The house looked different, all right, when Mrs. Anderson went home. We children didn't feel like moving anything: Mrs. Anderson might come back. It was lunch time, but she'd cleaned out the refrigerator, so we couldn't poke around in it and find something to eat that still smelled all right.

"After a while, Mrs. Anderson brought us sandwiches and a carton of milk and went back home. We ate the sandwiches off the floor—it was certainly clean enough—and passed the milk carton from mouth to mouth. Finally, when there were crumbs on the floor and the dogs were rolling the milk carton around and licking the sandwich wrappers, we felt enough at home to turn on the television."

"What a story!" Gunther said. "What did your folks say when they came home?"

"They yelled at us, because the house was still too clean. 'Just what's been going on here?' my stepmother shouted. The two other girls couldn't wait to tell her. 'Mrs Anderson made us wash dishes, and we had to pick up everything on the floor!' they told her. 'She washed the beds and towels and all our clothes!' They tried to outshout each other and be the biggest martyr, the way children do."

Gunther was laughing and I laughed, too. It could almost seem funny to me now, because I was in my husband's arms with my head on his shoulder.

I sent a postcard of one of the beaches to Rhody: "Dearest Rhody, if only you could lie on this beach in the sun with me. But I'll hope to see you when I can. Love from your Mary."

Beautiful days passed. Our last Mexican evening came.

"Let's show Mary the divers at La Quebrada," Gunther said to Ben after supper.

"Divers?" I said as we went downstairs.

"Men dive a hundred and thirty feet down to the water and rocks," Gunther said.

We drove along the light-studded shoreline of Acapulco Bay. "Our last honeymoon night," I whispered to Gunther.

Ben watched us in the rear view mirror as we kissed. Was there a woman in his life? I wondered. I might have asked Gunther, but I kept still. Whatever the two men had argued over still gleamed in their eyes and grated in their voices. I saw it and heard it, and pretended I didn't.

"They'll start diving soon," Gunther said as we walked from the car to a rocky cliff edge. Far below—so far that a bird flew between our ledge and the distant water—an inlet foamed with waves against sheer walls. High above us young men in swim trunks were poised at the brink of a cliff: tiny figures against the far glitter of the Pacific.

I stood in Gunther's arms. The air was cool. The small figures disappeared. "They're praying at a shrine," he said.

They would jump? That far? I could hardly look as one of the men appeared at the brink again. He carried a blazing torch in each hand. Suddenly he spread his torches wide and dove from the rock, poised for a moment on dark air before he fell.

Down he plunged, his torches the only sign that he was plummeting to the foaming surf. Then his torches went out.

"It's so dangerous!" I cried. "How can they do it?"

One by one, men dropped toward waves that surged and smashed on rocks.

"Dangerous?" Gunther said. "They learn young to take chances." The torchlight of the last diver glittered in his eyes.

T he next morning we waited for our flight at the airport. When it was called, Gunther slapped Ben on the back and said, "Wish we could stay forever. Thanks for a wonderful honeymoon."

"Yes!" I said, and kissed Ben's cheek. "Thanks, Ben—all the wonderful memories!"

"Come any time," Ben said. He was staring at Gunther. "Any time *at all. Please.*"

Ben wasn't begging me; he was begging Gunther. Ben threw his arms around Gunther as he had when we arrived, and I saw, for a second, sharp desperation in Ben's eyes as he turned away.

W e flew back to our Chicago apartment—Mr. and Mrs. Gunther Risling. I felt like a bird settling in a safe nest at last. I was home. Sometimes I dreamed of sending a letter to the Durfys: "I'm married to a graduate student. We have a lovely apartment. I'm going to college in the fall."

But most of my dreams were about Rhody. I sent her presents, but every time I called her, her voice was more plaintive, more hopeless.

"You miss her," Gunther said. "Should we bring her here?"

How kind he was, trying to give me what I yearned for. But Rhody was only five, and our apartment was so small. In September I'd begin university classes. We had to admit that we weren't ready for her yet.

Gunther went back to his laboratories and teaching, overworked and underpaid. He was so busy that he often called to say he wouldn't be home for supper. My days were long, but I filled them with cleaning and sewing and painting. Our kitchen floor shone five shades brighter. Our washer and dryer pounded and spun as "Mary Dirty" faded from my memory, like wash-water down a drain.

Over and over, I thought of Sophy Saul as I did my housework. Was she still alive, with her fuzzy white hair and her kind heart? I'd written letters, but they were always returned marked address unknown. Gunther praised my cooking, my sewing, my house-keeping. Who had taught me? Sophy Saul.

Guther praised me and loved me. I never doubted it. But as June came he began to stay on campus late into the night. He had a look in his eyes I remembered from our dating days: he was intent, single-minded and wound tight. "Time," he said. "Do you know how I'm working against time? But I count on you, Mary. You're the heart of everything. I count on you." He thrashed in his sleep, as if he fought time even in his dreams.

I worried about Gunther, and had my own dreams. The apartment wasn't finished yet, but when it was, I'd have Gunther's friends to dinner, and I'd invite Becky for lunch. And when fall came, I'd be a student at last.

One morning I was sick at breakfast. I didn't tell Gunther: he was still sleeping after a long night at his lab. I had a cold, I thought, or the flu. But the next morning I was sick again, and the next.

"It can't be," I said over and over, pacing our apartment wall to wall, back and forth. "It's impossible." I'd taken the pills Gunther ordered for me...we'd been so careful...I *couldn't* have a baby... not now...I ran out to buy a pregnancy kit.

It told me what I didn't want to know.

But pregnancy kits could be wrong. I went to see a doctor. He said, "You'll have a baby, Mrs. Risling. In February."

I went home to sob and wail, half-wild. I paced in and out of our small rooms, back and forth, yelling at the walls, hearing the doors of my future slamming shut. I'd learned what it meant to take care of a baby when I was thirteen—Rhody might as well have been mine! And babies cost money that we didn't have!

Could I bear to get rid of the baby—bleed myself loose like

a trapped raccoon I'd found once in the woods—never tell Gunther?

No—it was his baby, too. We'd have to decide together.

Gunther called me in late afternoon, as usual. "I've been sick…" I began, but all he said was, "Sick? You're sick? I'm coming home!"

I put on some makeup and my trousseau nightgown and robe, and waited the long hour while he drove home through rush-hour traffic. "Are you all right?" he asked the minute he opened our door. "What's the matter?"

When I tried to tell him, tears ran down my face. "I'm p-pregnant!" I wailed. "I've been to a doctor, and he says I'll have a baby in February! All our plans! We haven't got enough money for a baby!" I covered my face and sobbed.

"Mary!" Gunther said, holding me tight. "Oh, Mary! How wonderful!" His blue eyes shone.

"But we've been so careful!"

"A baby on the way!" He danced me around the room.

"But how can I ever—"

"I don't want you going to classes or taking a single chance!"

I pushed away from him. "You've worried about money. So have I. We've got so little. I don't have to have this baby, do I? We'll have others—I can—"

The smile on Gunther's face turned to horror. "No!" he cried. "Never!" He grabbed me and held me so tight that I struggled to get free, almost frightened. He saw it and loosened his arms and murmured, "Never…never…" in my ear. "I want you to take care of yourself."

I could see he meant it. "But I'll only have one semester, and then I'll have to quit my classes," I said.

Gunther didn't want me to go to the campus at all. I begged to have the fall semester at least. He wouldn't hear of it.

We argued, but he won, because I began to have spotting. My doctor told me to stay in bed until it stopped. I came home and told Gunther. "Maybe I *should* lose this baby," I said, and wished I hadn't.

Gunther stared at me. "You don't want it?" he said.

"It's *your baby*," I said. "Of course I do!"

Gunther put my breakfast and lunch beside the bed before he left each morning. He brought dinner home for us every night, with little gifts for me, as if I were the center of his world. The bleeding was soon gone. My dreams of college were gone, too.

Becky came for lunch on one of her afternoons off, bringing a pink sweater for the baby. I told her I'd been so careful not to be pregnant—I wanted to go to college!

"You will!" she comforted me. "Here you are in your own apartment with your own husband and a baby coming—I'd sure trade with you!" She hugged me. "It's as wild as ever at Dinty's— they fired the manager and we've got a new one, a mean old witch with a face like that barracuda we saw at the zoo—all teeth. And I don't have you to talk to! That's the worst of it."

Becky came, my morning sickness disappeared, and I could call Rhody any time I wanted on my own telephone. I should have felt so lucky, so happy—didn't I have my husband, and my own home, and a baby coming? Not even a year before I'd been sleeping under a hedge! But I was miserable. I felt trapped. No college for me.

Gunther understood, I think.

"Don't worry," he often said. "When I get a job, we'll hire a babysitter, and you'll start classes again."

He must have understood. He must have loved me...he made love to me so carefully and tenderly, and brought flowers, and one night he put a big box on the floor of our living room and said, "You've got work to do."

He ripped the top off the box. "You don't have to go to college to learn," he said, and piled book after book on our living-room table. He turned on a lamp. "Here you go: your textbooks and syllabus for the university's freshman Western Civilization course—all of them. Study!"

I kissed him over and over, and thanked him, and we opened and shut the books and read from the syllabus. The next morning he went off to work triumphantly, tossing a last "Study!" over his shoulder.

I was alone with a stack of textbooks.

Did I grab the first book on the syllabus list and begin to read? I did not. I put dishes in my dishwasher, and clothes in my dryer. I went grocery shopping, buying food we already had on our shelves. I called Rhody. I called Becky.

Finally I had to stop. I had to look at the stack of books on the living-room table.

There they all were, waiting: new and thick and mean.

I walked back and forth, not touching a single one. They watched me, pile after pile, I thought—they might open their pages and fly at me, screaming as scornfully as gulls over garbage: *You're that Dirty Durfy kid! What would you do with books like us? Those students at the university have read for years, but you? Do you even know enough to hold us right side up? Ever heard of a paragraph? A glossary? An index?*

I left them where they were for hours. I didn't open one.

But I love books. New books! Their inky, papery, never-touched smell. If there were such a thing as new-book perfume, I'd wear it. Sophy Saul bought me new books when I was a dirty little kid. I climbed in the shabby nest of her old recliner and buried myself in that smell. "Don't you love it?" I asked her cat. "Your nose is so good. Smell!"

And Sophy Saul said I was smart. "Smart as the smartest kid in town," she said. "Smarter than that. You've read every book I've got, haven't you? I thought so. Now tell me, what did you think of *The Ambassadors...Canterbury Tales...Don Quixote...My Mother's House...The Tale of Genji...*" and away we would go, talking and eating and talking and laughing.

I wanted Sophy. I'd never stopped wanting her. She'd loved me.

And Gunther loved me: he'd bought that pile of books, new, ink-smelling, never-opened books. He supposed I could read them. Didn't he?

Gunther had left papers on top of the books: the syllabus for the course. I read that course outline, beginning to end. The first book assigned was Homer's *Iliad*. After a while I found it on the table: a paperback, so new that its pages would hardly open.

A new book. I sat on the couch and smelled it. Yes.

A brawny Greek flourished his sword on the cover. I settled myself among couch pillows in the still apartment, opened the *Iliad*, and took my first step on its vicious, blood-soaked battlegrounds.

Beautiful Helen of Troy had been stolen by Paris, and the

Greeks and Trojans had been hacking each other to death for years. Now their leaders were quarreling over slave mistresses taken in battle.

So far away, so long ago—so many centuries before Christ—these heroes snarled and sulked like Chicago ghetto gangs, and they had the same code: shame and dishonor were worse than death. Women were objects to them: nothing but plunder, like shields or gold helmets. The priceless things they battled and died for were their gangs, their honor, their glory.

I was still deep in the *Iliad* when Gunther came home. He didn't even take off his coat—he rushed to me on the couch, hugged me, kissed me and said, "Our money troubles are over!"

"Over?" I thought he was joking.

"Ben called. He's got enough money now to give us a loan, he says. Enough money to see us through the school year and pay for the baby."

"Ben! Why? You've told me he needed money. Owed money."

"He's my best friend," Gunther said. "And his mother has died and left him plenty."

His eyes shone: we would have enough money.

So we had money. We were dizzy with the thought of enough money to buy a car, have a baby, hire babysitters, send me to college.

Dear Ben. I hadn't appreciated his kindness enough, or his friendship for Gunther! Now he'd taken most of our worries away.

I wrote Ben to thank him for his wonderful help. I told him how I loved my home, and how I was waiting for the baby by devouring the books for a college freshman course that Gunther had bought for me: Homer, Aristotle, Plato, Virgil, the Bible, Machiavelli, Dante, Boccaccio, Montaigne, Shakespeare, Jane Austen, Marx, Mill, Nietzsche, Beauvoir, Conrad, Woolf… I wrote him that I was making myself do all the assignments, writing them out in notebooks, saving them for the classes I hoped to take someday. I even tried to tell him how, book by book and month by month, I was being confused, thrilled, appalled, changed.

The slow weeks went by. Gunther worked on the campus late at night.

Thanksgiving.

Christmas. We gave each other baby clothes.

In January we made a "baby corner" in our bedroom; a crib waited there. Gunther was sure we'd have a girl. I wanted a boy exactly like him, for I loved him so, and saw how worn and worried he was: he began staying all night on campus to keep up with his work. He said four hours sleep was enough for him, and crawled into our bed at first light.

And then, one cold February day before dawn, we rushed to the hospital and our baby girl was born. Gunther was with me through every screaming, hard hour of birthing, and was beside me when my last yell brought our child into the world. In a few minutes she was cleaned up, wrapped snugly and laid in my arms.

Gunther hung over us, white-faced. "Maria," he said. "She has to be named Maria—she looks just like you. Let me hold her." He cradled Maria against him, staring at her. His hand shook as he touched her cheek. He gave her back to me and sat by my bed, his face in his hands. "She's the image of you," he said.

Was Maria the image of me? I couldn't see it. Her eyes were the undecided color of newborn baby eyes, and her hair was only a fuzz. "Her eyes will change to blue," Gunther said. I laughed at his decided tone. "And her hair will be blonde—a baby angel's halo."

Such a romantic picture! *He's a new father,* I told myself. I remembered dear Rhody. Babies were no pink and white dolls to me. Rhody howled in my memory, hungry and smelly and wet and mine.

But how helpless Maria was, there at my breast, her head lolling, her hands gripping anything she could find in this terrifying world. Sometime during our first night together, I began to shake and shiver with love for her, my newborn baby. I felt as if a cord ran back from me to my dead mother. She had loved me like that, and lost me as the bullet struck her.

9

One late afternoon our apartment doorbell rang. Maria hadn't slept well the night before, and both of us were napping at dusk. Half asleep, I looked through the door's peephole and saw a young woman. When I opened the door, she pushed past me into our dark living room.

"So this is where he keeps you," she said. A streetlight through the window hardly lit her black jeans and shirt. She came closer and stood with her hands on her hips and her chin thrust forward.

"What?" I said. "This is the Risling home."

She came closer yet in the dim room. Too close. "You poor thing," she said.

"What?"

"You poor little Nebraska bastard."

I couldn't speak. My mouth must have hung open. She laughed. "Did you suppose I wouldn't find out? Don't think I haven't known where you are." I followed her into the bedroom. She turned on a light, and I saw her long black hair almost touch Maria's face as she bent over the sleeping baby in the crib. "I thought so," she said. "Gunther's hidden you away to have bastards. You're his whore."

The woman didn't have the sense to dodge me—I shoved her into the living room and opened my front door, yelling, "Get out! Out!"

She laughed in my face. "A trucker's bastard from some hole-in-the-wall town, what was it? Plattsburg, Nebraska? A hamburger joint waitress? Gunther's going to be famous, and he's going to be rich! Will somebody like you be there beside him then—his whore? His little side dish?"

I gave her a push and she got out of our apartment quick, and spoke from the hall. "Not a chance," she said. "Here. Take a look at this. You'll find our *wedding picture* in it. And we've bought a new house in Oak Park. It's gorgeous!" She threw a thick newspaper section through the door. "Stay away from my husband! Go home to that shack in Nebraska!"

I slammed the door on her. Her heels click-clacked away.

Whore.

Bastard.

I locked the door I'd slammed. She was insane. She had to be insane. But she knew my mother hadn't been married and I'd been a waitress...she'd yelled about my father and Plattsburg...

The newspaper lay at my feet. I grabbed it and hunted through it, page after page, until suddenly—there was Gunther! He sat looking straight at me, while my nasty visitor, grinning in satin and lace, stood beside him, holding him down with a ringed hand on his shoulder.

Neola Renee Rand and Gunther George Risling exchanged wedding vows February twenty-fifth in Oak Park.

Parents of the bride are Dr. and Mrs. Arthur S. Rand of Oak Park. The groom's parents are deceased.

The bride is a recent graduate of the University of Chicago, and her husband is a research assistant at the University.

The Rev. Charles Snow performed the 2 p.m. ceremony at the United Presbyterian Church, Oak Park.

The couple reside in Oak Park.

I couldn't seem to take a breath. Who was I?

Who was Maria?

I lifted her from her crib, and shuffled through the newspaper pages scattered on our living room floor—a whole edition, too real not to be believed.

Gunther and Neola smiled in black and white under my feet. I was left with Maria—no name, no home, no marriage. We were alone, like two animals whose safe burrow had been clawed open to the light.

I don't know how long I stood there, while Maria made little sucking noises against my neck. At last small facts began to appear:

they perched in my head, one by one, like a row of harpies, waiting to be noticed.

My "wedding." Only three of us were there, and the priest. No friends of Gunther or Ben had come—not one. His parents were dead. "Almost all the people I know are in Monterrey, where Ben and I grew up—hundreds of miles from here," Gunther had said. "And our last-minute wedding plans kept them from coming."

The priest at the chapel? Was he a priest at all, or only someone in a black robe? Gunther and I might have knelt while he recited the market reports over us in Spanish. And our Spanish "wedding license"—what had it said? I couldn't read it.

Long ago, when I called Gunther, a man had asked: "Neola?"

And who in the whole city of Chicago knew I was a trucker's bastard daughter from Plattsburg, Nebraska? Becky knew. But she'd never tell someone like Neola.

Gunther knew.

Why had Gunther Risling courted me, flown me all the way to Acapulco and pretended to marry me?

"For the same old reason," I'd told Becky after a date with Gunther. "The old, old, obvious reason."

You poor thing.

His little side dish.

Where had Gunther been when he "worked late" so many nights? Why had he crawled into our bed at dawn so many mornings? Where were Maria and I when he put a ring on Neola's hand that Saturday afternoon? We had just come home from the hospital the week before.

I carried Maria back and forth, talking to myself and her.

I looked at the phone every time I passed it.

I'd never called Gunther at the university. He'd told me that if I ever needed to reach him, I should say: "Would you ask Mr. Risling to call this phone number, please, as soon as possible?" (Why? Why not say who I was?)

So stupid. So trusting. So needy that I "married" the first man who wanted me. So hungry for college that I'd taken the bribe of "classes in the fall." Gunther had told a few lies and I was caught. How Gunther and Ben must have laughed at me!

Thinking of those two men, those liars, I picked up the phone and called Gunther.

"Stay away from my husband!" she yelled in the dark. "Go home to that shack in Nebraska!"

It wasn't long before Gunther called back in that smooth, rich voice of his—it's been heard hundreds of times on television. I loved that voice. I loved that man. I would have lived in darkest Africa on the bare ground with him.

He sounded scared. "Maria's all right?"

"Yes," I said. "But someone's just been here. She says she's married to you."

There was silence on his end of the line.

"Your wedding announcement was in the paper," I said. "You married Neola Rand." My voice was steady, but my lips were trembling.

Gunther made a small sound like a moan.

All the breath seemed to leave my lungs, but I had enough left to cry, "We had a *wedding*! Ben was there! We had a *priest*!"

He didn't answer. I said in a fierce voice: "Don't lie to me any more! The wedding was a fake! We're not married!"

"No." Gunther only whispered, but I heard him.

Tears ran down my face; I was glad he couldn't see them. "You didn't want me. You didn't want Maria."

"You know I love you!" he whispered. "I love—"

"You married somebody else. When I'd just come home from the hospital with your baby."

"Yes, but—Mary—I'm coming home—"

I cut him off.

I didn't even say goodbye.

Oh, I was a wild woman! I was a little girl who didn't even know who her father was—I was Mary Durfy again, the bastard, the Mary Dirty of the Dirty family, the natural-born whore! My love for Gunther exploded into hate, like oil flaming under a match. Burning like that, I wailed. I shuddered.

I screamed. I dumped my "wedding dress" out of its box, and stabbed it with a kitchen knife through every lace medallion, as if they were memories I wanted to kill. I ripped that dress. I shredded it. I threw what was left of it on our bed, lay on it and howled.

Finally I heard Maria fussing at the noise I was making. Poor little bastard.

I splashed cold water on my face. I had to leave—I had to go! Where? Gunther might already be hurrying home.

My suitcase was in the closet. I threw some of my clothes in it, and the picture of my mother and me, and the clipping about Gunther and Neola, and Sophy's letters. I used the rest of the space for Maria's clothes, blankets, and diapers. Gunther had bought me a big backpack for my books; I filled it with more of Maria's things, and some bread and cheese for me.

When I locked the door of my home for the last time, I looked up and down the street for Gunther, then splashed through March slush with Maria, the suitcase and my pack. I withdrew all the cash from our account at a nearby bank—there wasn't much—and took a bus to the bus station to read the timetables on a wall. I felt like a fox escaping a hunter: what towns could we ride to, then double back to the south? Who could I run to but my grandmother in Florida?

Had I told Gunther where my grandmother lived? I didn't think so—he only knew she existed. We had shared our lives with each other for hours, but he had never once told me, even in his sleep, his own truths: "You're not my wife. You've never been my wife. I've married someone else."

The bus left in a few minutes, and seemed to take hours to leave Chicago. I couldn't put enough space between Gunther and us; no cities went by soon enough. We left Indianapolis at last, bound for Kissimmee and my Florida grandmother I hadn't seen for years. She had sent me Christmas cards; that was all.

Lies, I kept saying to myself. *Lies*. The lies I was running from swarmed after me. I heard Gunther telling lies with his velvety voice, watching me serve hamburgers behind the counter at Hal's Grille.

Lies. A "wedding" in Acapulco. Ben's cold, dark-eyed stare: he knew! He knew! A Chicago apartment far from the university and Gunther's friends—and Neola.

I still wore the "diamond" and "wedding" rings. Gunther had admitted that the diamonds weren't real, but never the marriage. I wanted to throw my wedding ring in some toilet, like Julia Roberts did in the movie, "Sleeping With the Enemy," but I wore it for Maria's sake.

Lies. Gunther had said he wanted Maria. He'd come from Neola's bed to watch me have his child. I looked down at Maria sleeping in my lap. She'd be called "bastard," the same name my "stepfather" had called me.

The big bus droned through the night.

How had that woman found where I was and who I was? Anger shook me; I leaned my forehead against the window and wished I'd yelled at Neola: "Gunther Risling would never marry somebody like you—a goose-necked, round-heeled, louse-scratching, flat-chested—"

Too late. Gunther had married Neola Renee Rand. Gunther had lied and lied and lied for her.

Indiana, Kentucky, Tennessee, Georgia. We had left a Chicago ugly with soot-gray snow, but now we were leaving winter behind. I ate the bread and cheese I'd brought, and drank water. Maria nursed and slept through hour after long hour. I couldn't sleep. Sometimes tears ran down my cheeks, but I kept my face to the window and wiped them away. At last we were in Florida.

Thoughts of Gunther had followed me all the way from Chicago. I remembered his long fingers in my hair. "Your hair's like corn silk," he'd whispered. Spanish songs he'd taught me jangled in my head. "I could never satisfy my father," he had said over and over. "When I'm famous, he won't know." *Famous... famous...famous...*he had said that word often, mouthing it as if he were eating delectable food—yet he was often so tense, so anxious, as if he were a man steeling himself to dive from a cliff.

Forget him, I told myself, and turned my mind to my grandmother. What would she do when she found me on her doorstep with a baby? "I'm not married," I'd have to tell her, the same words my mother before me must have had to say.

My grandmother. I'd seen her only once, when I was fourteen and so scared, because my "stepfather" and "stepmother" were out of town. When Granny came, I was sitting in bed with my father's gun in my lap. I had finally nodded off beside the two girls and Rhody. Then somebody tapped on the door.

"Who's there?" I called softly through the dark, Rhody clutched in my arms. "I'll kill you. I've got a gun."

"Mary? It's your granny. Fine welcome I get. Where's your manners?"

I unlocked the door and the old lady came in. The other girls were asleep. I put on the light in the other room, and we shut the door behind us.

Granny was wearing a worn shirt and wrinkled pants, and she was worn and wrinkled herself. Her hair was dyed no earthly color and her face was sour. "So you're grown now," she said, and put a hand on my hair. "Look like your mama."

I had a hundred questions I wanted to ask her, but before I could begin, she said she wanted a drink of water. "Are those people you live with away?" she wanted to know. I said they were, and she dropped her false teeth in the glass of water, lay down on our old couch, and went to sleep.

Rhody and I went back to bed. When I woke in the morning, my "stepfather" and "stepmother" had come home and were yelling at my grandmother. My grandmother yelled back at them. Then she ran to where I was sleeping, stuffed an envelope under my blanket, and was gone. I hid it until I could run outside and look at it. Granny's address was on the envelope, and there was a fifty-dollar bill inside. I'd never seen so much money. I buried it in a bottle under the roots of a fallen tree, and wrote my grandmother to thank her, but no answer ever came.

Our last day on the bus passed so slowly. I remembered parts of poems from my college textbooks...stories of people who were homeless and alone, especially Tennyson's *Ulysses*, the wandering hero of Homer. *I am become a name for always roaming with a hungry heart.*

It was almost dark when we reached Kissimmee. I gave the driver the name of Granny's street, and he said he'd tell me when to get off. He stopped. I carried Maria down the steps. The bus rolled away. There I was with a suitcase and a backpack and a baby on the Irlo Bronson Highway.

The night was hot, with no breeze but the rush of cars passing. I'd run out of my food the day before, and felt faint as I walked beside the highway. "Can you tell me where Paris Street is?" I asked a mechanic at a gas station. He waved a greasy rag to show me. "Two blocks down."

I'd given my granny a glass of water once. She'd at least give me a drink. At least she'd want to see her great-grandchild. At least she might have a bed for us.

I found her place a block from the highway: a small, dark house. The corner streetlight shone on a yard littered with old furniture and crumpled boxes. I picked my way through the litter, put my suitcase down and rang the doorbell.

The house echoed the ring. No one came. I rang again and again, and heard nothing but the roar of highway traffic behind me, and the sound of tires on concrete as a teenaged boy cycled up the driveway next door. "Does Mrs. Bryant live in this house?" I called to him.

"Bryant?" the boy said, straddling his bike. "She died. Al Roger's bought the place now, but he's on vacation."

"Died?" I said in a faint voice. He didn't hear me; he'd ridden his bike out of sight. A door slammed somewhere; that was all.

I felt dizzy. My head ached. I couldn't stay there. I tried to think, but no thoughts would come as I carried Maria and my suitcase out to the bright neon lights again.

How hot it was. I walked along the highway, then turned off into a parking lot on a side street. Only one car was parked there, and someone had left the doors of the car unlocked. I put my suitcase and backpack in the front seat, and lay in the back seat with Maria. We'd rest for a little while. Then I'd have to find a motel…

10

"Wake up!" a woman's voice said in my ear. "Are you all right?"

Someone was leaning over me and shaking me. I mumbled that I was all right and tried to crawl out of the car with Maria. I almost fell. "Watch out!" a woman said, and took Maria from me. "It's lucky I came out here to shut the car windows. Come on."

I slung on my backpack, grabbed my suitcase and followed her. She unlocked a door, and I blinked as we entered a bright, cool room. A line of people behind a railing watched us as the woman gave me Maria, grabbed a pair of black revolvers from a chair in the corner, and said, "Sit down here. You don't look good. Do you want a drink?"

"Yes, thanks," I mumbled, and stared at the woman. She was splendid in satin and feathers; the skirt ruffles of her southern-belle dress swept the fancy carpet. Before she disappeared through a curtain, I saw her dress was split up the back and tied together. Under it she was wearing a T-shirt and jeans.

What was I doing in a Victorian parlor? A high-collared gentleman with a mustache and watch chain stared at me from his portrait above the fireplace. In another corner a bathtub, balanced on three lion-paw feet and a brick, stood against peeling wallpaper. People standing behind a railing were watching Maria and me.

"Here's a drink," the Victorian lady said, sweeping back through the curtain to hand me a can of cold pop. A fancy bar from some wild-west movie ran along another wall, littered with whisky bottles and decorated with WANTED posters and a life-sized painting of a woman draped on a couch. She wore nothing but three kittens playing in strategic places, and looked very bored.

My aching head made no sense of anything I saw. Suddenly a teen-aged girl pushed another curtain aside and stood awkwardly by one of the bar stools, pulling her black net stockings up to meet her short red satin skirt. The heels of her shoes were narrow and high. She teetered over to a mirror and yanked her feather boa away from her very low rhinestoned bodice.

Somebody in the crowd whistled, and someone else called: "Hey! Look at that!" Maria stirred in my arms; she'd be hungry before long.

Then a teenaged gunfighter sidled from behind another curtain, bewildered by the leather chaps he was trying to belt around him. When the Victorian lady came to help him, he tilted his broad-brimmed cowboy hat over one eye and grinned at the crowd.

"Loaded for bear," said a bearded young man, coming through a door to put a pistol in the gunfighter's belt. The gunfighter said, "Yeah!"

"Sit on the bar stool, please," the Victorian lady told the girl, who managed to climb up in spite of her spike-heeled shoes. The lady slid a garter on the girl's thigh, then slipped an ace of spades under it. The girl wriggled her behind on the bar stool and gave me a preoccupied stare.

"Get close to your light-o-love, now," the bearded man said to the gunfighter, and watched him jingle his spurs to the bar and put his spurred boot on the rail. "One hand around your shot glass and the other near your gun," the bearded man told him. "Rough times in the Old West."

"Yeah," the gunfighter said.

Someone in the crowd crooned, "Ooh, look at that!" as the Victorian lady crowned the girl with a headdress of black feathers. "Hold this," she told her, handing her a whisky bottle. "You've got to sell whisky. Give the bartender some business."

"And *you've* got to have money to interest the lady," the bearded man said to the fellow with the gun and the shot glass, and tucked a wad of fake cash half in, half out of the gunfighter's pocket. People in the crowd giggled.

"Turn a little this way...raise your chin...give him a come-hither smile..." The Victorian lady and the bearded man walked from one teenager to the other, until at last they stepped back and away.

The watching crowd hushed as sudden light blazed on the gaudy pair at the bar, their young hands hovering over a gun or gripping a whisky bottle. For a moment they looked out at me from another time, while the naked lady above them had seen it all, and was bored.

Then one flash after another fixed them there. The bearded man stepped away from his big camera on its tripod. "Done," he said, and suddenly all I saw was two embarrassed kids at a bar, kicking off boots and high heels and disappearing behind curtains.

"Are you feeling better?" The Victorian lady came to me. "We've been busy all night, but we'll close now." The crowd was leaving.

"I'm all right," I said, though I wasn't.

"Sorry about the rush at the end," the lady said. "They all decide they want pictures at the last minute. And the two of you came in as hot as fritters off a skillet, so the air conditioning's a shock."

"You take pictures," I said, stupidly.

"Old-time portraits. Good business. If it rains at Disney, the tour buses come to our mall, you bet. Tonight the mall had a vintage car drive. That's why folks were lined up for hours waiting for portraits. But now we're closing."

"We just got off a bus. I feel so faint..." I said, staring at guns hung in racks, and a garden of feathered and flowered hats clustered on hooks. The guns and hats began to revolve before my eyes in streaks...

The Victorian lady snatched Maria from me and pushed me back in my chair before I fell. "Put your head down on your knees," she said. I did. The fancy carpet began to steady under my shoes, and before long the big hats and racks of fancy guns stopped going in circles.

"You've been traveling for a while?" she said.

"Days," I said, still bent double. "From Chicago."

"With such a little baby?"

"I was going to look for a motel after we rested in your car," I said. "My grandmother lived near here on Paris Street, and I found her house, but a neighbor boy told me she was dead."

"Are you hungry?"

"I ate a little yesterday morning," I said.

"Oh, my," Colette said. "I'll see what's in our fridge." She came back with a small carton of milk and three plastic-wrapped sandwiches. "Have these while we I lock up," she said. She laid Marie in a basket of ruffled petticoats, and rustled away.

How good the food tasted; I ate it all while I heard whispers, and doors opening and shutting. When the lady came back, the bearded man was with her, and her satin and feathers were gone. She was just a small, tired woman about forty, wearing jeans and a T-shirt. She said, "I'm Colette Jordan, and this is my husband, Jack. There's a motel a block away. We'll get you a room. You're exhausted."

I'd decided to change my name again. "I'm Mary Homer, and my baby's Maria," I told them. They helped me out of my chair, turned out lights, locked doors and carried my backpack and suitcase to the motel. Colette held Maria while I signed my new name at the desk.

"Come over tomorrow morning for breakfast when you're feeling better," Jack said as he unloaded my luggage in the room. "We're at the Old Town Mall by eight. Look for our shop on John Thompson Avenue—it's called 'Instant Ancestors.'"

"Thank you both so much," I said. "You've been so kind."

They left, and I put Maria on the bed and looked around the clean, cool room. The dresser had big drawers; I pulled one out, laid its Bible on the bedside table, and padded the drawer with an extra blanket folded in a pillowcase.

Maria was awake and hungry, and cried in her dresser-drawer bed. I washed my face and hands and nursed her, changed her, and bathed her in the sink. When I put her in her drawer again, she was already fast asleep. I climbed into the shower and soaped my hair and myself, gulping water as it flowed down my face. The rush of water cooled the wild thoughts in my head: *Why did I leave him? How could I stay? How are we going to live?"*

When I was clean and cool, I washed our clothes and hung them on the shower rod, crawled in bed to thank heaven for Colette and Jack, read a comforting psalm in the Bible, and fell down a dark well of sleep.

Bright sun filled the room when I woke. I opened my eyes. The clock beside the bed said it was seven in the morning. Gunther wasn't beside me, but something was familiar in a strange room—Maria was calling me with her small cry that was half chicken-cackle and half hopeless grief. I brought her into my bed to nurse her, cuddling her close for comfort, smelling her clean baby smell.

To think that I didn't want you, I whispered to her. *Maria Homer, you're all I have now, and it seems as if we'll always be roaming with a hungry heart.* She stopped nursing for a moment, and opened her eyes. Gunther had been right: her eyes had changed, and were as blue as mine now: the one thing about her face that would hardly change in a lifetime. How thoughtful those eyes seemed: serious, intent, familiar, watching me.

Sunshine, and a blue-sky morning. I put on clean clothes, dressed Maria, and walked to Colette and Jack's big store. It filled a mall street corner with its show windows of fake-antiques for sale. A painting of Jack's bearded face decorated the swinging sign above the door: THE OLD TOWN PORTRAIT GALLERY.

Jack's real smile beamed at me behind the counters and glass cases. "How's the mama and how's the baby?" he said. "She looks happy. Must not have minded riding all the way from Chicago."

I felt a twinge of fear. Had I said "Chicago" the night before? "We're both much better, thanks to the two of you," I said.

"Hello!" It was Colette, coming from a back room with a muscular young man. "Did I tell you last night that we're the Jordans? And this is Clem Grover. He's a restaurant manager here, but he used to work for us, and he comes now and then to help us out. Says he *enjoys it.* Imagine."

Jack brought a clothesbasket lined with blankets for Maria, tucked her in it, and carried her down the block to Clem's restaurant with the rest of us. The salty-sweet smell of sausage frying made my stomach growl. "If tonight's as busy as last night..." Colette sighed. She was small and pretty; her hair was as brown as Jack's, but curly and thick. "What'll we do?"

Here came the loaded plates: stacks of hot, buttered toast... eggs...orange juice...I couldn't say a word, my mouth was watering so, but after a few bites I asked, "Could I possibly work for you?"

Jack looked at Colette. "Until Dianne comes next week, anyway? If she does? She didn't sound very interested in a job."

"Have you used a cash register?" Colette asked me.

"I've rung up sales at a hamburger place," I said.

"You'd have to talk to customers," Colette said.

"She'd be good at it with that smile," Jack said. "She could wear one of the Victorian outfits. Or maybe a bar girl?"

"But what about Maria?" I said.

"She's too little to be any trouble," Colette said. "Let her sleep in her basket behind the counter where you can watch her."

A week's work! I tried to pay for my breakfast, but Clem wouldn't let me. "Come to Instant Ancestors at seven tonight," Jack said.

I went back to the room with Maria, knowing that I could pay for my food, at least, and the motel. I was so relieved that I slept most of the afternoon when I wasn't feeding Maria. At six I ate at Clem's restaurant, promising to pay him when I had my first paycheck, then went to the Instant Ancestors shop. Maria was soon asleep in her basket behind the counter, and Colette gave me a quick lesson in ringing up sales.

"What will you wear tonight?" she asked afterward, and took me into the dressing rooms. Rows of costumes hung on hooks, and along a hall were little closets that held nothing but a seat, hooks and a curtain. "How about the blue satin bar girl?" Colette asked. "Take off your jeans and shirt. We make everyone put on one of these clean tank tops. Do you mind unbraiding your hair?"

I hung my clothes on a hook, freed my hair from its braid and pulled on the tank top. Colette lifted a short ruffled petticoat over my head, and then a velvet dress with a very low neck and a skirt short enough to show most of my legs in the black net stockings I pulled on. I looked around for a mirror. "We don't have mirrors in here," she said, reading my mind, "Except for the little one where you can put on your necklace and earrings. We do that so the customers don't fuss or want a change: they have to take our word when we tell them how good they look, and we do. Lots."

She handed me rhinestone earrings and necklace. My long hair fell down my back from a band around my head, crowned with a feather that danced every time I moved. "Wow," Clem said when I came out to the counter.

"Except for the shoes," I said, and showed him my sneakers.

"When you've stood behind the counter for a while, you'll bless them," he said.

The dinner hour was over. Shoppers roamed the mall streets and clustered outside our shop windows, or came to stare at the floor of our shop. Under the floor's wide, clear plastic surface lay hundreds of Instant Ancestor portraits of Indians, cowboys, Confederate generals, corseted ladies of the evening, and a big poster for the movie, *Sleeping With the Enemy*.

"My mother wrote that book," Jack said, joining me at the shop entrance. We walked over pictures of fellows in pinstriped suits with machine guns, and frontier Daniel Boones. The Roaring 'Twenties were there with a 'twenties roadster...a desperado in the tub having his back scrubbed by a floozy...a father with a gun scowling beside a groom and his padded-front bride. "Bet you've never seen a floor like that," Jack said to me.

We divided the work. Colette would costume the women, Clem would dress the men, Jack would take the pictures and print them, and I would ring up the money and try to sell frames. "When I give you the finished pictures, always put them in the big gilded frames before you show them to the customer," Jack told me. "Once they see how good their portraits look in that gold, they'll want those frames, nine times out of ten."

"Before it gets too frantic in here, take a little time to study the stuff in the showcases, will you?" Colette said to me. "Then keep watching for people who stop and look at them. If you're not ringing up sales, go up to folks at the cases...talk about what's there. You can tell them you're going to buy this or that toy for your brother, or some of the jewelry for you mother or sister...you know...give it a personal touch."

I walked along the showcases, picking out selling points of Indian headdresses, fake guns, glittering jewelry, plastic ladies in swirling skirts, staring china-headed Victorian dolls. The mall beyond the windows was growing dark with night coming. Street lamps and neon signs began to glow. "Can I answer your questions?" I asked customers as they came into the cool store from the hot street.

Soon curious families and pairs of lovers gathered in the store to watch, to dress, to pose, to pay. I made up my sales patter as I went along, but my mind was often on Gunther. Was he chasing me? Had he already flown to Florida and driven to Kissimmee... found this mall so close to my grandmother's house? Might he just happen to look in the window of Instant Ancestors...

82

No! I told myself, and kept myself busy with chatter. "How you feeling today?" I asked the crowd, using their southern talk. "You come a long way? Where you from?"

"Where *you* from?" one fellow said, looking as far down my bodice as he could. "Heaven?"

"Iowa," I said. The fellow laughed at that echo of an old movie and said, "Figures."

Jack heard me. "You're not from Chicago?" he asked, going by with a pile of portrait frames. "Iowa? We're from Iowa."

The night was hot, but fierce air-conditioning kept the crowd from leaving. "The colder they get, the more they feel like putting on costumes," Colette said. I shivered in my skimpy dress, but Colette had the worst of it in the small dressing rooms crowded with hot bodies. Her thick hair stuck to her forehead; she slumped on a barrel beside Marie's basket to drink a bottle of water.

"You might like me to change places with you for a while," I asked. "You can work at the counter where it's cool. Could I learn to dress the women and girls?"

Colette sighed and considered. "Maybe you can," she said. "It's not easy. They've already chosen the time period they want, so tell them they're not allowed to change their minds. You have to be tactful. Sometimes I tell them the costumes they want are being repaired, or are in the wash. Put the fat ones in dark colors with interesting necklines—the light colors are for the skinny ones. Be sure they put on a clean tank top first, or they'll soak the costumes. When they pose for Jack, you can take turns with him, giving them extra little props: purses, fans, pretty pins, another flower on their hat, long gloves, rings—make the whole thing exciting. That's what they're really buying: the thrill. Dressing up. Being somebody else, like a movie star. It has to be a performance. The rest of them are watching, and you want to entertain them and make them want to do it, too."

I was glad to disappear into the dressing rooms. All day, busy as I was, I'd thought of Gunther. I remembered the desperate look he had sometimes. He'd said so often: *I count on you. You're the heart of everything.* But why would he follow me? He couldn't leave his classes. He had a wife. Why would he ever be among the crowds at Old Town, catching sight of me in my satin and feathers at a brightly-lit counter?

But now I was hidden in the hot dressing room lined with costumes. Half-nude, barefooted women pulled tank tops over their heads. I tied costumes at their backs: beaded flapper dresses...Annie-Get-Your-Gun fringed leather jackets...ribboned bloomers...checked gingham from the frontier...chin-high Victorian blouses with leg-o-mutton sleeves...hoop-skirts for the southern belles...

Some of them smelled awful. Some of them were babies, or toddlers: we had clothes for them, too. Little boys brandished their firearms. Little girls in shirts and shorts changed to Alices in Wonderland, standing patiently to be dressed in clothes of another century.

I put parasols in some hands, whisky bottles in others, and settled great feathered hats on their heads, or homespun sun-bonnets...curling feathers...beaded Indian headbands...flapper helmets. Skinny young girls needed padding. Fat ladies needed big fans. Praise and flattery, jokes, bits of made-up history—I did my best to follow Jack's lead. He was a master. Word by word, prop by prop, he drew whole families into the past. When I held up their portraits in gold frames, there they were, caught in the bright colors that such people would have had in the past, if any lens could have caught them.

At last, hanging up a batch of costumes, putting used tank tops in the bin, I realized the rush was over. The store was empty. It was eleven o'clock.

Had I done good work? I helped clean up and didn't ask; we were all too tired to talk. "Goodnight!" I called as I left with Maria. "Thanks for the job!"

"Thanks!" Colette called from the dressing room. "You saved our lives. See you tomorrow morning for breakfast!"

There was a breeze when I stepped into the street and walked to the motel with sleeping Maria. Just before I reached the motel drive, I saw a car coming from the Parkway. A streetlight showed me the faces inside—

Gunther and Neola.

Their faces seemed to hang before my eyes forever, and yet in a second or two I backed up in the dark, and ran for the Old Town Mall.

84

I ran back, clutching Maria, to pound on the gallery door.

11

Gunther! Neola! I ran to the mall and tried the door of "Instant Ancestors." It was locked. I pounded on it until Clem saw me through the window and let me in. "There are people chasing me!" I cried. "They're passing my motel, and they might go in! Can you call the motel and tell them to say they've never seen me?"

Clem didn't ask questions; he grabbed the phone, punched keys and said, "Gary? Listen—a party may come into your place in a minute or two and ask if you've seen a woman with a baby. They're after Mary Homer, who's staying with you. Say you've never seen Mary or the baby, will you? Act like you don't know a thing."

Hide…hide…I ran into the small, dark dressing room with Maria, and pressed my face in a ruffled petticoat on a hook. Jack, Clem and Colette followed me. "What's the matter?" Colette asked.

Maria was crying; she was hungry, and I was holding her too tight. "It's my ex-husband and his wife!" I said. "I can't let them find me, ever!"

"We'll turn out our lights, just in case they come looking here at Old Town," Jack said. "Folks may remember you're working for us."

"But we're always the last place in Old Town to close. They won't find anybody to ask," Colette said. "Don't worry. How'll they know you're here if Gary doesn't tell them, and he won't."

"Yes! Yes! Thanks!" I said. The shop went from light to dark. "These people aren't dangerous, are they?" Colette asked. "Guns. Anything like that?"

"I can't imagine they'd want to hurt anyone," I said. "I can't even imagine why they've come all the way from Chicago. He married me in a fake wedding, and then married her...I came here to stay with my grandmother." There I stood, nursing Maria among the costumes in that smelly little room, and crying.

"What a dirty sneak," Colette said.

The phone rang. Clem answered it, listened, and said, "Okay. Thanks." He came to the dressing room. "Gary says a man and woman did come in his place to ask about Mary. He told them what I told him to say, and they've driven off."

"We'd better stay here a little while," Colette said. "Mary shouldn't go right to the motel, should she? They might play a trick and come back."

All of us were very tired. I nursed Maria while we sat on chairs in the dark. "I don't know why he'd come after me—he's married to her," I said. "And why would *she* want to find me?"

"Maybe you've got something they want?" Clem said.

"Diapers?" I said. "Old clothes? A fake diamond and wedding ring?"

"The baby?" Clem asked. "He wants his child?"

"Maria? Well, yes, he does love her," I said.

"Maybe his wife can't have children, and she wants Maria because at least Maria's his daughter," Jack said.

"His wife came to our apartment and called me awful names," I said. "She threw a newspaper on the floor. It had their wedding picture in it."

"And you never knew? Never had a suspicion?" Clem said.

"No." I was crying again. "We'd had a nice wedding in Mexico, but I never met anyone but a friend of his who was his best man, and the priest who 'married' us." I wiped my eyes on Mary's blanket. "I was so dumb, so trusting! We went back to Chicago and a little rented apartment, and were both going to the university, but I couldn't—I had to stay in bed to keep from losing the baby. I thought that was why we never met any of his friends, but then the baby came..."

"Let me get this straight," Jack said. "You had a fake wedding?"

"He admitted it after his wife pushed her way into my apartment to tell me, and see Maria. He loves me—I know he does. And I love him...or at least I did."

"Then maybe…" Colette said, "this wife of his has some hold on him?"

"She's got money," I said.

We sat for a while in the dark, listening to the Parkway traffic.

"He can't leave his graduate work very long," I said. "If they can't find me in a day or two, I think they'll go home."

"I'll ring Gary again and ask him if the coast is clear," Clem said. He called. Gary told him he hadn't seen anyone around.

"Then I'll go, and let you get some sleep," I said. "And thanks for staying so late, and hiding us."

I said goodnight and went to the motel. I shut the window-blinds tight, and tried to relax as I bathed Maria and put her in her dresser-drawer bed, but I couldn't sleep.

Neola hated me. *Stay away from my husband! Go home to that shack in Nebraska.* And Gunther didn't want me—he'd married Neola when I was having his baby! They'd come to steal Maria? What other reason was there?

I shivered in my bed. They were after Maria. And…close to me…perhaps only a few miles away…Gunther was lying in Neola's arms.

The next day, and for days afterward, I could hardly eat or sleep. Gunther's face through a car's windshield—I saw it in my mind, over and over. And Neola sat beside him. At night every footstep that passed my motel room terrified me, as if I were a child again, staying on watch, clutching my father's gun.

Jack and Colette understood why I wanted to work hidden in their shop's dressing room with Maria in the corner—I had to have her always in sight.

A week went by. I felt safer. I began to work behind the counter again, dressed as a Victorian lady, or a frontier cowgirl, or a flapper from the roaring 'twenties. I sold frames and took money and costumed women and children.

The Jordans were short-handed. "Finding good people to work for us is the hardest part of this business," Colette told me one morning over breakfast. "We can't pay as much as a lot of stores do, but that isn't the only problem. It takes a special kind of employee to do our work."

I held my breath, afraid I was being fired, but Colette said, "That's why you're such a godsend to us right now. You're from

Iowa, maybe that's the reason. You do a good day's work. You want to learn. You come on time, don't drink, don't do drugs—"

"I'm not really from Iowa. I'm from Nebraska," I said. "But my grandmother was from Iowa."

"Good enough," Colette said. "Can you keep on with us? We don't mind having the baby in the store, she's so good. It's hard work, but you like it, don't you?"

"I do," I said. "And you've been so kind to me. But here's my problem: I need two jobs to pay all my expenses. How can I work two jobs with a baby?"

"Let me talk to Jack," Colette said.

We worked a long, hard, late Saturday: crowds, cold air, hot lights, bodies to be dressed and undressed. It was after midnight when we closed the store and stood on the mall street in a fresh breeze.

"Jack and I wonder if you'd like to have a second job with us—work every morning when business is slow," Colette said. "You'd be mending costumes. I haven't had time to sew for a month, and our repair pile is huge. Can you sew?"

"I've used a friend's sewing machine," I said, remembering Sophy's lessons. "Nothing fancy, but I can certainly mend."

"Great!" Jack said. We'll start you tomorrow on double pay."

So I mended costumes every morning, slowly working to the bottom of the heap. I sorted some into my mending pile, and put others in a second pile to be sent through the shop's washer and dryer. Maria slept in her basket beside me as the sewing machine thrummed. I began to feel almost safe. I had enough money. I could sleep at night.

Rhody was always in my thoughts. I called her over and over, until finally she answered. I asked her about school, about her sisters, about her mother and father. She only answered Yes or No in a small, cold voice.

"Maria likes it here," I said. "She reminds me of you every minute."

"You never come."

"And now I have two jobs and twice the money. I'll be coming for you before you know it."

I couldn't tell her I was hiding, but I asked her if anyone had come to Plattsburg looking for me. She said No.

I told her I loved her. She hung up.

One morning Colette pushed her chair back after we ate breakfast, and smiled at me. "Business is slow this week. Why don't the two of us and Maria take a day off? We never celebrated your birthday—you're nineteen! Let's go to Epcot! It's just a few miles away and you've never been there. They give us cheap tickets."

"Oh, yes!" I said.

Colette helped me dress Maria in her little blue shirt and pants. "You'll be as pretty as your mama," she told her. "Beautiful blonde hair. Beautiful blue eyes."

We drove to Epcot in the bright Florida sunshine, left the car in the parking lot, and went to turnstiles that crowds were streaming through. I carried Maria, and Colette carried the baby bag of diapers and blankets and wipes and bottles of water.

Disney's Spaceship Earth loomed over us, an immense silvery-gold ball. When I stopped gawking at it and looked around me, Colette was gone. Then I saw her, wheeling a rented baby carriage for Maria.

I must have looked frightened, for Colette said, "Let's agree on a place to meet, just in case we're separated. How about that rental place over there where I got the baby carriage?" We put Maria in her rolling bed and turned our backs on the huge silvery ball.

"What should we see first?" Colette asked, unfolding a map. We looked at it together. "It's your birthday party," she said. "You choose."

"The World Showcase!" I said.

So the three of us strolled in and out of famous buildings that had, as if by magic, lost the cracks and stains of centuries and shrunk to a fraction of their size. A scarlet temple gate from China…the Venetian campanile and Doge's Palace I'd seen in my textbooks… the Eiffel Tower…China's Temple of Heaven—even the "Mexico Pavilion." "I don't want to go in that one," I told Colette. "I've had enough of Mexico to last me the rest of my life."

How beautiful the "World" was—so old, and yet so new, shining in the sunshine around a blue lake.

I bought Colette an enameled bracelet she admired at a shop in "China." She said that my gift was too expensive, but I said: "What if you and Jack hadn't taken me in? You saved us!"

Lunch in Canada. A snack in Italy. Strolling players. Marching bands. "We'll have supper at a French restaurant," Colette said as we sat on a bench among flowerbeds.

After a while I thought Maria was hungry. "She's beginning to fuss," I said. "I'll feed her in the women's restroom over there."

"I'll meet you across the road at that soda fountain, and we'll have something cool to drink," Colette said.

There was another woman nursing a baby in the restroom. The four of us sat in companionable silence, our eyes closed, the babies hard at work. By the time I changed Maria, she was asleep.

When I came from the restroom with Maria, her baby carriage waited by the door. I put her in it, then turned to rummage in the bag of diapers and bottles on my shoulder. I turned back to the carriage—Maria was gone—

Ben Carlos!

Ben Carlos stood there with Maria in his arms!

I yelled "Ben!" and tried to take Maria from him, but he wouldn't let me. I had to follow him as he hurried away, leaving her carriage on the sunny path, her blanket hanging on the handle. I looked frantically for Colette, but she wasn't in sight. "Colette!" I yelled. "Colette!" People were all around me, listening to my screams, but none of them was Colette.

I kept close to Ben. What else could I do? The three of us looked like a family, and Ben was trying to make it seem that way. He carried Maria through strolling sightseers—he was a father with his small baby and his white-faced wife. At the edge of a crowd he stopped, holding Maria close, his black hair glinting in the Florida sun. "You'll have to trust me," he said. His dark brown eyes were stern.

I was afraid to say a word—if I made him angry, or shouted for help, he'd run away with Maria, before anyone could stop him.

We hurried past "Italy." Colette and I had leaned on a counter there only an hour or two before, admiring the Murano glass.

We passed the "Biergarten" of Germany; I heard the dancers in lederhosen stamping.

The Chinese gate—I had bought Colette's bracelet there. We went by "Norway" and "Mexico." Ben was heading for Spaceship Earth and the entrance plaza. He was almost running as I followed him into a covered passageway. A crowd of Japanese tourists was entering it behind us.

Gunther! I saw him, and gasped. Gunther was there! He stood against the sunshine of the Plaza ahead, then stepped into the light, and cries met him as he appeared: "There's Risling!"

"Get him!"

"Mr. Risling!"

Ben backed into the tunnel with me. Cameras aimed at Gunther. What was going on? The Japanese tourists around me didn't know, either, but they were taking pictures of whatever it was, right at my shoulder. "Gunther!" Ben yelled, and Gunther whirled and ran to us. The three of us and Maria pushed through the Japanese crowd, ran down the passageway, and sprinted past families, flowerbeds, and through an open door.

Shouts followed us. Someone yelled, "This way! They went this way!"

I raced after Gunther and Ben through one door and then another, past supply trolleys...workers in their Walt Disney shirts...surprised stock men...

"There they are!" shouted someone behind us. Ben took a flight of stairs two at a time with Maria tight in his arms and Gunther at his heels. We ran through a door at the top. A crowd was moving past, and the four of us were carried along.

"Blasting off!" a loudspeaker announced.

"Come on!" Ben said. "They won't be able to get us in this crowd!" People closed us in and carried us with them to a car. Gunther and I and Ben with Maria fastened seat belts, and the ride began—we seemed to be shooting through space, stars, planets—I shut my eyes and held my breath. A voice talked of "Jules Verne's cannonball flight to the moon," and told us we would see what no one had ever seen before our time on the world's largest picture screen.

Gunther's warm body pressed close to me, and his face was inches from mine: the handsome face and gleaming blue eyes, and a mouth I had kissed hundreds of times. He tried to take my hand, he tried to kiss me, but I leaned against Ben, as far away from Gunther as I could get. I was in my own "car of the future" now. I didn't want to kiss Gunther, or hold him, or be anywhere he was. Ever.

At last the ride was over, and the crowd surrounded us as went out to sunlit trees and sidewalks. "Give Maria to me!" I begged Ben.

Ben pulled me between a wall and some flowering bushes. "They're out there," he whispered. I looked through leaves and saw cameramen.

"This way," Ben whispered, and pushed through the bushes to another walk. As I ran beside Ben with Maria in his arms, I said, "What's the matter? Tell me!"

Gunther followed us as we ran. I kept asking questions. Ben wouldn't answer me. Neither would Gunther. We were out of breath. Maria began to cry.

"Get in here," Gunther said, and we stood in an angle of a wall, almost hidden, crowded close to a bench and a diorama labeled "The City of Tomorrow."

"Give her to me," Gunther said, trying to take Maria from Ben.

"No!" Ben cried. The men glared at each other.

"Give her to *me*!" I said, putting my bag full of baby equipment on the bench.

Maria was howling. "She's hungry," Gunther said.

I gave him a disgusted look. "She's not hungry. She's wet."

"I'll put her down on the bench," Ben said. "Don't either of you try to grab her. I'm holding her arms. You'll hurt her."

I found that she'd made a mess. "Maria…Maria," Gunther crooned, bending to kiss her. "Your mother took you away from me."

Anger shot through me, so fierce that I shook. I held a dirty diaper in my hand. Before Gunther could duck, I smeared the diaper on his startled face, wishing it were acid, not a yellow-brown mess, and I yelled: "She's mine! She's my *bastard*! I was your *whore*! Neola said so, and she ought to know—she's your *wife*!"

Oh, I was pleased to see Gunther's face! He looked so funny that I actually laughed when he cried, "I love you! I'm going to marry you—really marry you—as soon as I can get a divorce—"

"Do you think I'd *ever* marry you?" I yelled while Gunther wiped his face with a clean diaper. "A man who lied to me? Seduced me?" Gunther said nothing. I cleaned and diapered Maria while Ben held her small hands tight. When I finished I tried to take her, but Ben held her arms, and I had to let her go or hurt her.

There was martial music in the air. People were gathering near the wall we hid behind. "Photographers after you?" Ben said to Gunther. "Maybe the law! What do you think you're doing? Get out of here!"

I sobbed as I ran. I'd lost Maria.

Suddenly marching men with flashing brass and stamping boots were upon us. Ben gave Gunther a last appalled look and ran with Maria in front of the parade ranks, so close that the trombones almost hit him.

Gunther and I couldn't follow him; rows of red coats and stern faces made a moving wall. We couldn't break through. We couldn't go around.

The marching men sang, "The Girl I Left Behind Me" as they passed the three of us. Ben and Maria were out of sight when the marchers were gone.

Gunther said, "You'll have to trust me."

"Trust you?" I shouted.

"Come on," Gunther said. "There's only one way out of here. We'll get to the entrance before he does." We ran in and out of crowds, sprinting toward Spaceship Earth far across the lake. All at once a solid wall of people were in our path: a tour group, blocking the walk. I dodged along one side of the crowd; Gunther ran around the other. When the mass of people was behind me, I looked this way and that way, hunting for Gunther. He was gone, and so was Ben—and Maria! Gone.

12

I wanted to scream and howl as I stood with nothing in my arms but a backpack. The sky was darkening as lights began to glow. I raced toward the Plaza, sobbing softly as I ran. I'd lost Maria. Two men could hide her from me, perhaps forever.

I don't know how long I sat hunched on a bench at the Epcot entrance, watching every person leaving through the turnstiles as night fell.

Suddenly Ben was there with Maria!

I jumped up to grab her, but Ben wouldn't let me. "Come on!" he said, and I had to follow him through an exit turnstile, and climb into a tram bound for the parking lots.

Ben wouldn't talk to me. I panted behind him, shouting questions, begging for Maria. We left the tram, and he carried her along the ranks of parked cars. He never looked back; he knew I would stay close behind.

He found his car, opened the passenger side door for me, and slid behind the wheel with Maria. "Give her to me!" I cried, but he only flipped a switch to lock me in, and drove away with one hand on the wheel. We had barely cleared the parking lot when another car, parked at a curb, drove into our path so suddenly that we hardly stopped in time. Gunther jumped from the car and ran toward us, yelling.

Cars were waiting in our lane, but there was a gap in the other lane's traffic. Ben swerved around Gunther's car, swerved back. Gunther left his car and ran after us. We left him behind, his car blocked by other cars.

I kept looking back as we sped down a highway. Could Colette have seen us and followed? Was Gunther in one of the cars in the line behind us?

Ben drove fast, steering with one hand. "Where are we going?" I kept asking him. Lights of approaching cars lit his high cheekbones and black hair as he glanced at me, but never spoke.

Suddenly he swerved into a parking lot, turned off his headlights, and hid us among the dark cars. "Why do you want Maria?" I asked, trying to see his face in the shadows.

"I'm doing this for your sake," he said. "And Maria's. And Gunther's." For a moment he laid his cheek against Maria's blonde hair and whispered, "Our poor baby girl. Mixed up in this."

"Mixed up in what?" I asked, but he didn't answer, but pulled out of the dark lot to the highway again. I watched his grim profile as we drove in heavy traffic, mile after mile, then entered an expressway. Airport signs began to appear, and then the airport's flowerbeds and lights. Ben took a lot ticket, pulled into a parking space and said, "Follow me" as he left the car, Maria in his arms.

We entered the airport in silence, and hurried silently through the crowds. Ben's dark eyes looked in every direction as signs told me where we were going: to the international gates.

We were leaving the country.

I trotted beside Ben. My mind traveled faster than my feet—should I run to some guard and tell him, "This man is kidnapping me and my baby"?

How could I prove it? I couldn't even prove who I was. I didn't have a driver's license...

I didn't have a passport.

No passport. Ben stepped up to a counter and smiled at the woman behind it, and she smiled back at the father with his baby. He could say Maria was his! He could leave me behind! I opened my mouth to yell, but Ben put two passports on the counter. When the woman opened the second one, she looked from it to me, and back again. It was my passport! I had left it behind when I ran away from Gunther and Chicago.

"We don't have a passport for the baby yet," Ben told the woman. "But I was told her birth certificate would be enough."

He had Maria's birth certificate? The woman looked it over, handed the documents to Ben and let us walk through.

We were leaving the country.

I sat on a chair by the gate and put my hands over my face.

"I'm sorry," Ben said, sitting beside me with Maria in his arms. "You have to go with me, but you won't lose Maria." He looked down at her. "I'd never seen her until today. She's so healthy. What a beautiful child."

"Can't you tell me anything? Explain anything?" I said. "Where are we going? Acapulco?"

"The two of you will be safe there."

"Safe from whom? Safe from what?" I cried. The chairs in front of the gate were almost all empty. The few people sitting there looked at us: we were a family having an argument.

Ben got up with Maria. "We're boarding, and they're taking children first."

"How will I ever get home again?" I said. "What will my friends in Florida do when I've disappeared with Maria? I haven't even got my passport, or money!"

"You'll have to trust me," he said. He had said those words before that afternoon. So had Gunther. "I'm sorry. That's all you can do."

He was right—all I could do was follow him to my seat in the plane and buckle myself in. "Now you can have Maria," Ben said, and put her in my arms. She was wrapped in a blanket I had embroidered in the little Chicago apartment I loved...with the husband I loved...

The great plane lifted from the runway. I was shivering in my hot-weather shirt and shorts and sandals I had worn to Epcot that morning, walking with Colette in the sunshine. Ben said, "You're cold" and covered me with a blanket. He tucked a pillow behind my head. "It's a long flight. See if you can sleep a while."

We were thousands of feet in the air: no one could take Maria away. I fell asleep in a breath or two, wrapped in the blanket and the engine drone. Ben woke me when food arrived, and I ate everything, famished, and fed Maria, and slept again.

When I woke, Ben was asleep. Maria lay in his lap, her face half hidden in his shirt, and she made a little sucking sound in her sleep now and then, as if the warmth of his body promised her milk.

Ben's long eyelashes shone in the plane's overhead lights. Relaxed in his sleep, he might have been an actor playing some Spanish nobleman—he only needed a black mustache and a little beard to make him a "Don Carlos." His eyebrows had a curious lift: they arched, then feathered downward, as black as his dense black hair.

Maria kept a tight hold on Ben's silk shirt in her sleep. The leather of his shoes gleamed, and his suit was fine wool. He wore a gold ring with a crest on it, and when he half woke, his ringed hand moved over Maria to cradle her tighter against him. Every movement of his, every glance, every word he said puzzled me.

Hour by hour, I asked Ben questions he wouldn't answer. I ate the food. I fed Maria. The stewardesses hovered over us, admiring "such a good baby," and admiring Ben, too: I saw that. "Her daddy's in love with her, you can tell," one of them said.

I didn't look at Ben, and pretended I hadn't heard.

When at last we descended to Acapulco, Spanish chatter surrounded me once more. I had taken this same route with Gunther; we had gone through customs and walked into the Mexican sun, lovers waiting for our wedding day.

"Are we going to your apartment?" I asked Ben as we drove off in a taxi. I kept my voice low. "First I had a fake marriage in this place. Now I'm forced out of my new life and kidnapped back here. Can you imagine how I hate Acapulco, and Mexico?" I glared into his eyes. "And Gunther? And you?"

"You haven't been kidnapped," Ben whispered back. "You've been taken out of danger." He stared back at me over Maria's fuzzy head. "I didn't want that wedding. You saw how I fought against it. Gunther and I almost ruined our long friendship over it. I couldn't stop him."

"But why did he do it? Because I was young and poor and didn't have anyone to protect me? Because you didn't want a bride like that for him. He did it to spite you?"

"Who wouldn't want to be married to you?" Ben said. I barely heard him over the sounds of the taxi and the traffic. "He pretended to marry you in order to keep you. If he'd asked you to be his mistress, what would you have said?

"No!"

"Exactly."

I turned from Ben to watch the city from my window. There was the beautiful view again; I remembered Gunther's voice close to my ear: "Punta Diamante." Everything was changed for me now, but the Pacific was still as blue, the hotels were brilliant in the sun, and beaches were still swept by the same constant surf.

The taxi let us out at Ben's apartment house. "I'm sorry," Ben said as we went in. "It's the best I can do, this apartment. I've tried to have it ready for you." He handed Maria to me. "I live near the hospital now."

"You can't be sorry for me," I said, hugging Maria to me at last. "If you were sorry for me at all, I wouldn't be here. You've done what Gunther wanted. You've taken his 'mistress' and his 'illegitimate child' out of his new wife's way, haven't you? Out of the country!"

"I have to explain what's happened to you. Will you and Maria come to dinner with me tonight?"

"Dinner?" I said. "How can I? A dirty shirt and shorts—"

"Explore the apartment when I've gone," Ben said. "I hope you'll find everything you need. I'll come back at seven."

He closed the apartment door behind him, and then—to my horror—I heard a key turn in the lock.

"Ben!" I shouted, but there was no answer but the sound of his steps going downstairs and out. The door was locked; I put Maria on the couch and yanked at the door, pounded on it.

I was locked in. My jailer had the key. I was in prison with Maria. I looked in every drawer and closet for a telephone. There were none.

At least I could keep Ben out: I fastened the door's two chains. I shot the bolt.

We were trapped. But I had Maria. I picked her up and told her: "You're back where you began." I turned to look at the apartment, expecting to see the same worn rug, the swaybacked couch...

No. My frantic rush to find a telephone had blinded me to the rugs that were new and thick...new furniture...fresh flowers in vases everywhere. The kitchen had new paint, new appliances, and every new saucepan had a lid. Someone had bought a half-dozen mixing bowls. The new refrigerator was stocked with food.

How I hated to go in that bedroom! But our wedding-night bed was gone. Fine furniture stood on a new rug. I put Maria in a pretty pink crib. Stacks of diapers and baby clothes were piled on a changing table. "Maria," I said to the little girl kicking her feet in her new crib, "somebody's given you a new wardrobe."

I found the bathroom was all new, and there were rows of creams and sprays and soaps on the counter. Maria fell asleep, and I washed my hair and myself in the new shower. I'd have to put on my dirty clothes again, unless there was a bathrobe somewhere...

I opened the closet near sleeping Maria. A note was taped to a shelf edge: "MARY: Gunther gave me sizes for your clothes. Hope you can bear to wear these."

Astonished, I reached out to touch new dresses, blouses, skirts, swimsuits, robes, nightgowns, coats. I looked at the labels: the clothes were my size. So were the shoes, sandals and slippers still in their boxes. Drawers in the closet held stockings and frilly underwear.

A whole wardrobe. Enough for a long stay.

I sat doubled up on the bed, holding my still-damp hair in both hands. A long stay...sleeping with Gunther? Sleeping with Ben?

I put on some of the new underwear. I would do that. I put on my shirt and shorts and sandals again, and washed clothes. I bathed Maria and fed her. I waited, walking up and down, up and down.

At seven there was a tap on the door, and a key turned in the lock—Ben. My lock and bolt and the two chains stopped him. He set his weight against them, but they held.

I put my mouth close to the door crack. "I'm not going out," I said.

For a moment there was silence. Then his voice came close to the door crack, too, so that our mouths were only inches apart. "You're not feeling well?" he asked. "Is Maria all right?"

"We're well."

"Did you find everything you need? I did what I could on short notice. Can't I take you to dinner?" He shoved against the door again.

"Not until I know what I have to do in return for the clothes and furniture and food and flowers," I said.

"Do?" He sounded puzzled.

"I've been tricked into being a mistress once. That's enough."

Again there was silence on the other side of the door. Then a voice came through so heavy with scorn that I could hardly recognize it.

"Do you think I have no honor?" it said. "That I'd take the woman my best friend entrusted to me? The woman he loves?"

I could feel my face grow hot. "Honor? A man who'd take a woman and her baby—against her will—thousand of miles away from home? Lock her in like a prisoner…like a concubine…his property? His and his friend's *property*?"

"Gunther…and… I…want…to…keep…you…safe." The cold voice spaced out the words as if I wouldn't listen or couldn't understand.

"Safe?" I cried. "I want to be safe from you and Gunther! I'm not married to either of you, thank heaven, and I'd thank heaven if I never saw either of you again. I want to go *home*. I want to go home *with Maria*. I don't believe that 'safe' of yours. I don't trust Gunther and I don't trust you—why should I? I don't trust that 'honor' of yours!"

There was no answer but the click of a key turned in a lock. His steps went down the stairs and out.

When I ran to a window, I saw him. He was dressed in a dark suit and white shirt. He threw flowers in the back seat of his car and drove away.

13

Night in a strange country. I ate some fruit and drank milk and crawled in bed beside Maria's crib. Lying in the dark, I remembered a bridal bouquet hanging above me. Sounds from the street were the sounds I remembered: the windows were in the same places, and the walls and doors stood around me: the same, the same, the same.

How could I sleep? At dawn I sat hunched over coffee at the kitchen table. I'd made my best dinners in that kitchen for two men who spoke in Spanish. What had they said to each other in their language while they smiled at me and praised my cooking? *How stupid she is!* Was that what they said? *What a trusting fool!*

Maria woke. Her chirps and gurgles reached me where I sat with my face in my hands. I fed her and bathed her and talked to her, pretending that such a little baby could understand. Whenever her eyes met mine, they startled me a little, as if I saw something in them...did she have my mother's eyes?

I was diapering her when I heard someone unlock the door, then shove against the bolt and chains. "Mary!" Ben called.

"What do you want?"

"Let me talk to you. Please."

One by one I undid the chains and bolt. There he stood in blue jeans and shirt. "May I come in?" he asked.

I turned my back on him and went to the bedroom to finish diapering Maria. Ben didn't follow me; he sat on the living room couch like an acquaintance paying a polite visit.

"Have you had breakfast?" he asked when I joined him. I

shook my head. "No?" he said. "Would you make one for us? I'll help."

"You bought the food," I said.

He set the table. He poured the juice. He buttered the toast. We ate the scrambled eggs and bacon without speaking, until Ben said, "You've been chased and frightened and brought here, and you don't know what any of the reasons are."

"Explain, then," I said as we sat down in the living room with our coffee. "If you can." He eyed my shirt and shorts. I hoped he understood why I wore them.

"I have to start with Gunther." Ben looked out the window, not at me. "I think you've seen how driven he is. I've known him since he was six, and he's never changed: he's still determined to do what's never been done."

"Yes," I said.

"Ambitious." Ben sounded as if he were talking to himself. "And his father was behind him, always pushing, very proud. Very cruel. I've watched him beat Gunther. I can't forget that. I couldn't do anything—not against a grown man. Have you seen a child abused?"

"Yes," I said, thinking of Rhody, a hungry, screaming baby who nobody wanted but me.

"Gunther didn't want to be a doctor. He fought with his father, and his father cut off his money. Gunther ran away to Chicago to go into microbiology. Before long Gunther was the premier student in the department, and the dean of the science faculty was impressed. He saw to it that Gunther got grants…was able to start graduate work. And this dean had a daughter named Neola."

Neola was there in my memory: long black hair, furious eyes. *Stay away from my husband!*

"Imagine what Gunther was up against," Ben said. "He had to have Dean Rand behind him, because what he wanted to do was illegal. Work with embryos horrifies many people, so the government gives them what they want: laws."

Ben got up and walked back and forth. "And Neola wanted Gunther," he said. "I suppose it looked like the perfect answer for Gunther: marry the daughter of a man who could protect him and back up his research—and had plenty of money. Wouldn't a father-in-law stand by you? So Gunther and Neola were engaged.

106

But then, against his best interest, Gunther fell in love with you."

I gave Ben a bitter look. "He said he did."

"He did, believe me. So there he was: trapped. How could he jilt Neola when their fancy wedding was already planned and the Dean was calling him 'My future son-in-law'?"

"So he loved me, but he married her."

"I fought it," Ben said. "You must have seen how I fought, even if you couldn't understand our Spanish. You were exactly what he was looking for: a poor woman with no family to speak of who needed money. He brought you here to Acapulco in spite of everything I said—"

"You knew!" I cried. "You knew he was lying to me! How can you talk about your honor? The two of you enjoyed the joke, didn't you? He'd found a woman dumb enough to never suspect—"

"No!" Ben said, his dark eyes glistening with anger. "It wasn't funny. It wasn't honorable. He'd told me he'd given up marrying Neola, and would marry you. Then— the very first night you were here—he sat in this room and said he'd decided to give you a fake wedding and marry Neola. You saw how we argued, I think."

He saw the scorn in my eyes. I jumped up and stood at the window with my back to him.

"You were so innocent," he said. "So happy." His voice had shame in it. "You brought your wedding dress! So trusting. I tried and tried to change his mind, but he wouldn't listen. All I could do was give you the most romantic wedding I could."

I wouldn't answer him.

"He's my friend, but he's...wild with ambition," Ben said. "And he married Neola when he went back to Chicago! I couldn't believe it. He had to have his father-in-law behind him. And then Neola found out about you."

"How?" I said. "Gunther hid me away. I never met a single person he knew—of course I didn't!"

"Neola isn't just her father's daughter, she's her mother's daughter. Her mother's big, rich family has its thumbs in every Chicago pie. She has two brothers who never liked Gunther; they'll damage him in any way they can if he plays around. When Neola began to suspect that Gunther had a..." Ben hesitated. "...a love somewhere, she had you investigated. Her brothers had Gunther followed. Gunther didn't know it."

I kept my back to him as I said: "She called me a trucker's daughter and a hamburger joint waitress...I thought Gunther had told her about me. And when I called him, he admitted we weren't married."

"You left him," Ben said. "Of course. He chased you to Kissimmee because he knew your grandmother had lived there."

"But Neola was with him," I said.

For a moment I thought Ben hesitated, as if to choose his words carefully. "Neola wanted to hear Gunther tell you, face-to-face, that he couldn't see you any more. She insisted on that, I think—that's why she came with him. And maybe Gunther was going to warn you about Neola's brothers."

"I saw Gunther with her in Kissimmee. I hid."

"He called me to say he couldn't find you, so I flew to Florida to help him."

"Isn't the whole Rand family satisfied now?" I said. "I'm out of the United States. I'm trapped in a foreign country—for how long? Until the Rands forget about us, if they ever do? Until Gunther divorces Neola, which he doesn't even dare to think of doing?"

"No one wins," Ben said. "Gunther has this rage to be first, to get the Nobel, to be in the papers and on magazine covers and television shows: the Man of the Century. He was well on his way until he fell in love with you. Now the press knows about him. You saw how they chased him at Epcot. Perhaps he's in prison already."

"So that's why you wanted him to come to Mexico," I said.

"If he came with you and Maria, the four of us could be here together. We'd be safe to announce what the research had produced—no fear of prison. Maybe he's had time to think about it now. You and Maria are here..."

"So we're the bait," I said.

"You're the two he loves," Ben said. "More than anything, even fame, perhaps."

"So much that he'd hide me here with no life of my own? No freedom? No marriage, or love, or peace?"

Ben came close to me. "Do you love anyone now? Want to marry anyone?"

I stared at him. "I have Gunther's child."

"Then you'll wait for him? He's said over and over that he'll divorce Neola once her father sees him through this danger. There may be prison for him, and a fight to change the U.S. laws."

"Wait for him? How long?"

Ben's silence gave the answer.

"Years," I said. "I'm going to be trapped here for years with Maria. You'll keep us here until he decides to get rid of his wife?"

Again Ben was silent.

"And tell me this: who am I, compared to Neola?" I asked. "I can't do anything for his career—I'm a waitress, she's a college graduate with money. Why would he ever leave her for me?" I felt a gap, a blank, as if we had left out certain vital words.

"I have other things to tell you," Ben said. "You can have a college education here in Mexico. You can get your doctorate if you want it, and hire people to care for Maria while you do. You can live in a nicer place than this. In a few years you'll be a professional—a teacher, a scholar—whatever your dream is."

"And who's going to support me all those years? Gunther? How can he afford it? What if Neola finds out?"

"That isn't a problem," Ben said.

"Why isn't it?"

He didn't answer.

"It will be your money, won't it?" I said. "Because he's your friend."

"Because his father made it possible for me to be where I am."

"But *I'm* not your friend! You deceived me, you've put me here in a strange country with a baby and no husband." I didn't raise my voice. My words struck hard enough.

Ben stood close to me, but he didn't meet my eyes. "Now I want to say what Gunther would never want me to say. I'm not speaking as his friend. And I'm not offering to support you and Maria, educate you, protect you because I'm his friend, either—or because of all I owe his father." Morning sunlight fell on his hands he clamped together before him. "I'm asking you to marry me."

Ben? Ben Carlos? Marry him? Ben knelt in the sunshine falling through the window. He took my hands and looked at my rings—Gunther's rings—fake diamonds. He bowed his head on our hands. "Don't answer yet," he said. "You don't know me well. I'm only Gunther's friend to you. Worse than that: Gunther's accomplice."

He lifted his head to look in my eyes. "Let me make it up to you. Give you your own, honorable place. I'm respected, and you'll be respected, too: my wife who's been married before, and has a little daughter, and is going to college. My mother died last year, and I inherited money. I have a large practice now. I love Maria as if she were my own child, because she's yours."

His dark eyes glowed. I felt his hands tremble in mine. "I haven't said the last thing, the most important thing of all. I've loved you from the moment I first saw you. I'd never have told you, if you were Gunther's wife."

"You sent us money," I said. "So I knew you loved him."

"It made me feel close to you." His voice was low and embarrassed. "I know I'm awkward and unromantic, and I've caused you such grief…" He put his head on our clasped hands again. "But I have to ask you: will you marry me?"

He heard me take a breath to speak. "Don't say anything now," he said in a low voice. He stood up and looked into my eyes, still grasping my hands. "You locked yourself in and were so afraid of me—I had to tell you how I feel. Why you're safe here."

"And I'm supposed to believe you?" I said.

He dropped his eyes, but I'd seen the flash in them. "Yes," he said. "But give me time to show you. Wait and see."

"I don't want to wait and see. I want to go back to my own country with Maria."

"If you trust me—"

"Trust you? Why? What reason do I have?"

He stood silent, his head bowed.

"Let me go back to my own country," I said. "Give me money for the plane, and I'll take Maria back to Florida, back to my job and the few friends I have. If you love me, let me go."

"I can't," Ben said, almost in a whisper.

"You don't want to, that's it! You used Maria to trap me here! You trapped me here before! You found that fake priest, didn't you, and that hidden-away chapel where no one but the priest would see what you and Gunther were doing?"

"Yes. I did that."

"And you expect me to believe what you tell me now? You say

110

Gunther's in danger of going to prison—he's probably working happily at his lab and going home to Neola every night!"

"I can show you a few things you can believe," Ben said. He took newspaper clippings from his pocket. "You may be able to see the action on television here, but here's what U.S. papers say happened at Epcot."

I unfolded the clipping to see a picture of Gunther: a man looking wild and trapped. The photographer had caught Gunther as if he were turning back to a woman who was out of focus in the background, but the woman was dressed in the same shirt and shorts I was still wearing. I read:

STUDENT AT UNIVERSITY OF CHICAGO ACCUSED OF WORK WITH HUMAN EMBRYOS

Dr. A.K. Rand, Dean of the College of Science at the University of Chicago, held a press conference today, stating that Gunther Risling, a graduate assistant, had not had access to any human embryos, nor had he used any in experiments. "We have no records showing that Gunther Risling has done anything illegal," Dr. Rand said.

Risling is Dr. Rand's son-in-law, and resides in Oak Park. Authorities are still investigating an anonymous report of Risling's alleged unlawful work which was mailed to them last week. Risling was seen at Epcot in Orlando, Florida on Tuesday, but eluded authorities and the media.

"Gunther's in trouble," Ben said. "They don't know where the 'anonymous report' came from. You can see that Rand is trying to protect Gunther, but I don't know if he can."

I gave Ben the clipping. "Why should I care?" I said. "Gunther's made me a...what I swore I'd never be. And I've heard the name his wife calls Maria."

"Stay here a while," Ben said. "You're safe—even from me. I love you, and I'll wait for you forever, if I have to. If I can marry you, I'll marry you with the whole world watching, I'll be so happy and proud." His eyes were shining.

I turned away and said in a dull, hopeless voice: "I've been kidnapped with Maria. I have no money to fly back to Florida."

Ben said, "Being here doesn't have to be your jail sentence! Put on a swimsuit and bring Maria. We'll go to the beach—"

"We won't go anywhere," I said. "I don't trust you. If you love me as you say you do, leave me alone. Get out. Go away."

Without a word, Ben went out and closed the door behind him. He locked it. I watched from the window and saw him drive away.

Maria and I were in prison again.

I nursed her, bathed her, had my lunch, and roamed the apartment through the long afternoon. Colette and Jack were hunting for me...calling the police, probably...worrying. When I turned on the television, every person on the screen chattered in Spanish.

Maria slept. I opened the closet door beside her crib. A closet full of clothes. I wasn't going to wear them, but would they fit me if I did? At least I could try them on and have a style show for myself, forgetting for a while that we were prisoners.

The bathing suit was red: the same color I'd worn to the beach on my honeymoon. "Stop thinking of Gunther," I said to myself, and shoved the suit out of sight.

Had Ben shopped for the bras, panties, slips, hose? Had he stood at a counter, his handsome face bent over frilly underwear? I almost smiled, then scowled. He'd expected to see them on me.

A silk suit with a coat to match: they were as blue as the Pacific, and they fit. I posed in a mirror. Ben must like soft, feminine things: he'd hung them there, one by one.

How could he ever suppose I'd marry him? He had! So had Gunther! Two men had lied to me, tricked me! For a moment I was so furious that I stripped off the silk suit as if it were on fire, grabbed an armful of clothes, ran to the window and yanked it open. Let the dresses—coats—blouses—underwear—nightgowns go tumbling down to the dirty pavement! Let Ben come to find them under the wheels of passing cars! Let people on the street help themselves!

But the blue silk clung to my fingers. I'd never owned anything made of silk...such a beautiful, lapis-lazuli blue. I'd never had such clothes.

I put the clothes back in the closet.

A long, elegant black evening dress hung there: the kind of gown that men think of when they think "blonde." It was designed to show nearly everything above the waist, but its scarf was wide and long. I posed in the mirror: Mary Homer arriving at a nightclub, swathed in black crepe...Mary Homer, wrapped head and shoulders, only her eyes showing, a Far Eastern lady of a harem. For a little while, playing at "dress up" like a child, I could forget where I was.

The television chattered in the living room. I'd turned it on while I ate lunch, and left it on: it was company, a human sound without meaning. After I'd done the dishes and fed Maria, I lay on the couch, the television turned low, and fell asleep.

The room was growing dark when I woke. Maria was fussing. I brought her to the couch to nurse her, and watched a procession of identical pictures on television. I changed channels, but the same picture was on them all: a serious, bearded man holding a very small baby. He wasn't speaking Spanish, I thought. Was he speaking French?

Suddenly I heard English words in a voice I knew—Gunther's voice! There he was on the screen, looking at me and saying, "Dr. Girard of France is not the first man in the world to do this. I claim the honor for the United States."

Spanish voices and faces blotted him out. What had he done?

Hour after hour I sat before the television. All I saw was the bearded man, and then Gunther repeating his two sentences. Finally I went to bed. Ben must know what Gunther had done, but I had yelled at Ben: "Leave me alone! Get Out! Go away!"

The next morning I turned the television on as soon as I woke. I began to see pictures Gunther had never shown me: a small Gunther in grade school, a teenager dancing with a pretty girl, and a young man shaking hands with an older man—his father? Then the Gunther I knew turned his blue eyes on me; his brown hair, blond-streaked, gleamed. I saw the lips I had kissed as he said, over and over: "Dr. Girard of France is not the first man in the world..."

The day passed, slow hour after slow hour. At last it was night, and Maria had fallen asleep. I lay on the couch, and the television's constant flow of Spanish lulled me into a doze. Some of the stations showed a car wreck: the car was crushed against a wall like a smashed egg.

Gunther's picture appeared, and he said his usual two sentences. But the pictures that followed brought me to my feet. A man was being carried on a stretcher. As the bearers turned the stretcher to load it into an ambulance, the body had Gunther's face! It had a tube in its nose, and its head was swathed in white, but I knew him! I knew him!

What were the voices saying? The smashed car appeared again, then a building, then a doctor in a white coat, hardly visible in the crowd of reporters and cameramen, and then Neola! Neola ducked her head, hurrying in a door marked "Emergency Entrance."

Over and over again I saw the car, the doctor, Neola...

I slept at last. When I woke as the sun rose, I watched for Ben from a window.

I heard him say, *I loved you from the moment I first saw you.* Then I heard footsteps coming upstairs.

Ben's key turned in the lock. I shot the bolt back and unhooked the chains. "What's happened to Gunther?" I cried as Ben came in.

Ben saw the tears in my eyes. "Don't cry," he said, and put his arms around me. "I've just talked to his doctor at the hospital in Chicago. Gunther's calling for you. He was being chased by reporters, I think, and he drove too fast. I have to go there. I hope you'll come with me, but you need to be told some hard things first." He pressed his mouth against my hair and said softly, "I seem to be your bearer of bad news."

I pulled away from Ben and wiped tears off my face. "Is he dying?"

"He has broken bones. His abdominal wound is the most serious."

"Reporters were chasing him?"

Ben turned the television off. "Hard to say. He's wanted, of course—he's broken the law. You saw how he was being chased at Epcot."

"He yelled that he wanted Maria and me at Epcot, but you left him!"

"That's what I have to explain to you," Ben said. "You can't imagine what's going on in America just now. Gunther's on every front page. You've already seen how the television crews and press chased him. If he can prove what he says, he *will* claim the honor for the U.S., and he'll get every prize going."

"He's broken the law?"

"He'd have been arrested by now if he weren't in the hospital—and if they believed him," Ben said. "It's much more than simply breaking the law by working with embryos. There's the devil to pay." He went into the bedroom and stood by Maria in her crib. "Do you remember the three of us talking on the beach about Ian Wilmut? Wilmut had cloned a sheep in Scotland in the 'nineties. Soon after that, scientists cloned monkeys, and monkeys are very like us, but the greatest prize of all will go to the scientist who clones a human being. That race is on, all over the world."

Maria woke up. She opened her eyes, yawned, and looked at Ben. She seemed to recognize him; she gurgled as he picked her up. He said, "Gunther's claiming he made Maria."

I took Maria from him. "Well, of course he did."

"Maria's not his child." Ben's voice was low and strained.

"Not his?" My face felt hot. "I've never slept—"

"I know. Gunther and I...made sure..."

"Sure of what?"

"Maria's father is your father, whoever he was. People are already talking about the virgin birth...publishing religious articles..."

"I've never seen my father!" I backed away from Ben. "Maria's my baby!"

"Maria's your baby. Of course she is. You carried her for nine months. But you're not her mother."

A cold calmness settled over me. I had Maria. Ben had left the apartment door unlocked. Every alarm in my body shrieked: *Get away from him. Run!*

Ben came close to me. Too close. "Haven't you felt it?" he said. "Haven't you seen it in her eyes? Maria's mother is your mother. Maria is you, born again. Your clone."

I couldn't understand. He saw it. "Look at yourself in that mirror." He nodded at the mirror behind Maria's crib. "Maria will look exactly like you when she's nineteen...as beautiful as you are now: every lock of blonde hair, every fold of skin, every tone of voice." He stared at Maria and me in the mirror as if he were seeing ghosts. "No one on earth—until now—has ever been able to see themselves reborn. Never before. You are the first."

Maria looked up at me. Meeting her eyes, I said, "I can't believe—"

I never finished that sentence. I stared into Maria's eyes. How many times had I seen that look of hers: so serious, so intent, so *familiar*?

"I think you've already guessed," Ben said softly.

I carried my baby into the living room and sat down, holding her as carefully as if she were made of glass. "Will she grow up?" I said in a shaky voice. "Will she be all right?"

"We don't know. No one has ever produced a living clone. We know she'll be immune from the two most common defects regular children are born with. Maria's perfectly natural, made from living cells developing in a woman's womb: an ordinary child."

"Maybe she *is* an ordinary child. Gunther's and mine."

"No. Gunther has cells from you, and took cells from Maria after she was born. They're identical." He looked sheepish. "I kept a set of your cells, too, and Maria's. I had to be sure."

"My twin?" I said softly, looking down at Maria. "My real sister? My mother and father's baby?" I lifted Maria to kiss her, my hair falling over her, and looked up to see naked love in Ben's eyes. He saw my glance, and turned away.

"But how did Gunther do it?" I asked. "Why wouldn't I ever know, ever suspect…"

"We told you that you were 'sick' when you came to Mexico with Gunther. Remember? He drugged you the first night you were here—even while I was trying to stop him."

The champagne I drank while the two men argued. Days I couldn't remember: I was "sick with food poisoning."

Ben said: "Gunther had already helped to clone rhesus monkeys—the secret research his department was doing. They never imagined he'd try to clone a human, because Gunther wasn't a doctor: he'd have to team up with an IVF specialist—in vitro fertilization—and what specialist would work with someone who was only a graduate student who wanted to break the law?"

"You would," I said.

"Yes. He was my friend. And Gunther would need a surrogate mother to give birth to the clone. How could he afford one? They cost thousands of dollars. And he'd be breaking the law, so the woman would have to be kept in secret, and what woman would take kindly to being isolated somewhere for nine months?"

"I would," I said. "I thought I was married and living in our apartment, but I wasn't married—I was just hidden away?"

Ben nodded. "But you have to realize how driven for time Gunther was. He'd found out that several men in the U.S. and abroad were racing for this prize. If he were going to beat them to it, he'd have to woo you, win you, get you to Mexico, and begin the cloning. You can see he barely made it—less than four weeks ahead of the French. He was a wild man when he brought you here."

"So he pretended to marry me after you two had started my baby growing."

"Your first night you saw us argue and nearly come to blows. He wasn't trained to do any of the procedures. The only thing he could contribute was his experience with cloning—and, of course, he contributed you. But he described the new procedures to me, and I followed them. You'll hate us now, hate us both—"

"I don't remember anything! No memories! I thought I'd been sick, that was all, and when I was well we had such good times! But you'd drugged me!" I cried. "And you—the two of you—"

"Please!" Ben saw the horror I felt. He stretched out a hand and saw me recoil.

"The two men I trusted! You drugged me!" I cried. "You *raped* me!"

"Gunther and I...we risked everything," Ben said. "Together." His lips trembled. "We were both in love with you by then. We 'walked the crumbling floor...'"

"I recited that," I said, so appalled that I could hardly speak. "There in the sun, between the two of you. I was so proud. I was going to be Gunther's wife. But I wasn't! You both knew it! I wasn't anyone you could respect! While you sat with me on that beach, you could remember me naked and helpless! Both of you!"

He said nothing.

He stared at Maria and me in the mirror as if he were
seeing ghosts.

I was trembling all over. "Where did you and Gunther do it? In your clinic?" Ben nodded.

Tears spilled down my cheeks. "I thought I knew the worst thing Gunther did to me," I said in a choked voice. "I thought there could be nothing worse than being made a whore…having a bastard. What could be more terrible than that?"

Ben brought newspaper clippings out of his pocket: the front pages of newspapers with headlines:

WILL AMERICA BE OUTDONE BY FRANCE?

Dr. Jean Girard, a French embryologist, has proven that he has produced a human clone, born to a surrogate mother a week ago. The mother and baby are identical, though born twenty-five years apart. They are said to be twin daughters of the surrogate mother's parents. French law, like U.S. law, prohibits such work, and Dr. Girard has been imprisoned pending trial.

A microbiology teaching assistant at the University of Chicago, Gunther Risling, claims that he has produced a living, month-old human clone, thus giving the U.S. the honor of this historic, though criminal, first. Risling has broken the law and would have been arrested, but on Monday night he was seriously injured in a car accident near Chicago.

Another headline said *THE SORCERER'S APPRENTICE CLONES A WOMAN.*

"I have to go to Chicago," Ben said. "Will you come, with Maria? Gunther's in pain and trying to tell his story. No one believes him."

"They'll believe him if you say so?"

"No." Ben folded up the clippings and put them in his pocket, not looking at me. "There's only one person in the world—and her baby—who can be tested to prove without a doubt that Gunther's not lying. Our evidence could be faked, but not yours."

"But what did Gunther really do?"

"What?"

"You said he only brought me to Mexico and told you how to do the cloning. You did it. He didn't."

"I'm his friend."

"Maybe you are," I said, "but you're not mine."

"I'm trying to be," Ben said. "You're so angry and hurt, but don't decide whether to go to Chicago or not until you take time

121

to think. Think what this means to all of us."

"You want me to make you and Gunther famous—by exhibiting Maria and me?"

"You'll be mobbed. You'll be merchandized. Think of the Dionne quintuplets—they were nothing compared to you and Maria. I want you to realize what your life will be like if you go to Gunther. You'll be hunted. So far you can't be recognized. No one has pictures of you, except the one at Epcot, and you're blurred in the background behind Gunther, so no one has noticed you. Gunther and I were careful never to take your picture. So you have two choices. You can hide here, or you can come with me."

"Is he going to live?"

"The doctors aren't hopeful."

"And he could die without any of the honors he's worked for?"

"Yes."

Neither of us spoke for a while. Finally I said, "I'll go."

"I'll book our flight," Ben said. "I'll try to get us there as soon as I can. When can you be ready?"

"In an hour," I said.

"I'll be back then." Ben ran out my door and locked it, took the stairs two at a time, and drove off.

I pulled on a black shirt and jeans, then packed all our clothes I could jam in two new suitcases. I put makeup and the long black evening dress and scarf in Maria's small bag with her diapers and bottles. Ben came in less than an hour, but I was ready.

We left the apartment that was full of memories: a place I never wanted to see again. *Goodbye* I said to the trusting girl I'd been at eighteen, so proud to cook in that little kitchen…so in love, lying in the bed where my "bride's bouquet" hung.

We had first-class seats in the plane. Maria had a baby bed. The plane roared down the runway, and I felt the wheels lift and leave Mexico behind.

The seats around us were empty. An attendant brought us magazines and newspapers. Gunther was on front pages of the papers in black and white or color with the headline: THE SORCERER'S APPRENTICE.

122

"Gunther didn't tell you he was bringing me to Mexico before you first saw me?" I asked.

"Only a day before," Ben said. "You were just a girlfriend of his, I thought."

"You didn't like me," I said. "I felt that the minute I saw you."

Ben turned his expressive dark eyes on me with such love in them that I looked away. "Gunther told me: *She's mine. I want her and she wants me. She doesn't even like you. Keep away from her.*"

"So you helped him pretend to marry me."

"I hated it. That first night, I tried every argument I could think of to change his mind. He told me he loved you, but he had to marry Neola in a few weeks. I told him that if he married you and stayed in Mexico, he and I could announce the cloning without going to prison. But he said he could never do that: he wanted Neola's father on his side, and the Rand money. And he had to pretend to marry you in order to watch over you for nine months. You might abort the clone. He called me when you mentioned abortion—he was frantic."

"Of course," I said in a bitter voice, staring through the window at the floor of clouds below. "He might have lost all his work."

"He loved you, I'm sure, and he worried about you. I did. I sent the money so you'd be cared for."

"It was your clone, too. Your chance at fame," I said.

"Yes."

"You looked desperate when Gunther and I went back to Chicago."

"I was so in love with you, and I had to watch him pretend to marry you...watch you go back with him, so happy—a new bride, you thought. You never dreamed that in less than nine months you'd be a new mother, with no husband. And I suspected Gunther wouldn't care if you were paraded in the eyes of the world, an unwed mother! He wouldn't care if he went to prison. He'd be famous. And I'd thought he was my friend."

Suddenly I saw what I'd never noticed. I said, "Gunther's claiming he made the first human clone, but he's never mentioned you."

"No. He never has."

"But you came to Epcot to help him catch the baby and me—take us to Mexico..." I stopped, seeing another new thing.

"You came, but you took us to Mexico without him. He yelled, 'Give them to me!' but you didn't."

"I was trying to use you and Maria as bait, as you've said. Tried to make him...be my friend, I guess, and come to Mexico and be safe, not in prison. But now it's too late."

"So," I said. "You're taking Maria and me to Chicago to prove *you* did this, not Gunther. *You* are the one who deserves the prizes and fame."

"No," Ben said in a quiet voice. "I can't do that. Now you know everything, and it's you who will choose. You've chosen Gunther, I think, because you love him. You're the only one who can prove he's the one who made the first clone in the world. If he's not going to live, you may be able to give him the fame and praise before it's too late. But I hope I can save you and Maria from the worst. I can try."

"Oh!" I cried, and bent double over Maria in my lap, my hands pressed against my ears. "I don't want to hear any more!"

Gunther's voice came from a television set above me, speaking of human clones and honors. Maria lay in my lap, sucking her fist like any baby, wetting her diaper, falling asleep.

At last we were through the customs at O'Hare and stood among the airport crowds. "I'll make a reservation and send our luggage to a hotel," Ben said. "That way we can go straight to the hospital." He gave me my passport. "You sit here with Maria, and I'll claim our luggage."

"What if something happens—I don't have any money," I said. "I'd better go with you."

"No. You sit and rest," He took out his billfold and gave me a thick wad of bills. "Here. Keep this. And why do you think I'd ever let anything happen to you?"

I put the money in my pocket. "I'll go to the women's restroom and change Maria," I said, and walked away with Maria and the bag of her things. At the restroom door I looked back. Ben was already lost in the crowds.

Run! Run! I ran with Maria in my arms and her bag thumping against my back. I found a taxi stand outside and said to a driver, "The train station, please."

Now I was in my own country. I had money. Sitting in the taxi with Maria as Chicago streets went by, I looked at what Ben had given me: hundreds of dollars.

At last we came to the busy train station. I paid the taxi driver, and found the nearest women's restroom.

There was a restroom stall with a sink and a changing table. I locked the door and spread paper towels for Maria to lie on. When I'd changed her, I hurried to change myself into someone new.

Ben had left every kind of cosmetic in his apartment for me, and I'd thrown a few handfuls into Maria's bag. I smeared dark tan makeup on my face, and penciled thick black eyebrows over mine. The long evening dress Ben had bought slithered over my black shirt and fell to my shoes. I had played with the long black scarf—now it covered every hair on my head and hid my bare arms and low neckline. My eyes disappeared behind dark sunglasses.

I hung the bag on my back, picked up Maria and looked in the mirror. A Far Eastern woman stood there with her baby, swathed in black from head to foot.

When I carried Maria into the busy train station, my skirt clung to my ankles at every step, and I began to swelter in my black cocoon. I bought a one-way ticket to Boston.

A woman dressed like me in hot, thick, swaddling black passed the ticket counter. She carried suitcases; the man with her carried none. She walked behind him like a slave.

15

The train to Boston was half empty. I settled with Maria on a double seat, and pretended to read a discarded newspaper. Had Ben found someone to check the restroom at O'Hare, then managed to find my taxi driver? I watched the platform from my train window. Was he asking someone: "Did you sell a ticket to a woman with a month-old baby—a young woman with long blonde hair and blue eyes, wearing a black shirt and jeans?"

I smiled a little. Let them try to find me. Hadn't I earned my Master of Disappearance degree by now? Each time I'd run away—from my father—from Gunther and Neola—from Ben—they hunted me, but I wasn't there, like T.S. Eliot's "Macavity, the Mystery Cat." I listened to the rhythm of the train's wheels as we pulled out of the station, and remembered Sophy Saul in her little house next door, feeding me, teaching me, loving me, chanting: *MaCAVity, MaCAVity, MaCAVity's not there!* to me and her old cat.

After a while I began to read the newspaper. The headline said:

SORCERER'S APPRENTICE PROMISES
TO REVEAL CLONE

Gunther Risling, graduate assistant at the University of Chicago, is gravely ill after a car accident, but able to talk to reporters. He claims that the baby he cloned, born last February three weeks before the French clone, will soon be available with her mother for medical tests.

"Oh, no, they won't," I said to myself. But I looked at Maria, sleeping in my arms, and the wonder of what Ben had told me seemed to gather around her, as bright as the setting sun. *Nothing like you and Maria has ever existed. Never before.*

It was dark when the train pulled into Boston. Its lights showed me my reflection in my train window: a woman wrapped in black with a baby in her arms.

At least I wasn't penniless. Never before had I had money when I came to a strange city. I climbed into a taxi with Maria, yanking my long skirts out of the way of the door. "You want Belmont?" the driver said. "Yeah."

I was too tired to have any thought in my head but Sophy Saul. Was she still alive? Was she still living with her daughter? If Sophy were gone, would her daughter remember me? I stared through the taxi window at a heavy fall of rain.

"What's that address again?" the driver asked after miles through city streets. Finally he pulled up at a big frame house on a corner, its spread of gables white against a starry sky. I paid him and said: "Will you wait until I see if my friend still lives here?"

I ran with Maria to a side door and put out my hand to ring the bell, then stopped. Through the door's sheer curtains I could see a big kitchen, and just as I looked, a tall woman with flyaway white hair turned from a stove and I saw her face.

"It's all right," I called to the taxi driver with a wave. He drove away. I rang the bell, and heard slow steps. Sophy Saul opened the door: an older, thinner Sophy. The sight of her brought tears to my eyes, and I couldn't speak. Sophy stared through the rain at a woman hidden in black from head to foot, a baby in her arms.

"Do you know me, Sophy?" I managed to ask. "The girl you helped for years in Plattsburg, Nebraska?"

"Mary!" she cried. "And a baby?"

"It's Mary and Maria," I said. "Though you'd never guess. I'm in disguise."

"Come in, come in! I know that voice!" She was as tall as ever, but slower on her feet; she led me into a kitchen that smelled of simmering meat and onions.

"There," I said, taking off my scarf. "You'll know me now, though my black eyebrows and brown face must look funny. And here's my daughter, Maria."

127

Sophy hugged us both, and pulled the baby blanket aside to see Maria. "Pretty little thing. You look just like your mother."

"I've come here to hide," I said. "There's nowhere else in the whole world I want to be, if you're well enough to take me in—again. I won't stay long; I have to find a home and a job."

"You're so welcome—so welcome! Sit down. Let me take Maria—you must be exhausted."

I sat on a kitchen chair and shut my eyes. "You don't know what that voice of yours means to me," I said. "I could sit here and listen to you all day. I lost you! You weren't well, and then you didn't write, and then I ran away from Plattsburg after high school. Did you send letters there?"

"I was sick for so long, and couldn't write to anybody. And when I finally sent you letters, they came back. You must be... nineteen? Six years!"

"Your daughter's here?" I asked.

"She died last December and left me this big old house."

"I'm so sorry."

"Yes, she's gone and at peace, I hope." Sophy's voice was brisk, not sad. "Are you hungry? I'm making our old favorite: roast beef hash. Bring your bag and Maria first; I've got a bed for you." I followed her down a huge hall and into a bedroom. "Maria can sleep in a clothesbasket until we get a crib out of the attic."

The room was lined with shelves like the Schatzles' old storeroom, but it had a black marble fireplace, a big bed, a high ceiling, and a thick rug. We made a bed for Maria in Sophy's clothesbasket.

"Could I take a shower?" I said. "I'm tired and sweaty and dusty—from the playground, you know!"

I had echoed her long-ago words to Mary Durfy, home from school. We laughed.

"I *am* tired from the playground," I said. "The playground's a mean and dirty place."

"Tell me about it, when you're rested. When you feel like it," Sophy said.

She left me to shed my hot clothes and step into her shower. Down the drain went my eyebrow paint, tan makeup, Mexican dust and the sweat from a black crepe cocoon. In a little while I was clean and smelled of flowers, and laughed with delight to see a hand come through the half open door with a pink nightgown in it.

"Do you know me? The girl you helped for years?"

"Now you look like my Mary," Sophy said when I came into the kitchen. She wrapped a bathrobe around me and dropped a pair of slippers at my feet. "Maria's asleep?"

"Yes. She already feels your mother-aura," I said, and yawned. "Can you yawn when you're trying to escape…being chased… scared to death?" (I was with Sophy; I could say anything that came into my head, and I was light-headed with relief.) "I've never thought about it. I haven't yawned for days."

We loaded our dinner plates. "Do you have a television?" I asked. "I have to watch the news."

"Bring your plate and we'll watch while we eat," Sophy said. "And then I'll show you this place. I don't use the second floor. It's a big old house of the roaring 'twenties: two parlors, servants' rooms on the third floor, butler's pantry…high society."

The huge hall we crossed divided the house in two; it was wide and long, with a front vestibule at the end. Sophy went through a door to pull heavy drapes and turn on lights. "This was the dining room, once upon a time," Sophy said. A glass chandelier sparkled high above white paneling. Half of one wall was a buffet with glass doors; a marble fireplace was on another.

"It's lovely," I said, and sat down on a couch with my supper, but I hardly took a bite: I was watching the television she had turned on. In a moment, there was Gunther's face.

"The Sorcerer's Apprentice," Sophy said. "We've been hearing about him for days now. Poor boy. He looks awfully young…"

"Oh, Sophy!" I cried. "I was married to him—I thought!"

Sophy's mouth fell open. She stared at the screen, then at me.

Gunther's face was pale and drawn. An off-camera voice said: *Gunther Risling continues to assert from his hospital bed that he is the first man to clone a human being.*

Gunther's tortured face filled the screen. His lips moved, and I could read them. He was saying, "Mary…Mary…"

Tears ran down my face. Safe with Sophy Saul, I think I cried for everything, from my childhood to my first sight of Sophy in her kitchen an hour before.

Sophy came to sit beside me on the couch, hugging me and never asking a question. When I finally subsided to hiccups and sniffles, she warmed up our supper. We ate together, as we had hundreds of times, and I nursed Maria.

"She needs a bath, poor little thing," I said. "She flew from Mexico, and then she was stolen away by a mysterious woman in black, and brought all the way from Chicago on a train."

"We've got the very thing for her—a sunken bathtub," Sophy said, and opened a door to a butler's pantry. It had a sink just Maria's size: a basin with high-arching silvery faucets under cabinets with silver knobs.

I ran warm water and bathed little Maria. "She's your Rhody all over again," Sophy said.

"I miss Rhody so much!" I said. "I've wanted to bring her from Plattsburg ever since I left, but I never could. I call her every week or two, and send presents, but she won't believe I'll ever come for her."

I rinsed and dried Maria, and she lay on towels in front of the pantry's serving slot, kicking her plump feet. She was full of milk and clean and sleepy. Sophy fastened one side of her diaper; I fastened the other.

"Neither of you can stay awake," Sophy said. "Bedtime. Come on."

That night I was tucked into bed thousands of miles from my prison in Acapulco, with no tears left to cry. I slept as soundly as Maria, safe with Sophy Saul.

In the morning I watched television news. Gunther was still alive. I called Colette and Jack in Kissimmee before they went to work at Instant Ancestors. "It's Mary," I said when I heard Colette's voice. "I've got Maria and we're all right. You must have been so worried—"

"Mary!" Colette yelled. I heard her shout for Jack. "Where are you? I hunted all over Epcot!"

"Gunther and his friend stole Maria out of her baby carriage," I said. "I turned around and she was gone! I had to go with them or I'd have lost her. They wouldn't let me use a phone, or I'd have tried to call you. But now I've escaped with her, and I'm hiding with a friend."

"You're both all right? We didn't know what to do. We didn't want to go to the police, because we knew you were hiding—"

"I can't come to Kissimmee right now. I'm so sorry that I had to leave my wonderful jobs with you without giving you any warning. I won't tell you where I am, because it makes me feel safer, and you

132

can honestly say you don't know if anyone asks you. Will you keep the few things I left at the motel until I can give you an address to send them to?"

"Of course. Call us again. We want to know you're all right."

"Give my love to Jack and Clem. You're my dear friends. Goodbye."

April sunlight fell through high windows in Sophy's diningroom. She brought our breakfast and I nursed Maria. Sophy asked no questions; she told me how her daughter had been a bitter woman, a schizophrenic, who had thrown herself in the Charles River.

"I've wished every Massachusetts day that I was back with you in my little Plattsburg house," Sophy said. "When did you leave that awful home of yours?"

So I began the story of my last three years—started with the Andersons cleaning our house...then Rhody stealing the money I'd saved, and begging to leave Plattsburg with me. I told about nights under the hedge in the Schatzlers' back yard, and then I jumped up to rummage in my suitcase.

"Look at these," I said, coming back to give Sophy a pack of letters. "I've carried all your letters to me...slept with them when I crawled under those bushes. When I was lying on those chair cushions, I put your letters under my head for comfort. And they traveled to Mexico. I couldn't ever leave them behind, ever."

Sophy had tears in her eyes. I said: "And the ones that aren't opened are my letters to you that were "returned to sender."

Sophy rubbed her wet eyes. "My daughter," she said. "She didn't want me to have any friends...wanted me all to herself. She was so unhappy in her mind, and wouldn't go for help. No matter how much I'd loved her for years, she said I hated her. She must have sent these back to you. I never saw them. And then I was too sick to write."

"I'm so sorry," I said. "So sorry. But now you've got my letters, at least. You'll see how much I missed you."

Sophy and I talked every morning beside her old-fashioned stove, or on window seats in her big bedroom at the front of the house, or while we rummaged in the immense, cobweb-shrouded attic to find a crib for Maria. Sophy could hardly believe my fake marriage to Gunther in Mexico, and what he did to me with help from Ben Carlos.

She couldn't believe the cloning.

"Maria isn't Gunther's child," I said. "She's my mother's child, and my father's child, whoever he was."

"Not Gunther's? Or Ben's?" Sophy stared at me. "Having a baby *does* require a man, doesn't it? Always has?"

"Her father is my father," I said.

"But you don't even know who he was! You told me you'd never seen him!"

"I don't know his name. I've never seen him. But Maria is his child, like I am. She's my absolute twin. More than a twin. In fact, she's me, born again. My parents are hers."

Sophy looked dumfounded.

"My mother is her mother," I said. "I'm not her mother. I'm only the body she grew inside. That's what a 'clone' is."

Sophy flung her hands out and shook her head. "I don't understand."

"You will, I think, in a little while," I said. "What I don't understand is why I was so stupid. Why did I trust Ben—and Gunther?"

"Stupid?" Sophia said. "You checked to see who Gunther really was. And it certainly seemed as if he could do what he promised: marry you in Mexico and pay your way through college. If you'd asked me, wouldn't I have said, *Marry him?*"

We left the attic to have lunch in Sophy's kitchen. April sun turned her African violets into jewels on the windowsill: ruby, amethyst, sapphire.

Sophy said, "When Ben took you back to Mexico, Gunther announced he'd 'created the first clone'?"

"But he never mentioned Ben!" I cried. "A double cross! It took me so long to see it. The last person he wanted to see at Epcot was Ben, but Ben came to help Gunther. *I had thought he was my friend*, Ben told me."

Sophy sighed. "Let's get away from our troubles. Let's go out and walk for a while. It's a beautiful afternoon for you to see Belmont and Cambridge."

I covered my hair with a scarf, and put on dark makeup and sunglasses. Sophy and I carried an old "perambulator" from the attic to Sophy's car, and she drove the three of us to Cambridge.

"This old car is about to die," Sophy said. "And I can't afford another. In fact, I don't think I can keep the house."

"If I can get a job here…" I said, and knew what that meant: no chance for college.

New England was halfway into Spring, but winter chill was still in the ground, and the Charles River was icy blue. Harvard Yard was white stone and red brick, and students dodged through traffic. We parked and walked along "Tory Row" to Longfellow's house, where he had seen his young daughters one evening:

> *From my study I see in the lamplight,*
> *Descending the broad hall stair,*
> *Grave Alice and laughing Allegra*
> *And Edith with golden hair.*

Sophy and I recited his poems in snatches, one remembering what the other forgot. We had lunch in a little patisserie near where the village smithy had stood "under the spreading chestnut tree." When we were tired, we sat on a bench in a cemetery near the Square.

The graveyard's round-shouldered gravestones leaned on each other in a tranquil space surrounded by traffic, but I couldn't be at peace there, even with Maria in my arms and Sophy beside me. "I go over and over everything's that happened," I said, staring at a stone that read "Washington Alston." Its worn letters were dappled with sun and shadow. "And I think about the future. Maria will talk to me with my own voice! How can I teach her what's right when she'll have all my weaknesses?"

"I can't imagine all this…but if she's really you, she'll have your strengths, don't forget," Sophy said. "You've got plenty."

"She'll be in her twenties when I'm in my forties, and I'll see myself young again—and she'll look at me and see the way she'll look when she's eighteen years older!"

"But she'll have had so much more than you had," Sophy said. "She won't be the same. She'll have a happy childhood, for instance. If you marry a good man, she'll have a father. A real home. Love."

I saw that Sophy was beginning to believe that I wasn't crazy— that clones could be possible. "I turn everything that's happened over and over in my mind," I said. "I think Ben wanted Maria and me to be safe in Mexico, away from the spotlight."

"I think so," Sophy said.

"But now I think Gunther wouldn't care about safety. He wouldn't even care if he went to prison, as long as he was The First Man To Clone. He wouldn't care if reporters called me a prostitute, or said Maria was illegitimate. He wouldn't care about Ben." I felt sick at what I had said, but I couldn't stop. "Gunther wanted me as his little 'side dish.' Neola was right. And Ben saw it all, and wanted to save me. Didn't he?"

"What happens if they never find you?"

"Ben said it was my choice: to go to Gunther or..." I stared at Sophy. "Or run away?"

"Ben left you at the airport," Sophy said. "He gave you all that money."

"To make it easy for me if I wanted to run? He did that?" I got up from the bench with Maria, and walked back and forth, my mind turning over everything we knew. "Why?" I said, "If Ben wants the fame, he'd have taken Maria and me to Chicago! He could have shown us to the whole world: poor little Maria, the Guinea-Pig-Baby...and me: the stupid, seduced Bimbo who didn't even get paid!"

Sophy gave me a slight smile. "They call Gunther 'The Sorcerer's Apprentice,' but you're like a sorceress yourself. And you're no apprentice, either. It seems to me that you're the only one who can give Gunther and Ben fame and fortune...if you please."

"But I don't please!" I cried. "No! I'll never do that to Maria!"

"Then you can make Ben and Gunther nothing but fools," Sophy said. "People will snicker behind their backs, year after year. Where will Gunther and Ben find work? What will they do? Who'll believe anything they say?"

16

Gunther was still alive when we watched television that evening, but movie stars and politics had crowded news of him to the end of broadcasts: he was only the young Sorcerer's Apprentice—some wild-eyed man who had claimed what he couldn't prove.

We settled Maria in her crib for the night, and sat by the fire in Sophy's parlor in our nightgowns. "I'm supposing this Ben Carlos of yours isn't too attractive?" Sophy said. "A bit uncouth, maybe? Short and stout?"

I said, "He's certainly not 'mine,' but he's older than Gunther, and half Spanish and half Mexican, and he looks like a Spanish nobleman: dark eyes, and hair so black that it has blue sparkles in it sometimes. He's tan and tall and slim...he's really quite..."

Suddenly Ben was on the television screen, as if he'd heard us say his name. "That's Ben!" I said.

Ben looked tired, sad, severe; his dark eyes were narrowed against the bright studio lights. He said: "I want to corroborate that Gunther Risling has, indeed, been first to clone a living human being. This clone is a little girl named Maria, born February of this year. I have seen her and examined her in the last few days, and have taken identical cells from Maria and her surrogate mother."

An interviewer's voice asked: "You performed this 'in vitro fertilization' in Acapulco, Mexico?"

"Yes."

"But you can't produce this 'clone,' or the surrogate mother?"

"No," Ben said.

"Why?"

"The surrogate mother intends to keep her child, and she is concerned about the effect of publicity on her daughter's life," Ben said. "She has a perfect right, of course, to remain hidden."

"Then you're asking us to take your word, and Gunther Risling's word, without any absolute proof?"

"We have substantial proof," Ben said. "But Mr. Risling's condition—"

"You can't produce the surrogate mother and the clone?"

"It's the surrogate mother's right to protect the child. I'm doing what I can for Gunther Risling. He is my friend. If he should die, he will die with the knowledge that he is the first in the world to produce a living human clone, and has won this honor for his country."

Ben disappeared from the screen.

"He's trying to imply that it was all Gunther's work," I said. "That he simply followed Gunther's directions and produced Maria."

"So he wants to give everything to Gunther: the prizes, the famous name…"

"Yes," I said.

"We're both tired," Sophy said. She turned off the television. "Go to bed. We'll watch television at breakfast."

I went to bed and lay in the dark listening to Maria's steady breathing. The house around me creaked: an old house settling for the night. Over and over I heard Ben's voice as he faced the bright studio lights.

Suddenly I sat up in bed. The Ben Carlos on television wasn't the Ben I thought I knew. He had looked at me with cold brown eyes the first time I saw him, but he had told me later: *You were innocent. Happy. You brought your wedding dress…so trusting. I had to give you the most romantic wedding….*

Ben had redone his apartment for me, bought me clothes, handed me hundreds of dollars and left me free to run away from him. He'd said: *Do you think I'd ever let anything happen to you?* He had argued and fought for me. I remembered two angry men standing in the surf of a dark beach.

And I had just heard him call me "the surrogate mother." Not a flattering name, but not the nasty names Neola had used. He

He had argued and fought for me. I remembered two
angry men standing in the surf of a dark beach.

was letting the world think I had been paid to have children for others, as many other women had done with no shame. And he had described me as a mother who wanted to keep her child.

Thinking of Ben, I left my bed to stand in Sophy's wide, silent hall, hundreds of miles from Chicago, and couldn't believe what I felt: Ben Carlos was my shield, my protector. He always had been.

The house was dark. Above me were empty bedrooms. A century before, parents, children, nursemaids, and servants had filled that darkness with their sleeping breaths. The breaths had stopped long ago, and their choices. The only sound was April wind singing faint tunes in old chimneys.

"Mary?" Sophy came out of her bedroom in her long flannel nightgown. "You can't sleep?"

"Ben asked me to marry him," I said. "I didn't tell you that."

"I rather suspected he had. You weren't married to anyone else, after all."

"He asked me before I knew about the cloning. He wanted to give me an honorable life, and pay for any education I wanted."

"And you said No."

"Marry a man who raped me?"

Sophy sighed. "I'll make us some tea," she said, and we went into her kitchen.

"Sophy," I said. "You've done so many, many things for me. Do you think you could do one more big thing?"

"Just ask. "

"Will you go to Chicago with me?" I said. "But not *with* me. Only on the same flight: be a grandmother traveling with your little grandchild? Will you stay in a different hotel room from mine, so I can use your room as a hiding place if I need it? Who'd ever connect me with Sophy Saul and her granddaughter?"

"Of course I'll go. But you could stay here with Maria and be safe."

"I have to see Gunther. While I can. I have to help Ben. Can we fly to Chicago tomorrow?"

"Are you going to bequeath fame and glory?"

"Me? Mary Dirty of the Dirty Family? I don't know," I said. "I don't know."

141

When I followed Sophia and Maria into the plane for Chicago, I stayed far behind them, a newspaper in my hand. The headline said: MYSTERY MOTHER AND CLONE ELUDE SORCERER'S APPRENTICE. My seat was far from Sophy's; I tried not to notice when the "grandmother's" baby howled as the plane took off. Maria didn't approve of milk coming from a store-bought nipple. She slept at last, but she yelled at the end of the trip when we left the plane at O'Hare.

I followed the white-haired grandmother and baby into an airport restroom. Half an hour later the grandmother carried a full, dry and quiet Maria out of the restroom and into a taxi, and I followed her in another. I wore dark glasses; my hair was covered in a scarf.

Sophia checked into our hotel as I stood beside her, impersonating a stranger. Our rooms were on the same floor. In a few minutes Sophy and I relaxed at last on Sophy's hotel bed, watching television with Maria propped between us.

A news program told us that the Sorcerer's Apprentice was still alive.

Someone knocked. "That's the crib I ordered, I think," Sophy said. I shut myself in her bathroom until she called, "All clear."

"I'll feed Maria and then go to the hospital this evening," I said. "Maybe about suppertime, when most people may not visit. They probably won't let reporters camp outside his hospital room, but they'll be in the hospital lobby. I suppose only his family can see Gunther."

"Except for Ben."

"That's what I'm counting on," I said. "And the fact that no one knows what this 'surrogate mother' looks like. If I sit in the lobby where Ben can see me as he comes or goes, he'll find a way to take me to Gunther."

We had an early supper in our room. The snug safety of Sophy's house was gone. I took a cab to the hospital wearing dark glasses, my hair wrapped in a scarf. When I went through the big hospital doors, I felt as if anyone might yell: "There she is!"

No one did. Photographers and reporters were in the lobby: bored men waiting for news. They looked me over, then looked away. I sat as close to the outer door as I could and picked up a magazine.

An hour went by. Suddenly, there was Ben coming from the elevators to the lobby, hurrying to the door.

The reporters ran for him. The flashes of cameras caught him quite close to me. I took off my dark glasses and looked at Ben, and he stopped. "Nothing new to report, gentlemen," he said to the reporters clustered around him. "I've got to go back to the fifth floor—I've forgotten to speak to the nurses."

I watched him go. I waited until he disappeared. When I walked slowly to the elevators, no one was nearby. I punched the "up" button with a hidden hand as I walked past for a drink at the water fountain—until the elevator door opened. In a few seconds I was on my way to the fifth floor before anyone could catch me.

Ben was waiting there. "Come on," he whispered. "Quick." He opened a door close to the elevator.

Gunther's hospital room was almost dark, except for the blinking of red-eyed machines reflected on metal and glass. The air smelled of medicines mixed with roses, for roses stood every- where in tall vases, walling off the bed from the door.

Ben murmured "Mary," and took me in his arms.

"Is Gunther…" I stopped, feeling Ben's suffering as clearly as I felt his breath on my cheek.

"Going," Ben whispered. "He's going." His arms tightened around me as if he could keep Gunther there by keeping me. "But he might hear your voice and know you."

I went to the bed and leaned over Gunther. His arms were in casts; his head was bandaged. I took off my scarf and my hair fell around his face on the pillow as I whispered, "Gunther. It's Mary." I had kissed that pale face so many times. The lips had kissed me. The body lying there had leaped through surf in the sunlight… made love to me… "Gunther," I breathed. "Gunther."

The blue eyes opened. Could he hear me? "I've come," I said. "It's Mary."

Now he was trying to speak. I put my ear close to his lips. "I made another…" he said in a voice that was hardly a breath…"one of you. Because…I love you so. You left."

"I love you, too," I said. "But I had to leave."

"Too late," came the ghostly whisper. "Too late."

"You'll have the honors and the prizes," I said. "Get well and you'll see." Tears were running down my face but I didn't feel them. "Get well."

"Give them…" He was trying to summon up breath. "To Ben." Then, fighting for more breath: "Kiss me."

I kissed him with a tear-wet mouth. When I drew away his eyes were open. Could he see me? I turned to Ben; he leaned above me. "He can hear you," Ben said.

I stroked Gunther's face. "Remember the little passageway at Hal's Grille, and our first dinner together—my first restaurant dinner?" I asked him. "You told me you wanted to amaze the world, and you have. Remember the Art Institute that afternoon, when we walked away, engaged? And my first birthday cake with the pink roses? And your diamond ring?"

Gunther's pale lips formed the word Yes.

"Ben's here," I said. "Remember how he welcomed us to his apartment with champagne? Remember…" I was babbling, as if I could keep him alive with words, nothing but words. "I've got the silver necklace you bought for me. Marie will wear it someday."

I couldn't talk about a sham wedding, or the baby that wasn't his. "Remember our first apartment?" I said, kissing his white face. "How we pounded nails with the heel of your shoe? Remember shopping for a chair, and finding the blue one we wanted after hunting all day? And the big bowls of beef stew that tasted so good afterward?"

Ben was sitting nearby now, his head in his hands. I sobbed. Gunther's eyes were shut now. "There's so little to remember," I whispered to Ben. "We weren't married long—and we weren't even married!" I covered my wet face with my hands and cried.

Ben lifted me into his arms. "Let him rest for a while." The dim light showed us the outlines of the room and each other. I tied my scarf around my hair again, and we stood by Gunther in the constant robot-click and purr of machines around his bed.

No one knocked. Tall urns of roses hid the door: a fragrant fence. Footsteps came and went along the hall. "You've spent days here," I murmured.

"Three," Ben said. "You came. I couldn't have found you, not in time."

"I watched you on television," I said.

Death seemed to prowl that room, breathing with the scent of roses bunched on a dresser, clustered in vases on the floor, drooping already in the close, dim air…

The door opened. Someone snapped on a dim light—

Neola!

I saw her between urns of roses. Behind her were two men.

Everything happened before I could snatch my breath to yell. Ben shoved the wall of urns against Neola and the men. Flowers and wire and pottery smashed over the three of them as they staggered against the open door, their feet tangled in broken vases and stands. Ben dragged me into the hall, into the open elevator. The elevator door shut behind us, cutting off Neola's cry: "That's her! Mary Bryant!"

The elevator sank so slowly. Ben stopped it at the second floor, and we left it and ran down stairs. In a moment we were in the cold night wind, racing for Ben's car, jumping into it, and swerving through parking lanes, the car tires squealing, to join passing traffic on the busy street.

"Where are you staying?" Ben asked as he glanced in the rearview mirror. I told him the hotel, and my room number. "But I've got a friend with me in another room—room 303," I said. "We can go there. It's not under my name—I call myself Mary Andrews—and no one has seen me in it."

"A friend?" Ben said.

"A wonderful woman who helped me when I was a child," I said. "Sophy Saul. She's got Maria. We traveled separately. We're pretending she's just a grandmother with her granddaughter."

"I don't think they followed us, but we'll have to make sure," Ben said. "Your hair's covered. You've got dark glasses. I'll leave you around the corner from the hotel. You go up to your friend's room if you don't see anyone suspicious. I'll park and come to you if the coast is clear. If it isn't, they'll follow me to my hotel. They've been following me all day. You can call me there." We were waiting for a green light; he scribbled a hotel name and some numbers on a card and gave it to me.

Ben dropped me on a corner. I lingered there a few minutes, then went into my hotel and crossed the lobby. No one seemed interested in me, or moved closer as I went to the elevators. There was no one in the hall when I reached our floor.

"Mary," Sophy whispered when she'd heard me knock five times and opened her door. "What happened?"

"Ben was there. I talked with Gunther, but he's...he won't live long. And then Neola came—just walked in with two men I suppose are her brothers. Ben and I ran out before they could catch

145

us, but Neola was yelling, 'That's her! That's Mary Bryant!'"

"You got away?"

"I think so. Ben's coming here to your room if there's no one following him."

"Everyone's seen him on television now."

"Reporters went after him in the hospital lobby. He won't come if there's any danger. I can call him."

"He doesn't want them to find you?" Sophy said. "Because it's too late now? Gunther isn't well enough for awards and honors?"

"Ben knows I couldn't stand what he's going through—reporters and photographers on his trail day and night." I felt cold, and sat down on the bed, shivering. Sophy put a blanket around me.

17

Someone knocked softly at the door. I hid in the bathroom, until I heard Ben say politely: "I'm Ben Carlos, and you must be Sophy, Mary's good friend. Has Mary come?"

I stepped into the room. He saw me and said, "I think we escaped them. For now."

Sophia said, "I'm so glad to see you, Ben. I'd stay and talk, but I think the two of you have plans to make." She smiled at us. "Mary, if you give me your key, I'll spend the night in your room, and you can have this one with the crib. That way you'll be here with Maria, and you and Ben can decide what to do."

"Thanks," I said. Sophy began to pack her clothes in her suitcase, and I helped her. "I'll bring your things from the other room, and knock five times," Sophy said.

By the time I'd changed Maria, Sophy was at the door. "Nobody's around," she whispered. "Goodnight."

Ben lifted my suitcase to a rack. I nursed Maria with a blanket around me. The muted sounds of Chicago traffic came from the street below. Voices passed in the hall outside.

Ben said, "What will you do?"

"You're giving me my choice again," I said. "You let me choose in the airport, didn't you? You put the money in my hand and left."

"I had to know."

"And I didn't choose Gunther."

There was the pressure of hope in Ben's voice. "Then why did you come?"

147

"I saw you on television trying to give all the honor to Gunther. Everything."

"He's dying."

"You could have let him die without proving anything. You could have kept me locked up in Mexico and waited, and had the fame and awards and honor."

"Yes."

"You didn't," I said. "That's why I came."

Ben bowed his head; I couldn't see the expression in his eyes. "I'll go on living," he said. "Gunther won't. I tried to be like a big brother to him, but he didn't want advice."

"You tried."

"You can see that?" Ben asked.

"Yes," I said. "Now I can."

"But it's not my decision, it's yours. What will you do?"

I looked down at Maria, who had fallen asleep in my arms. "I don't know."

"I've got to go back to him," Ben said. "I'll make sure no one sees me here, and I'll come to you when he..."

Ben gave me a last look, and was gone.

"Dies," I said to no one but a baby asleep.

In the deep night a sound worked its way into my restless doze. I opened my eyes to a dark hotel room. Someone was tapping at the door.

Like an echo from my prisoner days in Acapulco, I whispered into the door crack: "Who's there," and another echo answered: "Ben."

He came into my arms as the door closed behind him. I held him there in the dark. "Gunther's gone," he whispered.

He swayed in my arms. "You're exhausted," I said. "You've gone days without sleep." It wasn't hard to ease him down on the bed. "You're too tired to dodge reporters any more, or drive. Rest here for a while."

He hardly seemed to hear me. I helped him out of his coat and suit coat. He lay on the bed and I took off his shoes. He said: "I've brought your suitcase you left at the airport when you ran away. It's there by the door. What time is it?"

"Three-thirty." I leaned over him and he pulled me into his arms. For a moment his hands were on my breasts through the thin silk of my gown. "Mary," he whispered. "Mary."

148

"Go to sleep," I murmured, and ran my fingers through his hair on the pillow. He caught my hands in his, and felt my left hand with its fake rings. "Go to sleep," I whispered once more. He didn't answer; he lay as still as a dead man.

I hung up his coats and turned on the bathroom light long enough to see Maria asleep in her crib. Then I crawled under a blanket at the far side of the bed.

Suddenly I heard Ben's cold, hopeless voice. "You only think of me as a man who would rape you."

I didn't answer; I felt the bed shake. A man was crying beside me in the dark.

Morning had come when Maria woke me; she was hungry and wet. Ben lay sleeping beside me; his face looked young and peaceful. If he woke, he would remember Gunther.

Maria gave her first little chicken-clucks of warning: she would cry soon. I grabbed my clothes, scooped her up and shut us in the bathroom. Before long she was clean and asleep, and I was dressed.

I unpacked my suitcase Ben had left by the door, shaking out the wrinkled clothes he'd bought for me in Acapulco. Ben never stirred. I called Sophy and said, "Gunther died last night. Ben's here in bed. He hasn't slept for days, and I imagine he hasn't eaten much, either. Come here and we'll order breakfast."

Sophy came, tapping five times at my door. When I let her in, she looked down at sleeping Ben. "A dinner is what he needs, not a breakfast." So we planned a feast, and called in the order. When it came, we covered Ben with blankets. I hid in the bathroom as the room was filled with the smell of sausage and bacon and fruit and steaming coffee. When the door shut behind the waiters, Ben sat up in bed, blinking at Sophy and me. "Time for breakfast," Sophy told him.

Watching Ben's eyes, I saw reality come back to hurt him, and Sophy saw it, too. "Gunther is gone?" she said in a gentle voice.

"Last night about two." Ben said, and went in the bathroom.

"Poor Ben," I said. "He was too tired to try to escape the newsmen at his hotel. He never heard Maria yell this morning."

"It takes the smell of coffee and breakfast to do that," Sophy said. We pulled the table covered with food close to the bed; one of us could sit on the bed while the others used the chairs.

A crisp newspaper had come with the breakfast. I unfolded it to see a headline: GUNTHER RISLING DEAD. MOTHER OF AMERICAN CLONE FLEES. Sophy and I stood together reading the short article. It quoted Neola: "I've seen the surrogate mother of the clone here in Chicago: Mary Bryant. Gunther Risling must be given credit for this."

Ben came from the bathroom with his face still damp and his hair combed. He looked at the breakfast table. "We thought you might like a snack," Sophy said.

Ben sat down and put a napkin on his lap. "I've never seen food look so good," he said. We were all hungry; we hardly talked until we sat enjoying our coffee beside the empty plates. I handed Ben the newspaper; he read the news of Gunther's death.

"I shouldn't have gone to the hospital," I said. "I should have known Neola would come."

"You made Gunther happy," Ben said. As he spoke, I saw Sophy watching him intently. "He talked about it just before he..."

The unfinished sentence hung in the sunny air from the window. In a little while Sophy asked in a low voice, "How did the accident happen?"

"He was just outside of Chicago, coming from Florida and Epcot. It was raining, and perhaps he couldn't see the road well, or else he was being chased. The law was after him, of course, and the media were mobbing him at Disney World. I don't think we'll ever know. You've seen pictures of the car? There wasn't much left of it."

Sophy and I put the breakfast dishes on trays and set them outside the door. "I'm a pallbearer at the funeral," Ben said as we came back. "But you three should probably fly back to Sophy's house, wherever it is. The reporters are on Mary's trail now."

"We're in Belmont, Massachusetts near Boston," Sophy said, writing her address and telephone number on hotel stationery. She gave it to him. "I've known Mary since she was a child, and she's as dear as a daughter to me. Anyone who hurts her is my enemy."

"I'm your enemy then. I hurt Mary. Gunther did, too," Ben said.

"Yes. You did," Sophy said.

"I did it because I was ambitious," Ben said, his voice low and ashamed. "And I did it for my friend. But that's no excuse."

"No," Sophy said. "It isn't. When Mary was a child, she was called every filthy name a child can be called; I saw her try to live through that."

Ben got up suddenly as if he couldn't bear to be in the room any longer. He put on his suit coat and his overcoat. "I'll try to come again today, but you may be gone." He stood with his hand on the door knob and said to Sophy: "We both lost Mary—Gunther and I. That was our punishment: to break our hearts."

He opened the door, looked up and down the hall, and shut it behind him.

I packed my clothes and Maria's, then stood at the window of our room watching Chicago streets in the April sunlight, waiting for Sophy to tap at my door. We would travel to Boston as strangers again, with Sophy bringing her "grandchild," Maria.

The phone rang. Ben said, "Reporters caught me coming out of your hotel. Now they think you and Maria are there. Don't go out or try to fly home, or you'll be on every TV screen and newspaper front page. You're registered under a false name—that's good. Don't open your door for anyone but somebody with food. Put a 'Do Not Disturb' sign on the outside of your door. With any luck, they'll get tired of staking out your hotel. You've got my hotel room phone number—I'm hiding out here as well as I can. I'll try to call you soon."

Sophy and I cancelled our plane flights, and put "Do Not Disturb" signs on our doors. "Poor Sophy," I said, as we ate breakfast the next morning. "You ought to be in Belmont watching your tulips and daffodils come up."

We turned on the television. A commentator was saying: "Crowds are expected at Gunther Risling's funeral at ten o'clock. The cloning of a woman in France, and the story of the Sorcerer's Apprentice, has drawn world attention to the problem of replicating human beings."

Authorities were interviewed, and they disagreed with each other. "People will want clones," one man said. "They're already paying high prices for in vitro fertilization."

But a lawyer said: "Our universities are producing graduates every year who can work with IVF specialists like Ben Carlos to provide 'clone service' to the world. Is this what we want?"

"The Sorcerer's Apprentice may have cloned Mary Bryant, but he didn't make an exact copy of her," a third authority said. "The clone would always be a generation younger than Mary Bryant—not Mary's twin, but a child with one-of-a-kind consciousness and soul and memories. Nobody can clone a soul, or character, or personality."

A woman scientist said: "If we've cloned a woman, then single women can now clone themselves and have themselves copied as their own baby—no man involved."

Sophy groaned. "I can't believe it. I can't believe any of it. 'Oh, brave new world, that has such people in it.'"

"But you're beginning to believe that Maria is my clone?" I took Sophy's hand and smiled at her, then went to bring Maria from her crib.

I sat close to Sophy; Maria was awake and she looked up at me with eyes that had become bluer and bluer.

"Hold her up," Sophy said. "Put her face next to yours."

I lifted Maria in her little pink shirt and diaper and put her cheek close to mine.

Sophy stared at us, and her expression deepened as if she were seeing something new. "It's her eyes," she said in a faint voice. "There are two Marys looking at me."

"Yes," I said. "I remember the first time I looked hard—really hard—at Maria and me in a mirror."

"The eyes," Sophy said. She seemed to be almost talking to herself, not me. She looked stunned, almost frightened. "It's the eyes," she said, almost whispering. "You're there. Looking out of her little face."

Sophy and I watched Gunther's funeral on television. We saw his casket carried down rain-slick steps.

Ben walked in the line of pallbearers; I could see his tall figure, and his black hair sleek with the falling rain. "America has taken Gunther Risling to its heart: this young pioneer who claims to have done what no one has ever done," a commentator said. "Time—and a woman and her baby somewhere—may prove that he was right."

Neola followed the casket, and two young men had their arms around her. An older man and woman followed. "Those must be Neola's parents," I said. "And her brothers."

"He's lost his best friend," I said, and thought of divers falling from the cliffs to the sea.

"The brothers who tried to keep Gunther away from you?" Sophy said.

"They stalked us at Epcot, I think. They might have chased Gunther until he drove off the road. Killed him," I said. One of the brothers was dark-bearded. The other's head was bald, though he was young. Both were short and heavy, with broad noses; they half-carried their weeping sister between them.

The pallbearers in their dark suits brought Gunther's casket to the curb, then tried to wrestle the heavy coffin into the hearse. The big, gleaming box would not slide.

For a moment the camera gave us a close-up of Ben's face. "He's lost his best friend," I said, and thought of divers falling from the cliffs to the sea. "They took a great risk together."

Sophy watched as the casket slid into the hearse at last. "You do have a way to comfort Ben, I think," she said. "If you can."

I didn't answer. I remembered a man crying in my dark bed. The doors of the hearse shut, and it pulled away from the curb.

Ben stood alone watching the hearse go. His black suit and hair shone with the driving rain.

18

It was almost dark the next day when Ben tapped at the door of my hotel room.

"How tired you look," Sophy said, taking his coat. "Did you get any sleep last night?"

"Not much," Ben said. "You've had to wait for me. I finally took the subway because the reporters were easier to lose there, and I came here through the hotel's service entrance."

"We have some nice hot coffee for you," Sophy said.

Ben sat down with us, and I saw him stifle a yawn. "We watched television, and saw you at the funeral," Sophy said, pouring his coffee.

"So many people," Ben said. "They crowd around you, put notes in your pockets…"

"What kind of notes?" I asked.

"Oh…" Ben looked embarrassed. "Notes about the cloning."

Sophy had laid his coat on the bed near me. I reached into a pocket, found rustling paper, and read some of the notes aloud: "You are a true friend to the Sorcerer." "You are my ideal man." "Find the clone, help Gunther Risling."

"They're all pretty much like that," Ben said, hanging his coat in the closet. "How are we going to get the three of you out of here?"

"Sophy and Maria won't be any trouble," I said. "If reporters stop her because she has a baby, she can just be outraged, and say it's her grandchild, and yell at them until they leave her alone." Sophy laughed.

"But what about you?" Ben asked.

It was my turn to look embarrassed. "I still have the Far Eastern costume I wore... to hide from you when Maria and I ran away at the airport."

"A costume? You didn't have to go to all that trouble. I wouldn't have chased you." Ben gave me a tired smile.

"I put dark tan makeup on my face, and black eyebrows," I said. "And I wore that black evening dress you bought for me, and the scarf wrapped around me, and turned myself into a Far Eastern woman," I said.

"I hoped I'd see you in that dress someday."

"Put it on," Sophy said. "It'll cheer him up. And I'll go to my room and finish packing if we're going to Boston."

"Sophy—you can help me, if you will," Ben said. He gave her an envelope. "I wrote a note for you inside it. I won't be able to be with you this evening or tomorrow. I can't even take you to the airport. I don't know when I'll see you again."

Sophy hugged him, said goodbye and left. I took the black evening gown into the bathroom. It was wrinkled, but I put it on, and twisted my hair on the top of my head. I had found a box among my closet-full of new clothes in Acapulco—a jewel box holding diamond earrings. Now they dangled from my ears.

Ben's dark eyes shone when I came back. For a moment he looked like the man who had told me he loved me. Then he hid the look and said: "Beautiful. I always knew how beautiful you would be in that dress. And the earrings were my mother's. I wanted you to have them."

Neither of us knew where to look, or what to say. We stood by Maria's crib and watched her wave her hands and kick her pink feet. "Sophy is beginning to believe in cloning," I said. "She told me that Maria has my eyes."

"I noticed that the first time I saw Maria," Ben said. "When I stole her from you at Epcot. A perfect little girl. The first of her kind."

"Unlucky little girl," I said.

"But I want her to mean happiness for you," Ben said. "Give you your education. Support you afterward. She can do that."

"Show her to the public, you mean? Like some kind of freak?"

"Of course not. You can both live a normal life," Ben said. "She's the reason for so much of your unhappiness. So am I." He took one of Maria's small feet in his hand, letting her kick against his palm. "I've inherited a fortune from my mother. I've asked Sophia to set up a bank account for you. I want you to have—"

"No!" I shook my head and his earrings struck against my skin.

"I know you don't want me!" Ben's voice was tight with feeling. "But my money hasn't lied to you, or raped you—take it!"

"From you?"

"You ran away from me at the airport. How could I ever have found you again? But you came! You came! Let me try to make up for what I've done, and what Gunther did."

We were very close, there at Maria's crib. Ben's eyes went over my face, my hair, my bare shoulders and arms. "If you ever need me," he said. "If you're in any trouble, any trouble at all, call me! Call me! Come!"

I remembered his words to Gunther: *Come any time. Any time at all. Please.*

He had begged Gunther. He was begging me.

"Goodbye," Ben said. He opened the door to look up and down the hall, then closed it behind him.

I rubbed my wet eyes, and felt his earrings against my neck. I opened the door. Ben was still in sight. "Ben!" I called softly.

He heard me, and came. "I've forgotten the earrings," I said, taking them off and holding them out. "It's not right to keep them, if…" I couldn't go on.

"I want you to have them. Wear them," Ben said. "Because I love you. Count on it." A last look from his dark eyes and he was gone.

The next morning a convention crowd filled the hotel lobby. Harried clerks hardly glanced at a Far Eastern lady shrouded in black. Tired reporters and photographers sat in the lobby watching for a woman and baby.

A bellboy carried my suitcases to a taxi, we drove away, and I gave a long sigh. If Sophy and Maria could escape as easily as I had…

"Nobody stopped us," Sophy said when we met in the airport near our gate. "Some fellows in the lobby looked as if they might be trouble, but I glared at them and they left me alone."

The media were hunting for us. I watched television on the plane to Boston. Our escape was exciting news, and the commentators loved it. *Where's the mother?* they asked. *Where's the clone? Why did the Sorcerer's Apprentice do it? Was he lying?*

They caught Ben in Chicago. Sophy, Maria and I had barely reached Sophy's house when we saw Ben at bay on our television screen. His face was on the front page of the paper: MEXICAN DOCTOR INSISTS THE SORCERER'S APPRENTICE CLONED.

Interviewers grilled Ben: *Why hasn't the surrogate mother come forward? Won't you be a laughing-stock in your own country, Dr. Carlos?*

Think of the money all of you could make—books, talk shows, even a movie deal!

It's reported that you may be kept from medical practice in Mexico.

How can you think of creating babies without souls, Dr. Carlos?

Will people buy cells from movie stars and sports celebrities? Will we put our cells in storage when we die? Could a rich person—or a genius— live from clone to clone forever?

Ben smiled a little at some of the questions. "I'm sure the movie producers and science fiction writers will try to answer those questions for you," he said politely.

But other questions were difficult for him: *You've said the process is expensive,* an interviewer said, *But this won't stop rich people. How will we decide who gets cloned?*

Ben said nothing for a moment or two. There were dark circles under his brown eyes. "You ask important questions," he said courteously. "I can't pretend to have answers. If, indeed, we have made a normally-developing clone and I'm able to continue my practice, I'll need expert advice in order to be fair."

"So you'll play God."

Ben's face reddened. "Only as much as every doctor must. Today we save those who would have died a hundred years ago. We give barren couples babies of their own. If we are allowed to use cloning in all its forms, we will be able to commute death sentences for millions of people in the future, creating new organs and new knowledge."

"So you *are* playing God."

"I don't think it's playing," Ben said. "I think God invests us with this power. If it's so life-saving and life-giving, where could this power come from but from God?"

The interviewer gave Ben a disgusted glance. The program switched to a race with cars careening against a fence, but the look in Ben's eyes stayed with me as Sophia turned off the television. "What did Ben mean by saying: *If, indeed, we have made a normally-developing clone?*" I asked her.

"Maria's an experiment, I suppose," Sophy said. "Who can tell if she'll grow up? But that's true of any baby. She certainly seems healthy to me."

"Yes. She does." I rubbed my tired eyes.

"I know we're all exhausted," Sophy said, "but I want to give you this envelope Ben gave me. It's really for you."

I opened the envelope to find a check made out to Sophy. The signature was Ben's. The amount was unbelievable. I gasped.

The note with the check was typed, and wasn't signed: "Please be so kind as to deposit this check in a bank account for our friend to pay for education and any other expenses. If more is needed, let me know."

"He told me he wanted to do this," I said. "I told him I wouldn't take his money."

"Then you hurt him pretty badly, I think."

"It's like being paid for...for being used!" I glared at her. "Or is it hush money?"

"Was that part of the agreement? That you take the money and give him the fame?"

"He never mentioned that."

"Then the money's yours without any conditions, I think. Just his way of saying he's sorry—"

"Let him *be* sorry! He hasn't been made a prostitute with an illegitimate child! He's got all his mother's money! What has he got to lose?"

"Pretty much everything, I'm afraid," Sophy said. "I read an article on the plane. It said that Ben might be banned from practicing in Mexico. His new medical center would be closed. The authorities are even going so far as to call him mentally unstable."

"Insane!" I cried. "Ben?"

"He's made outlandish medical claims he can't prove."

"He'll lose everything he's worked so hard for?" I said. Sophy shrugged.

I took Maria into my bedroom to change her and put her in her crib. I put Ben's check on the marble mantelpiece. If I used Ben's money, it would support Maria, Sophy and me, and give me a college education. Maria could grow up as just another little girl living with her mother and her grandmother...hidden.

Reporters and cameramen stalked Ben. Before the next day was over, he boarded a plane for Acapulco, and was the butt of sniggers and jokes. He was pictured as "Mister Mac-Clone," blindly groping around him to find a squalling baby. He was "Doctor Two," not "Who," creating twin people in outer space.

Sophy and I set up my account at the bank. "Did you ever think you'd be the richest woman in Plattsburg, Nebraska?" Sophy asked me.

The discussion of cloning filled television programs. A French doctor spoke from his prison cell, appealing for legal freedom to clone.

"If Gunther were still alive, he'd be in prison now," I said to Sophy.

"He'd be fighting, like the Frenchman."

"He'd be happy," I said. "He told me over and over: *I'm going to amaze the world. I'll make my mark.*"

"Poor man," Sophy said, her eyes on the television screen. "And look at that! Poor woman. Poor little clone."

We watched the French mother trying to shop for food. A crowd of reporters knocked over store displays to get at her. The baby's visits to the doctor were a media free-for-all. A commentator said: "French authorities are asking if the world's first human clone should be guarded as the Dionne quintuplets were: she and her mother could be kept in a special home where the public would be able to see her from a distance."

"Ben warned me!" I cried. "He said the whole world would be after us—we'd be mobbed—displayed—merchandized."

"Ben was right," Sophy said, and turned off the television. Neither of us wanted to see another picture of the frantic mother and crying child.

"But someone has made you a different person from that French mother," Sophy said. "Somebody keeps stating that you are 'a courageous surrogate mother who intends to keep her child safe from publicity and commercial use.'" Sophy smiled. Ben had done that, of course, day by day, describing the woman no one could find.

"Yes," I said. "Ben."

We were safe in Belmont, I thought. I should have been able to relax with Maria and Sophy, but I couldn't.

"Would I dare go back to Nebraska?" I asked Sophy the next day.

"You want Rhody."

"I left her behind so long ago. She'll be seven years old in September! She's waited and waited and waited for me, and lost heart."

"It's so dangerous," Sophy said. "I could go."

"I did think of that," I said. "I know you'd do anything for me. But I know places to hide in Plattsburg, the way children do. I know every stick and stone of our neighborhood, and how to get her away."

Sophy looked worried. "If those Rands are looking for you anywhere, they'll be in Plattsburg."

We sat for a while, thinking.

"Ben gave me so much money," I said. "I keep thinking of people who don't have any, like Becky in Chicago. I could go through there on my way. I'll have to wean Maria first. Could you take care of her for a little while? And could I borrow your car?"

"Of course. But you're taking such a chance."

"No one has a picture of me yet, and I won't be traveling with a baby," I said. "Don't you think they've nearly given up looking for us? It's the French clone and her mother they're mobbing."

"I'm afraid they're still after you," Sophy said. "The Rand family craves the fame for Gunther—won't they do anything to get it for him? And this country wants to take the prize for the first clone away from France."

I didn't want to think about the danger. I thought of Rhody and the clothes she would need. I gave myself a different face with makeup, hid my hair, and took the subway to Boston. How happy

162

I was, buying a wardrobe for Rhody, guessing at her size for jeans and shirts and dresses and shoes. I packed a suitcase for her, and added all the games, puzzles and books it would hold.

Maria was weaned with no trouble, and Sophy and I enjoyed our days together. We explored the attic, and found boxes of books. Sneezing in the attic dust, we were our old book-loving selves. "Here's a set of Jane Austen!" I said one morning.

"Montaigne," Sophy said, wiping off an old book.

"I'll read him all my life," I said, and picked up a paperback that was losing its pages. "Have you read anything by Sigrid Undset?"

"*Gunnar's Daughter*," Sophy said. "Read that. A woman in Norway in the Middle Ages. You'll find she's your sister."

We carried books downstairs. "Rhody will want to sleep with me," I said.

Sophy opened a door to another big room with another marble fireplace. "We'll put all three of you in this front room, next to mine," Sophy said. So I bought Rhody and me rose-covered sheets—for "Rhoda" is Greek for "a rose,"—and I filled a bookcase with books for her. The next day I said, "Maria's weaned and I'm ready to go."

Sophy was worried. "You've got to be so careful."

"I'll go to Chicago first," I said, "and then go back to Plattsburg as...what? A widow? A widow at nineteen? Oh, Sophy!" (I could tell her anything) "How I would *love* to park your car in front of that Durfy shack and walk in wearing the nice clothes Ben bought for me—with my wedding ring on my finger!" I hugged her. "But I can't. I know what I have to do. I'll go there at night! I'll sneak and I'll hide, but I'll bring my Rhody home!"

19

At seventeen I'd run away to Chicago, scared, sleeping on a bus, gnawing a loaf of bread, carrying all I owned in a plastic sack. Now, not even two years later, I drove Sophy's car, slept in comfortable motels, and came at last to a Chicago street I knew so well.

But Hal's Grille was gone. I parked across the street and saw a dry cleaner's sign in the front window. The narrow passage between buildings was still there. Two lovers had kissed in that narrow space once upon a time. I followed the memory of Gunther into the sunlight at the passage's end.

The hedge was there, but two lawn chairs and their cushions were gone; the grass was a patch of weeds.

I went into the dry cleaning shop. A clerk stood behind the counter, bald and bored. "I'm looking for the Schatzels," I said. "Did you know them? They ran a little restaurant called 'Hal's Grille' in this building."

"Never heard of them," he said. Behind him was the hall to the storeroom where I had slept. For a moment a memory showed me Gunther Risling, leaning on that counter and saying: "You're as lovely as a Madonna."

"Thanks," I said to the clerk, and closed the Grille's old door behind me. I walked to Dinty's Hamburger Heaven. A "Servers Wanted" was in the window, and servers in their green shirts were still running back and forth.

I sat at a table gingerly—didn't I know how the grease spread in that place?—and hoped I'd see a dear, plump woman with a double chin, very black eyes and very big teeth. Once a handsome man had sat at the nearby table and asked Becky Warren for my name...

"Mary!"

It was Becky—Becky herself in her green shirt. "Mary! It's you!"

We hugged each other in the midst of rush and clatter. "When can we talk?" I asked her.

"It's my afternoon off today—after I eat lunch—one-thirty," Becky said. "Look at you!" She held me at arm's length. "Just look at you!"

I hugged her again. "Don't want to lose your job for you. I've got a car—I'll come back for you at one-thirty."

She gave me a last squeeze and rushed off. I drove past the little restaurant where a waiter might still remember a diamond ring...a birthday cake...and lovers too much in love to know it was closing time...

I drove to the Art Institute to eat lunch, and walked through rooms of beautiful objects, hearing Gunther say: *You'd help me? Marry me!*"

The gilded Madonna still hung in her place on a wall, watching me with sad eyes: a virgin with a child, like me. My footsteps echoed, leaving that lonely room.

When I went back to Dinty's, Becky was waiting at the door, a big grin on her face. "How beautiful you look," she said. She was a plump as ever, but tired and pale. "I recognized Gunther Risling right away on television," she said as we got into my car. "Then they showed his wife, and it wasn't you! *Something awful has happened*, I thought. And then Gunther died! I'm so sorry!"

"I ran away from him," I said. "We had a fake wedding. He only wanted me for one thing, I found out—just what I was afraid of. And now I've got my dear baby girl."

"Sorry again, but good for you," Becky said cheerfully.

"I may come back to Chicago to work, and I need your help. Again."

"Ask away," she said, giving my hand a squeeze. She wasn't asking questions. She never had.

"Are you still sleeping in that bread truck?"

165

"Yes, but I'm afraid there's no room for you just now. A new girl at Dinty's is sharing with me. She might be leaving, but it's going to be too hot in the truck when summer comes."

"Do you know of any nice apartments near Dinty's—cheap ones, but clean and safe? I could rent a place in advance."

Becky's black eyes lit up. "There's an old place a few blocks away that's just been taken over and modernized. It's pretty expensive, but the apartments are furnished. Let's go look." We drove away under city trees that were beginning to cast shade. "You've got a car, and such beautiful clothes!" Becky said, and gave me directions. "You've found somebody who loves you, I can tell." She teased me, but she didn't pry.

The apartments near Dinty's were for rent, newly-decorated and clean. We walked through some of them, and sat down to rest in the last one. "What do you think?" I asked Becky. "Do you like this place? Would you like to live here?"

"Would I? When I'm sleeping in a bread truck?" She looked around the apartment wistfully.

"Could I afford the rent?"

"Maybe," Becky said. "If you had two jobs. They'd have to be awfully good jobs." She sighed. "To have a cool place to sleep all summer, and a warm one in winter!"

"I think I like this one the best, don't you?" I said. "We like its nice view of some back gardens. But I have a problem. Can I rent it in your name? I know it's a lot to ask, but I want to keep my plans secret for now."

"Well...sure...go ahead."

"You'll have to pretend to rent it," I said. "And can you live in it and take care of it until I come back? I've got quite a bit of cash." I took a roll of bills from my purse. "Will you say you're renting it, and pay the deposit and six months rent, and get rid of this money before I lose it?"

"Live here?" Becky said, staring at the money I gave her.

We went downstairs to the office, and Becky hardly seemed to notice as the apartment manager took the money and gave her a receipt for the deposit and the rent. "You can move in now," he said.

Becky took the keys he gave her and followed me out to the street. "Mary?" she said as we drove off, "I can live there while your gone? In that apartment?"

166

"That's right," I said. "It's another favor you can do me. And there's one more."

"One *more*?" Becky echoed.

"I've got to have a bank account here, but I don't dare use my name on it, either," I said. "Can I put a couple of thousand dollars in the bank under your name?"

"A couple of thousand?" Becky looked stunned. "And I take it out for you when you come?"

"That's right," I said.

"And you trust me with all this?"

"Do I trust somebody who was a friend to a hungry girl from Nebraska, and taught her to work at Dinty's, and gave her a bed when it rained? Why on earth would I trust somebody like that?"

"Oh, Mary! A real apartment to stay in!" Becky's pale face turned pink. "I can't believe it! I can't believe any of it!"

Becky opened an account in her name at a bank near Dinty's, deposited my thousands of dollars in cash, and asked no questions as we stopped at a shopping mall to buy sheets, pillows, blankets, towels, and food. By seven that evening we were having supper in the apartment.

Becky kept exclaiming at new delights there: the air conditioning, the television, the little kitchen…we took turns taking showers in the shining-new bathroom. When it was late enough, we found the bread truck in the motel parking lot, and Becky dragged out her sleeping bag and some clothes. I peered into the truck's cramped space where I'd slept, thanks to Becky, safe from cold rain.

The apartment was waiting for us, and we crawled into the big bed with its new flowered sheets. "When I come back," I told her, "you know you'll be welcome to live with me here."

Becky's voice had a sob in it. "I can't believe it!"

"You're my dear friend," I said, and kissed her. "Don't tell anyone a thing about me. You'd better get to sleep. As I remember, Dinty's always opens way too early."

"You'll be here when I get back late tomorrow night?"

"Afraid not," I said. "But I'll call you when I can."

"Goodbye, then," she said, kissing me back. "I can't ever thank you enough, but I'll pray for you."

She went to sleep. I lay in the dark listening to the sounds of Chicago. *Keep moving*, I said to myself.

Sunlight filled the apartment when I woke. Becky had left a breakfast for me in her small kitchen.

I found a piece of paper and wrote a note while I ate, then propped it on the kitchen table where she would be sure to see it:

Becky, my dear friend,

> *Thank you once more for being so kind to me.*

> *The apartment and the six months rent and the bank account are yours.*

> *I meant them to be yours, but I didn't want to tell you because I was afraid you wouldn't take them. They are in your name—it makes me so happy to give them to you. I'm not involved, and you can do anything you want with them.*

> *Sorry to be so sneaky about this. Don't mention me to anyone. Not one word. I'll call you when I can.*

> *Love,*

> *Mary*

I was crossing the living room, my suitcase in my hand, when Becky's phone rang. I answered, and could barely hear her voice over the clatter of the kitchen at Dinty's. "Mary!" she said in a sharp whisper, "A girl at Dinty's just told me! A fellow who said he was a detective came to Dinty's yesterday afternoon asking about you! The boss told him you'd been here yesterday talking to me, but I won't tell anyone anything! Love you—bye!"

I got in my car. I went west to Nebraska like a fool. "Fool! Fool!" I said to myself and the slow Chicago traffic. "If Neola or her brothers have tracked me to Dinty's, they'll be waiting for me in my home town!"

But Rhody was there.

I kept watch in all directions, mile after mile. No one seemed to be following me as I crossed Illinois...crossed Iowa...stopped at last to sleep all day in an Omaha hotel, waiting for dark.

I left the city for narrow country roads, thinking of Rhody, so close now. I'd fought to keep Maria, and I'd fight to keep Rhody.

Only a few cars and trucks met me or followed me for miles. By the time the moon rose, Plattsburg was over a slight rise in the cornfields.

168

I remembered a lonely stand of trees along the road, and found it. At one side was a meadow of weeds and bushes. Sophy's car was black, and the meadow undergrowth hid it when I drove in backward to give myself a quick getaway.

For a minute I stood beside the car, listening to the cheeping and ticking of insects in the night. A breeze brought me a familiar rustling sound—the "Grandmother" cottonwood tree that Rhody and I had climbed so often. The tree was talking to herself with all her leaves in the dark field.

I hurried away. Moonlight cast shadows across the empty road. Now I heard the sound of traveling water, and there was the creek, and the fallen tree where I'd hidden my money long ago.

The Durfy shack was dark. No truck was parked behind it—was my "stepfather" out of town? Surely no one hunting me would stake out a shack at night. Was everyone asleep?

Junk was piled in the yard, just as it had always been. I didn't need to switch on my flashlight: moonlight showed me the path. My stepfather's rusty motorcycle was still propped against the privy.

I heard some animal skitter under a heap of old tires as I picked my way to the house. No television light flickered inside. But surely our dogs would hear me or catch my scent any minute, and bark.

I held my breath to listen. No dog's yelp—only a thin singing came through a window. The sound was as breathy and light as the breeze blowing on me, but it sang an old folk tune, and I knew the words:

> *The water is wide, I cannot go home,*
> *Nor have I any wings to fly.*
> *Lend me a boat that will carry two...*

The words hovered in the air like a ghost.

Our front porch creaked, as it always had. The door swung open on a black room.

The faint song had stopped. I snapped on my flashlight and covered half the beam with my hand, looking for girls asleep on one bed, Rhody in another...

The room was bare. No stove, no refrigerator, no table. My father's big chair was gone. No dogs came to meet me, only a trail of trash across the floor...

169

Something flung itself on me from the other room! The flashlight spun out of my hand. I fell on my back with a weight on my chest, the flashlight's beam on the wall, and a scream in my ears.

Arms would not let go of me. Legs twined around me. Long hair covered my face. When I sat up, struggling, eyes were inches from mine: Rhody's.

"You came!" she screamed. "I knew you would!"

I got my breath back, hugging and kissing her. We mixed our breaths with tears and wild words. "You came!" Rhody said over and over, shaking me hard, wiping her runny nose on her shirt.

"What's happened?" I said finally, staring around me at bare walls and trash.

"Mom and Dad got killed last week," Rhody said. "Smashed up on the highway in that truck."

"Killed?"

"I knew you'd come! Yesterday those girls took everything— one of them's married."

"But who's been feeding you?"

"They left some stuff for me. I knew you'd come!"

"Oh, Rhody, Rhody, I'm so glad to have you!" I rocked her back and forth in my arms.

"I was scared, but I didn't care."

"How I've missed you. You've grown!"

"We're going, aren't we?" Rhody sprang out of my arms. "Right now! While it's dark! Those men won't see us!"

"What men?"

"I don't know what men. They keep wandering around, talking about a baby they've lost, and her mother named Mary Bryant, whoever that is."

"Here? Now?"

"They said she'd stolen some baby. They tell everybody in town she did that, and they even come here at night—they were here last night…"

Her voice trailed off as we heard a car motor. It cut off. A car door slammed.

"The back window," I whispered. "Quick."

We'd climbed out that bedroom window many times. I dropped to a bare spot in the junk pile, lifted Rhody down, and we ran through old tires and rusted chicken wire and shadows cast by the bright moonlight.

Rhody and I ran away from the men through moonlit
bushes.

Men shouted behind us. I looked back and saw a bearded man at the bedroom window. Moonlight gleamed on the bald head of a man yelling behind him.

We raced along the creek. "I've got a car!" I yelled. "Run!"

The moon showed the way through familiar cornfields and over a fence. We heard pounding feet behind us; we couldn't hide from the bright moonlight...

The Grandma Tree whispered to us as we ran past. A gate in a fence. The car. We yanked two doors open—leaped inside—slammed them shut. Just as I gunned the car out of weeds to the road, the two men reached it—so close, so close—their fingernails scraped along the car before we left them in moonlit dust.

"Just let them try to catch us!" I cried. "Their car is way back at the house!"

I knew the farm paths for miles around, and the shortcuts from one to another. The moon lit our way through a farmyard, then an orchard. Cows watched our bucking car bounce among a meadow's cow-pies to a gate Rhody jumped out to open. I drove through, she shut it and climbed in beside me. Now we were speeding down a one-lane gravel road that looped over the hills without another car in sight.

20

Rhody was scared, delighted, excited. We followed narrow gravel roads for miles in the moonlight. After she had chattered a while, she amused herself with the car radio. I took minor roads to miss Omaha. When we made a stop in Iowa, she crawled into the back seat, tired out at last, and slept.

It was very late when I found a small motel between Des Moines and Davenport. I parked and looked at Rhody. She sprawled on the back seat in shabby jeans and shirt. Her dark hair stuck to her forehead in sweaty wads; there was mud on her forehead.

"Rhody," I whispered. She opened her eyes, staring at the car roof above her, then at me.

"We're going to sleep at a motel," I told her. "I don't want them to know you're with me. Hide on the car floor here, will you, until I rent a room? Then I'll sneak you in."

Rhody's eyes shone. "Just like a movie!"

She'd never been in a motel. The moment we closed the door she had to take the coffeemaker apart, and try the television, and pull tissues from the wall and a hair dryer from its rack. We unwrapped a bar of soap for her shower and a pack of shampoo to wash her hair.

"I've brought clothes for you," I said when she came out of the wet bathroom with a towel around her middle. "Here's your nightgown."

She loved the pink nightgown. She loved the pink slippers. She loved having her long, clean hair brushed. While I brushed

174

I said, "I haven't had time to tell you much about my baby. Her name's Maria."

"And you're married?"

"Not any more. He died."

"Do you have a boyfriend?"

Ben had told me: *I love you. Count on it.* "I guess so," I said.

"And he wants to marry you?"

"Yes. I'm afraid he does."

Rhody yawned and crawled into bed. "Most of all I love sleeping with you," she said as we curled together in bed in the dark. "I always knew you'd come."

"When I came, I heard you singing *The Water Is Wide*."

"I was scared, lying there," Rhody said. "The men might come. The one with the big black beard, and the other one with that kind of dead head, all shiny. Sing like you used to."

Her voice sounded muffled and sleepy. I sang:

> *Down in the meadow the other day,*
> *A-gathering flowers both fine and gay,*
> *A-gathering flowers both red and blue,*
> *I little thought what love can do.*

"That song's got boats in it," Rhody murmured. "We don't need a boat that can carry two. We've got a car. Sing some more."

> *I leaned my back against an oak,*
> *I thought it was a trusty tree.*
> *But first it bent, and then it broke,*
> *And so did my false love to me.*

I stopped. Rhody was asleep. Her face was almost buried in a pillow. How could she have slept all alone in that hot, dark shack, scared of the men?

The Rands were on my trail, hunting Maria and me.

The next morning I called Sophy from our hotel room to tell her the good news: I had Rhody. While we talked, Rhody tried on the clothes I'd brought her, jumping up and down to see all of her new wardrobe, piece by piece, in our dresser mirror.

She chattered as we ate breakfast, and sang as I drove, her lap full of the games and toys I'd brought. When we passed through cities, she looked at them with the awe I'd felt two years before, escaping to Chicago.

"You came…you came," she said now and then in the midst of her busy chatter. "I told them you would." But sometimes I caught her looking back along the highway. She moved closer to me in restaurants if she saw a bald man, or a man with a beard.

I was as jumpy as she was. Why had I underestimated Neola Risling—again? Her brothers had followed Gunther. She'd found our apartment and newborn Maria. She'd seen me with dying Gunther in the hospital, and alerted reporters. The Rands had staked out my hometown—surely they would have asked the names of my neighbors there, past and present. Now they'd use all-knowing computers to hunt me with ones and zeroes, and find every Sophy Saul in the country.

Rhody explored each new motel as we drove the long way to Massachusetts and Sophy. At last we drove into Belmont after dark.

Sophy's door was open the minute we parked at her curb. She hurried down the steps and hugged us both. "Maria's fine," she said, "and here's Rhody! What a pretty little girl." She kissed her. "Mary's sister! And do you know that you're an aunt?"

"Me?" Rhody said, her wondering eyes on Sophy's beveled glass doors, high ceilings and huge kitchen.

I brought Maria from her crib. "Here's Maria," I said. "She's your niece, and you're her Aunt Rhody. Sit down and you can hold her."

Rhody sat in a kitchen chair, and I put Maria in her arms. Maria dribbled on her bib and arched her fat stomach. "She likes me," Rhody said in a serious voice. "Does she smile?"

"Not yet," I said.

Sophy had a late supper waiting for us. We carried our suitcases in, washed up, ate the good food, and were in a safe place at last: home with Sophy Saul. Then Rhody climbed into our new bed with the rose-covered sheets and books on the shelf above our pillows, and was asleep in a minute or two.

When I went downstairs, Sophy was watching television. "It's the French clone," she said as I sat down beside her. There on the screen was the surrogate mother, a young, skinny girl with her clone only a few weeks younger than my Maria. Long blonde hair fell over the mother's face as she tried to cover her baby with a blanket; her eyes were big and frightened. As she carried her clone from her small house, she had to bend almost double to shield her baby from shoving, yelling people. In one picture, she shouted into the cameras, furious. In another she looked harassed and pleading.

Sophy gave me a look and turned the set off. I rubbed my tired eyes. "Go to bed, have a good rest, and you can plan what to do tomorrow," she said. "The Rands have probably lost your trail after this many days—it's cold."

Our trail was cold. I let the thought comfort me as I went to sleep: the Rands were hunting us, but our trail was cold.

The next morning I was jerked awake by small, clinging arms and legs—Rhody was plastered to me as if I were a log in a rushing river and she was drowning, but she was fast asleep. She never woke as I slid out of her arms. Every morning I found her hugging me tight in her sleep.

"It's because you had to abandon her," Sophy said one night when Rhody had gone to bed.

"I couldn't help it," I said. "I telephoned her whenever I could."

"But you left her the way your mother left you."

Sorrow struck at me from the past: my mother was gone, and I never knew whether she loved me... "Yes. Oh, yes," I said in a choked voice. Maria lay in my lap, kicking and chirping. She had toes like mine: the second one longer than the first. Her eyes were watching me: those haunting eyes that made me shiver, because they were the ones I saw in the mirror.

Sophy said: "Rhody's so terrified that she'll lose you. Do you think she needs to know me much better...feel as if I'm someone she can count on, too?"

I knew she was right. So the next days belonged to Rhody: days as peaceful as a picnic hidden in a jungle clearing while the wild beasts kept their distance. Sophy was always with Rhody as we explored the house, and ducked our heads under the attic eaves to drag out Victorian toys for her. Once more, a patient Sophy taught a little girl how to cook: how to break eggs, cream sugar and butter, and mix flour and water without lumps. As long as I stayed in the kitchen, Rhody stirred and beat and spilled valiantly, her long, dark hair tied back with ribbons.

Maria watched Rhody learning to mix and measure and bake in Sophy's kitchen. Sometimes Rhody gave Maria a taste of sweet things, and Maria waved her arms and kicked her feet and blew bubbles.

The next morning Sophy and I watched television as we ate breakfast. Suddenly we both gasped—Rhody's dirt-smudged face glared from the television screen.

A voice said: "The brothers of Mrs. Gunther Risling, widow of the Sorcerer's Apprentice, say they have seen the surrogate mother of the American clone, Mary Durfy, in her hometown of Plattsburg, Nebraska. Her half-sister, Rhoda Durfy, six years old, is missing and believed kidnapped by Mary. A large reward is posted for anyone locating this child, who was last seen with Mary Durfy in a motel near Albany, New York."

"Close to Boston!" I cried. "What if someone saw us coming to Belmont?"

"You came here after dark—"

"Look!" I cried. "Oh, look!" Rhody's face disappeared from the screen, and a newspaper clipping was there instead: a picture of me, a fourteen-year-old "Mary Dirty," wearing too-big pants and a T-shirt charred by her stepmother's cigarettes. Behind her was a rusted motorcycle parked in a trash heap.

"That's my picture!" I yelled. "From the *Plattsburg Citizen!* After you left Plattsburg, my 'stepfather' reported our neighbors to the police, and the *Citizen* put our whole family on the front page." I burst into tears. "What will Maria and Rhody and I do—run forever? Spend our lives dashing and dodging like rabbits?"

"But they don't know where you are," Sophy said.

"They'll find me! They've got my picture now, and they've tracked me down in Florida and Chicago and Nebraska...and now New York. Maybe I should just give up? Couldn't Maria and I be happy in a cozy jail with visiting hours for the public, and a gift shop selling Maria-and-Mama dolls, and T-shirts with Mickey Mouse as the Sorcerer's Apprentice—with Gunther's face?"

My picture faded from the television screen. "Why did the *Citizen* put your picture on the front page?" Sophy said.

"I've told you how my father and stepmother left home for days, and our neighbor, Mrs. Anderson, made my 'sisters' and me help her clean our house? My 'stepfather' said he'd sue the Andersons for setting foot on his property like that."

"For being neighborly?"

"Yes. The newspaper headline said: Local Family Claims Trespass. A photographer caught us Durfy children on the way to school. 'Let's have the one with the long blonde hair!' he yelled. My 'sisters' ran off, and there I was the next day on the front page of the *Citizen* in my stepmother's old jeans and a T-shirt she'd burned a cigarette hole in. Behind me were a trash pile and a rusted motorcycle. I can't forget that picture. I think it hurt me worse than my father and my stepmother calling me a bastard."

"I wish I'd still been living next door to you then!" Sophy said. "What did the Andersons do?"

"They were 'shocked,' according to the newspaper. They reported that Mrs. Anderson was crying. She told the reporter: 'We were only trying to be good neighbors and good Christians.'" My 'stepfather' went all over town, drunk of course, and told everybody what he thought of people who came into a man's house when he was gone, and took things that weren't theirs, and made his little kids cry. Was this a free country or not?

"The Andersons prayed with their minister, and sent a letter to the *Citizen* saying they would come to our house and apologize. So the *Citizen* wrote about *Apology Day*, and the next day the Andersons came to our house, along with as many folks from town as it could hold. When it was over, everybody took a last look at our house and then filed out in a hurry, as if they might be caught trespassing, too.

"'Good pictures!' my father said when they were gone. 'I told 'em to save a dozen of every issue. I'll be damned! The law was on my side, for once. Let's all go down to Dairystop for icecream.'

"'Mary shouldn't get any icecream!,' one of my 'sisters' said when we got to the Dairystop. 'She helped Mrs. Anderson clean— she did! Mary made us do it!'

"My father scowled, but never had time to speak, because I jumped out of his truck and ran home. I hid by the creek, and didn't go home until morning. My father never said a word to me about the Andersons, except: 'I hope you've learned a lesson from all this.' And I certainly had."

179

"I guess you did," Sophy said. "At least one."

"Well, I certainly found out what it was like to be followed and photographed and given nasty names and see your picture in the papers." I glared at Sophy. "And some people think that being 'famous' is fun!"

We heard Rhody come downstairs. She took a chair between Sophy and me at the kitchen table, alert to every word.

My hands shook as I buttered some bread for Rhody. "It'll have to be Ben." I said. "I don't know where he is, or who to call." I was keeping my voice matter-of-fact for Rhody's sake, and so was Sophy.

"I have his card," Sophy said, and gave me a slight, mischievous smile.

"But can you possibly help us again?" I said. "I hate to ask. Could we fly separately again? Could you go with Maria and Rhody, while I travel alone?"

"Tomorrow?"

"Yes," I said. "If we can."

Sophy went to her phone. In a while she came back. "All clear," she said. "Tickets will be waiting for us at the airport. Ben says he can get passports for Rhody and me in a day or two." She smiled at me. "He's very happy."

"Where are you going?" Rhody asked. She looked from Sophy to me, suspicious, her bread uneaten in her hand.

"Rhody," I said, "the four of us are moving far away, where it's safer."

"I'm going with you?"

"All of us are going," I said. "All of us. But we have to fly in two groups, and meet there. Sophy is going to bring you and Maria. I have to go alone."

"Why?" Rhody's eyes were wide and frightened. "You won't take me?"

"Do you think I'd go anywhere without you?"

"You did it before!"

"But now I have enough money. We can all go."

Rhody slid off her chair and flung herself in my lap, bread and butter and all. I hugged her and said, "Don't you see how everything is different now? I've never promised you anything I didn't do, have I?"

"Couldn't we hide in this house?" Rhody said, her face pressed against me. "It's got rooms and rooms—whole floors of rooms!"

"We're going to a new home you'll like," I said. "And if Grandma Sophy will buy you some clothes, we'll dress you as a boy—a special costume for you. Your name will be…what do you want your boy's name to be?"

Rhody's face was alight with the thought of costumes and secrets. "Peter!" she said. "'Cause I'm going to fly! Peter Pan!"

"Peter *Saul*, because Sophy Saul is your grandmother," I said. "If your grandmother will buy you the boy's clothes, we'll call you 'Peter' from now on, so you'll get used to it."

"Peter Saul! Peter Saul!" Rhody cried. "I'm Peter, and I'm flying! We're all flying!"

O nce again we packed suitcases, and drove to the airport. Rhody bounced up and down on the back seat of the car in her boy's jeans and boy's shirt, her hair cut short. Her name was Peter, and she was going to fly.

We would leave Sophy's car at the airport. I climbed from the car, and leaned to kiss Maria and Sophy. When I reached for the boy in the back seat, his face turned pale. "We say goodbye here, Peter," I said. "I'll see you again in a—"

"No!" the boy grabbed me, sobbing. "I won't let you go! I won't! I won't!"

I was stronger than a screaming little boy; I struggled out of his arms and out of the car, and grabbed my suitcase from the trunk while Sophy held him as he yelled. I must have run into the airport, but all I remember is Rhody's cries.

My ticket was waiting for me. I strapped myself in my plane seat with Rhody's screams still in my head. The plane was in the air before my trembling stopped.

I told myself that Rhody was with Sophy and Maria. Poor Sophy, her hands full of a baby and a yelling "boy." They would fly to the Mexican border, stay in a hotel there, and wait.

Ben had money, I told myself—he'd find a way to hide us. I had no one but Ben to run to, but he had terrible troubles of his own. How could I bear to make his life worse than it was? *I love you*, he had said. *Count on me*.

When I tried to sleep, surrounded by the plane's drone, I closed my eyes and saw a man sprawled on the sand near Gunther and me, his bare shoulders glowing with sun, his dark eyes as inscrutable as the waves coming ashore. He sat with me in an airplane, cradling Maria against him. He put his head on our clasped hands and murmured, "*Marry me.*"

21

Acapulco in the evening. I stood at the luggage carousel in the familiar airport, seeing no familiar faces.

Then a young, nervous-looking man stepped from the crowd around the carousel. "Miss Bryant?" he said. He saw the fear in my eyes. "Ben Carlos sent me."

At the sound of his voice I recognized him. "You were the minister at my fake wedding, weren't you?" I said. "Now you're Ben's courier?"

"Si. Here is a note from him."

The note was short: "Dear Mary, sometimes reporters follow me. I'm sending Fernando, my good friend, to meet you."

Fernando carried my suitcase to his car. "The media are still after him," Fernando said as we left the airport lot. "They call him names, because they say he has brought shame to Mexico with his lies. He had to close his clinic. There is nothing for him to do but hide, and hope that they forget him. He mourns for his friend."

I looked at the view I remembered so well: Punta Diamante's beach, its huge hotels descending the hill, tiers of glowing light. "Where are we going?" I asked, dreading the thought of a small apartment...

"To Ben's home."

"The big house? But it was almost a ruin, Ben said."

"He has rebuilt it," Fernando said. "His mother died and he inherited it, almost two years ago. For a while the tv and the newspapers came, but not so much any more."

We left the city, and soon the dark road ran through trees and looped upon itself. There was the long, low Spanish house I had seen on my "wedding day." I caught a glimpse of the chapel beyond, a roof against starry sky.

Weeds were gone from the flagstone courtyard. Once the gardens had been abandoned and overgrown—now they were masses of color where lanterns shone on the paths. Far away the lanterns stopped at the stone wall where I'd sat in my white dress and veil, drinking champagne with Gunther and Ben.

Every window of the house spread yellow light toward us. The door swung open and there was Ben, a tall silhouette, waiting. "Mary," was all he said when I came to him. His eyes were always on me, even when a very tall, very broad Mexican woman and three other women in their teens appeared behind him, and Fernando brought my luggage in.

Ben introduced the women: Mrs. Alvarez, his aunt, and her daughter Carmela. "Carmela is just married," her mother said, and the very pretty young woman giggled.

"Mrs. Alvarez brought friends from her town to work here," Ben said. "Lilia and Rosa Braga." The two women were small and dark and very much alike, except that Rosa had dyed her dark hair mahogany-red.

The women left, and Fernanado shut the door behind him. Ben and I were left to look at each other in silence.

"Your beautiful house," I said at last, looking around me.

"I meant to save it, repair it, live in it…"

"You're giving it up?" I cried.

"Selling it. I'll sell my laboratory and clinic and practice, too. Until Sophy called me, I was planning to fly to Spain next week. My mother's family is there. Perhaps I can set up a practice in Barcelona, in time."

"We've come to ruin your new plans."

"I told you to count on me," he said. "I'll have passports for Sophy and the children by tomorrow, and they'll be here tomorrow night."

"Poor Sophia," I said. "Two children to care for. Rhody cried and cried at the airport; she didn't want me to leave her."

"Yes," Ben said. "I know how that feels."

Mrs. Alvarez came to take me to my room and bring me tea and little cakes. I hardly remember going to bed that night. But

I woke in an hour or two. My bedroom had a wall of windows; I looked out to see a swimming pool like a slab of turquoise. Patio lights sparkled above their doubles in still water.

The house was dark. Ben stood at the pool's edge, his shoulders hunched and his hands in his pockets. I watched him for a long time. He was thinner, and his face was grim. At last he stepped back into the shadows. The pool lights went out.

Sunlight and laughter woke me. Where was I? A huge bed, a huge room, scarlet curtains glowing in the sun. There was no Rhody in my bed, her arms and legs wrapped around me, her head under my chin. Sophy and the children were on the Mexican border, and in danger. I crawled from bed, worry and fear flooding over me.

My western window showed Ben's gardens, and men at work there in the early light. I heard laughter. Another window looked down on the swimming pool.

Ben floated on the water there, his almost bare body shining. A pretty young woman swam beside him, one hand in his hand, her hair streaming in a dark underwater cloud, as if ink were leaching into the blue. She pulled Ben close and kissed him.

Someone knocked on my door. The newly-married Carmela came in with a breakfast tray, smiled at me and left. After breakfast I put on a shirt and jeans. Bookshelves beside me were crammed with books. If I had to stay hidden and wait the long hours until Sophy and the children came, at least I could read, I told myself. But I was listening to voices below my window: the girl's teasing voice and Ben's laugh.

Only when the swimmers left the pool did I look at the books, and found they were textbooks—textbooks for the classes I had never been able to take! What were they doing in Mexico? I lifted the heavy Western Civilization volume to the bed, and remembered Gunther bringing the books home to me. "Your freshman books," he had told me. "Study!" When I opened the *Iliad*, there were my notes scribbled in the margins, and the Greeks and the Trojans at war again, obsessed with glory, honor and plunder.

An hour later Ben knocked on my door. He was dressed in a shirt and shorts, and he said, "Good morning."

"My books!" I said. "You must have saved them from Gunther's apartment."

"Yes. I think I've read every one of them now," he said.

"Why?"

"A medical education leaves out wonderful things. I didn't know how starved I was for them until I listened to you quote from them." His voice dropped lower: "More than a year ago. When you and I and Gunther..." he didn't finish the sentence, but said, "I read your books here." He sat on the scarlet-covered bed beside me. "Slept here."

How still the room was. I could hear birds singing in the gardens.

"You've given me so much," I said. "Sophy gave me your money. I don't think I can ever thank you enough, but that money has already made someone so happy. When I went through Chicago on my way to steal Rhody, I spent some of that fortune to help Becky Warren."

"Your friend when you ran away to Chicago?"

"I was only seventeen. I'd never seen a city. I was sleeping under bushes in a back yard, and working at a hamburger place with her—"

"Under bushes! On the bare ground?"

"I had some chair cushions for my bed. And Becky taught me what to do at my job, or I would have lost it. When it rained and I couldn't lie on the ground, she let me sleep with her in the back of a bread truck in a motel lot."

"So you wanted to help her?"

"She was still sleeping in that bread truck! So I told her I thought I might come back to Chicago, if we could find a furnished apartment for me. We found a nice one, just a few blocks from where she worked! I paid the rent for six months, and put several thousand dollars in a bank account—in her name, because I told her I was in hiding. But when I left for Plattsburg to get Rhody, I wrote Becky a note in her new kitchen saying that everything we'd deposited and rented and bought was all hers for good."

It was good to see a smile on Ben's face.

"Your money," I said. "Your kindness. I should have written to thank you." I put my hand on his. "But how can anything make *you* happy when they call you a liar and say you've disgraced Mexico?"

Ben looked down at our hands on the scarlet silk. He shrugged his shoulders.

186

"We can't live here for long, can we?" I asked. "When they don't find us at Sophy's house, won't your home here be the next place they'll look?"

The phone rang. Ben answered, said a few words in Spanish, and turned to me. "It's Fernando. He's talked to Sophy at the hotel in Brownsville, and told her we have their passports. They're fine. She can call Fernando if she needs help. They'll come over the border tonight. He'll bring them here."

He left me then.

How businesslike we were.

In Chicago, his hands had been on me. He had cried in my bed.

Carmela brought lunch to my room. The house was still; I dared to explore the rooms around mine. Ben had given me the largest suite: the master suite.

The banister's wood was warm and satiny under my hand as I went downstairs. Windows were open to the gardens, and bird song and the scent of sea air and flowers filled the rooms.

I walked about the house from one cool room to the next. An inlaid box on a table held ivory dominoes. A spray of deep red orchids glowed against polished wood. I passed bookshelves of leather-bound books, and deep leather sofas. A dining room's rows of chairs stood at attention around a glossy table.

The patio beyond French doors was in shade. I sat on a patio chair where a television chattered in Spanish, and watched the French mother and her clone walking across the screen. She carried her baby from room to room in what seemed to be a home, but she looked frightened, like an animal shut in a new cage at a zoo. Reporters elbowed each other and yelled; crowds were packed against a high steel fence.

I couldn't bear to watch any longer. I hurried into the gardens to lose myself in flowers and the long, long view from the stone wall. Gunther, Ben and I had sat on that wall to sip champagne, and look at a wedding license in Spanish that I couldn't read and would never have believed was a false one. The fountain was clean and repaired now; rainbows hovered in its rising and falling spray. Its two naked marble ladies had new heads.

Beaches, hotels and blue water lay far below. Were Neola and her brothers down there somewhere, hunting for us?

I turned to look back at Ben's house, and felt for a moment like the heroine of Austen's *Pride and Prejudice*, visiting the luxurious home of the man she has rejected, saying to herself that it might have been hers.

But none of this place would be Ben's for very long.

The chapel roof showed through the trees. I went down paths and through a gap in a hedge. Two weathered angels still guarded the chapel door, their ruined faces as ghastly as they were when they watched me walk between them, a make-believe bride.

Ben had said: *Is this romantic enough?*

No candles burned in the chapel now. I walked toward the altar, my eyes adjusting slowly to the half-dark.

The altar was bare stone. I had knelt there beside Gunther. A fly buzzed and beat itself against stained glass.

He was giving you a fake husband, Ben had said. *I could give you a real one.*

It was dark when Ben found me on the patio. The moon threw a second moon on the surface of his swimming pool: a rippling silver coin.

"Don't stir," he said when he found me. "I'll have my supper with you." Rosa brought us salads, slices of roast lamb and an apple cake. We might have been any couple after a long day, together in the light of lanterns and the moon. The lonely, preoccupied look on Ben's face slowly faded, I thought. He poured wine for me, and we sat as quietly as if we understood each other too well to need polite talk—that thought startled me.

"What did you find when you got to Plattsburg," he asked.

"Neola's brothers had told people there that I'd kidnapped a baby. They were terrifying Rhody—stalking a child! After their parents were killed, my other 'step-sisters' took nearly everything from the house—Rhody slept on the floor. She jumped on me when I crept in, and scared me so. And then Neola's brothers came, and we ran for it. We took back roads and slept in little motels, and Rhody was in heaven. I'd brought her clothes and books and toys. She'd never seen a city, or slept in a real bed!" I hugged myself in delight.

Ben's eyes sparkled, and he grinned. I jumped up and walked back and forth by the moonlit pool, laughing at myself, glad that Ben could understand my happiness.

"He was giving you a fake husband," Ben had said. "I could give you a real one."

22

Ben and I were still smiling at each other on the patio when Lilia hurried to us. "There is a car in the drive," she said.

"Run upstairs," Ben said to me. "We don't know who it is."

But I heard Rhody's voice—she yelled, "Mary! Mary!" Before I reached the front door she dashed in and flung herself at me, her short, dark hair standing on end. "You're here!" she said between sobs. "You're here!"

Sophy held pink-faced sleeping Maria. "There you are," she said to me, and put Maria in my arms.

"We flew!" Rhody cried, her face wet with tears. She gripped my arm so tightly that it hurt. "We flew, and then we flew again."

"No trouble?" Ben asked Fernando.

"Not at the airport, or customs," Fernando said. "I drove with the children hidden on the floor of the car until we were sure we weren't followed."

"Are you hungry," Ben asked him.

"I must get home. My wife worries," Fernando said.

"Thank you," I told Fernando as he left. Rhody grabbed my shirttail. "I've got something for you in my suitcase! Sophy let me bring it!"

"Rhody," I said. "I want you to meet Ben Carlos."

"How do you do, Mr. Peter Pan," Ben said, holding out his hand. Rhody looked Ben up and down from his dark hair and white smile to his polished boots, then put her hand in his and said that she was really a girl and her hair would grow out.

191

"Come with me, and we'll find you a bed for the night," Ben said to Rhody, leading the way upstairs with a suitcase in each hand.

"Oh, Sophy," I said as I hugged her. "I'm so glad you're here."

Ben and Rhody climbed ahead of us on the wide stairs. Sophy whispered, "Is *this* his *house*?" She was too polite to stare at my huge bedroom that had a crib for Maria and a bed for Rhody in it now.

I put sleeping Maria in her crib. Rhody flung the lid of her suitcase back to throw jeans, shirts, books and toys on the rug. "Here!" she said to Ben, yanking off the top of a crayon box. "Sophy hid them. She said nobody'd find them in a box of crayons."

A glitter spilled from the box to the rug: the diamond earrings. Rhody knelt at Ben's feet, dangled an earring before her, and stuck out her tongue to lick it. "They're like the water in our creek at home. Rainbows, rainbows, rainbows."

I took the earrings, and she dug in the suitcase again, burrowing to the bottom, pulling out an armful of black crepe, and then a long black scarf. "It's a dress," Rhody said to me. "I'm supposed to tell you to wear it. That's what Sophy said."

Before long, the tired travellers and I climbed into our beds. I slept well that night with Rhody and Maria close to me, and Sophy just down the hall. But I woke in the morning in the grip of Rhody's arms and legs, with her head under my chin.

"Get dressed while I change Maria and feed her," I told Rhody, prying her loose. "Remember Ben told us last night that we'd have breakfast in the garden?"

Sophy was already downstairs at a garden table, looking over the wall into the huge, misty view. Sunlight turned her dandelion-fuzz hair into a silver halo. "Sophy," I said, sitting beside her. "What would any of us do without you?"

Ben came through his gardens to us, and introduced his aunt and cousin and the two maids to Sophy. They brought our breakfast, but Rhody wanted to explore, not eat; she took a sweet roll and disappeared down a path.

Ben sat at the table and looked at birds circling above beaches and surf. "I'd like to suggest a plan to the two of you," he said. "I can't stay here. You can see that. But I can go to Spain, to

Barcelona, and set up a practice. My mother's family is there. I'd like to ask you two and the children to go with me."

"Spain?" Sophy said in a shocked voice.

"Please don't think you have to come, Sophy," Ben said to her. "No one is stalking *you*. But Mary and I and the children must hide where we can, and I think we'll be safe in Spain. You're welcome to come too."

"Oh, my!" Sophy said. "I didn't think I'd ever be able to travel! Spain!"

Ben looked at me. "What do you think? When we're settled in Barcelona, England and Europe won't be far away, so we'll go traveling with Sophy and Rhody."

"The Rands won't follow us there?" I said.

"Spain is a long way from Illinois," Ben said. "And the Carlos family has considerable roots in Barcelona. I don't think the Rands would get far trying to make trouble. We'll have to decide about this soon. It will take time to make all the arrangements, and the Rands may very well be on our track."

Rhody explored her new home. Mrs. Alvarez showed us her kitchen as if she were a duchess conducting us through her duchy. "Your food is delicious," I told her. "You'll make me fat!"

"You young ladies!" Mrs. Alvarez said, screwing her mouth up and glaring at me. "So thin, like piecrust. A little more here..." (she cupped her ample bust in two hands), "a little more here..." she slapped her ample hips). "The gentlemen, they like that!"

Rhody was delighted to have grownups constantly available to cut and paste, tell stories, play games. She ran and slid on the shining tile floors. And she found Ben irresistible: a big man who would let her comb his hair, explore his pockets, tie his shoestrings in knots and beat him in card games. She filled the house with her happy chatter, but she had nightmares, and slept in my bed, pinning me down. All of us were listening for a phone call...a knock on the door...

I often talked with Ben after Sophy and the children were in bed. We strolled in his gardens, or sat by his pool. The tall man with the quiet voice kept space between himself and me—a careful, courteous distance. But his eyes, dancing with lantern light, were on me, always on me.

"I can't imagine I'm here," I said to Ben one rainy night. His study windows, streaked with a shower, were a glittering crystal curtain between us and his garden lights. "To be here, so safe from the rain!" I said. "Rain dripped through our roof at home. And the winters! That Nebraska cold blew over the ice and snow outside, and stabbed through our clothes. The house smelled of coal smoke and six people under old blankets wearing their coats and, on the bitterest nights—caps and boots. I kept a bottle of milk warm between Rhody and me in bed, and woke up to feed her when the stove was out and wind blew snow through cracks. And then those rainy nights in Becky's bread truck..."

"But you saved Rhody," Ben said. "With the little you had, you saved her."

"The worst thing I ever did was leave her," I said. "She's a constant talker and snooper and complainer, but smart. And so hungry for love."

Ben's eyes were on his rain-soaked gardens. "My childhood was everything yours wasn't. My father was Mexican and died young. My mother was Spanish, but she liked Mexico and she stayed here, and I had everything a child could want, except a father, so I borrowed Gunther's."

We talked about safe things: his brotherly love for Gunther... my "Dirty Family"...Jack and Colette...his father-son closeness with Gunther's father...Mrs. Alvarez as his second mother, loving him when his own mother was unloving. Our safe talk brought us closer together, but we were hunted people, with weighted silences between us. One night I said, "You lied for Gunther."

"For his father's sake," Ben said. "You've talked about what a friend Sophy has been for you. What would you do if Sophy asked you to help her with an illegal, dangerous, underhanded thing—a thing only you could do?"

"I'd..." I stopped. "I don't know," I said.

"And imagine you had to make up your mind almost at once. Suppose a lovely young woman stood before you at an airport. Happiness made her even more beautiful—she was going to be married to your best friend. But you knew she was going to have a false wedding, because your friend was fighting two terrible forces: the lack of money and the lack of time. Suppose you were his best friend and his only hope."

"So he planned it all, cold-bloodedly," I said.

"Except that he didn't expect to fall in love with you."

"*Did* he love me?" I asked. "Did he ever really love me? Did he love you? Wasn't he planning to exhibit Maria and me like circus freaks—and double-cross you? Do you call that love? Can you even call it friendship?"

Ben stared at me, his eyes narrowing as if he were in pain. "All that Gunther seemed to see was the fame and the money," he said. "I fought with him for a week, but I couldn't find a way to help you—unless you'd marry me." Ben's voice sank so low that I could hardly hear him. "And that was impossible."

"Well," I said, my voice as hard as his voice had been soft, "it was too bad for me, and too bad for you, too. Gunther was planning to keep the clone and her mother, and marry Neola for her money and her father's prestige, and take the fame and the prizes. I think you suspected it. I saw the look in your eyes when Gunther and I left Mexico."

"I told myself that you loved him, and he loved you, so he was taking you back to Chicago, even though it was so dangerous, so foolish. And when he married Neola, I couldn't believe it. I almost came to Chicago to make him tell you everything."

"But you didn't."

"He promised he'd divorce Neola and marry you as soon as he could. I wanted to trust him. I knew you loved him. But then he called me in a rage—Neola had found out about you and had gone to see you and Maria. He called me every name he could think of."

"Why? What had you done?"

"He was sure I'd told Neola about you and his baby—he said I'd betrayed him because I wanted you—had always wanted you. I told him I'd never do any of those things. He told me to prove it. So I promised that I'd come to Florida to catch you and Maria."

"And you used us as bait to get Gunther to Mexico and save him," I said.

Ben looked as stricken as if I'd slapped him. "If I hadn't done that, he might be alive now."

"Someone was chasing him in the rain that night," I said. "They might have been chasing the three of us, if he'd caught us at Epcot. Maria and I would have been killed, too."

"Perhaps," Ben said. "But now all I can do is to take you and Maria and Sophy to Spain before the Rands find us."

When I said goodnight and left him, Ben still sat on a garden bench, his head bowed. The fountain played near him, its silvery arch of water sparkling with starry spray.

Rhody's watchful eyes missed very little. She asked questions I couldn't answer: "Why do we stay here and never go anywhere? Are those men still after us?" And she caught the reserve between Ben and me: our careful politeness. "Why don't you like Ben?" she asked me.

"I do," I told her. "Look how he's hiding us—"

"No! You don't like him! You're mean!"

She meant it. She began a complicated, amazing show: she scorned me. She pretended to see no one but Ben, pulling down his smiling face to be kissed, twining her arms around him, her face hidden against his shirt. She had been my shadow for years; now she was Ben's, with no shame and no mercy. "I like Ben," she told me many times a day. "You don't."

Ben said, "Rhody, you can't be mean to Mary! She took care of you when you were born. Just look how helpless Maria is—what would happen to her if we didn't feed her and diaper her and love her? Once you were a new baby like Maria, and Mary was only a child, a sad, neglected child, but she chose to be your loving mother."

Rhody was shamefaced for a moment, then her eyes filled with tears. She crouched in the corner of a couch and cried, though Ben hugged her.

We worried about her. She had nightmares, and nothing would comfort her. She attacked me one evening after supper. "You won't even wear that black dress Ben likes. I brought it. I brought the earrings, too. He likes them—Sophy said he likes them." She began to cry. When I tried to put my arms around her, she shook me off.

Ben said, "It looks as if you'll have to wear that dress. Her heart's set on it."

Rhody sat up and wiped her eyes with the backs of her hands. "Put your hair up," she said. "Way up, so the earrings will show."

Sophy laughed, watching me go upstairs. I had hung the wrinkled evening gown in a closet, but found it had been nicely pressed—Lilia's work, I imagined. It was a little tighter that it had been when I wore it in a hotel room in Chicago, thanks to Mrs. Alvarez's cooking. I fastened the icy, flashing earrings in my ears. *Keep them. Wear them*, Ben had said at the hotel room door. *Because I love you.*

"Oh, *beautiful!*" Rhody cried as I came downstairs. When had she ever seen me in such finery? "Just like a princess!" She pulled me into the living room. "Ben! Look at Mary!"

I didn't look at Ben; I'd seen his eyes when I'd worn that dress in Chicago. Rhody cried, "Isn't Mary the most beautifulest thing you've ever seen?"

"She is," Ben said. "The most beautifulest."

"But look at you," Rhody said to him. "You can't dance with a princess in those jeans! I know you've got a black coat with a shiny collar, and a fancy white shirt like men wear when they dance on television. Go put them on."

Sophia and I couldn't help but laugh.

"You've been sneaking into my closet, young lady," Ben said sternly.

"There's no lock on the door," Rhody said.

"Do I have to?" Ben said. "That collar's tight."

"Yes," Rhody said. Ben shook his head and went upstairs. "Put on a bow tie!" Rhody called after him. "And black shoes!"

I sat on the couch and took Maria from Sophy—happy little Maria. Such a good baby. She noticed shining things; I had seen her reach for my fake diamond ring. Now she was looking at the genuine glitter hanging from my ears. Those strange eyes of hers that were my eyes, looking into mine!

"Maria is you," Ben had said to me the night before. "Perhaps I should lay claim to what I helped to make, and marry Maria in twenty years? Old Spanish families used to betroth babies still in the cradle."

He had smiled a little, and so had I, but there was Maria lying between us: the unearthly child, the first of her kind. Her face was losing its infant look. Sometimes I saw the shape of my head… the curve of my cheek…I shivered now, wearing my low-cut dress. My diamond earrings shivered, too, like a fall of broken glass.

"A prince!" Rhody cried. I looked up from Maria, startled. "Oh, look! Isn't he a prince?"

Ben was coming down the stairs, so handsome that I couldn't help but stare. He knew it. He laughed.

"A prince," I managed to say. "A prince of a princeness quite extreme."

Now Rhody laughed: I was using words from a poem she liked. "Stand up," Rhody said to me. "Give me Maria. Dance with him!"

"Dance?" I said, giving Maria to her and joining Ben in the doorway.

"All right," Rhody said, settling herself with Maria. "Ben, put your arm around her."

Ben did as he was told. "*Yellow bird*," Rhody sang, but she sang in Spanish. Ben and I were pressed close; I felt him pause in surprise. "You've taught her Spanish?"

"Not really," I said. "We don't know what most of the words mean. Gunther taught it to me. She just likes the song."

"Dance!" Rhody commanded.

The rooms were huge, the floor was smooth tile; Ben took me into the tango he had taught me on my "honeymoon," when he'd whirled me around his little apartment while Gunther clapped to radio music. We had danced to the front door, then into the kitchen, out of the kitchen, past Gunther grinning on the couch, into the bedroom and around the bed, and back to the living room again.

I looked into Ben's smiling face. "I've never danced with a man in a tuxedo."

"I bought it when I bought your dress," Ben said. "When I stole you away from Epcot. I wanted you to forgive me…Gunther and you and I would go dancing…"

I couldn't answer. His lips were close to mine, and I caught the hopeless undertone of his words.

Yellow bird. We danced to Rhody's thin, sweet voice. Ben twirled me, and Rhody stopped singing to cry, "Whirl her again!"

Ben did it again. *Yellow bird.* As I came back to him from my twirl and his arm closed around me, he murmured, "Do you know what those words mean?" and he sang along with Rhody: "*Yellow bird, you sit all alone like me…*"

I was in Ben's arms, so close that the tendrils of hair around my face brushed his cheek. I felt the hum of his singing thrum in his chest against me. *Yellow bird…*

Then a fist pounded on the door.

Rhody screamed.

Yellow bird. Ben twirled me, and Rhody stopped singing to cry, "Whirl her again!"

23

Someone beat on the door over and over. I ran to screaming Rhody to hug her tight, and Sophy took Maria, who was crying at the noise. Rhody and I sat on the couch, and she crawled in the cushions behind me and held me tight.

Ben went upstairs three at a time, and when he came down again he was loading a gun. He put it in his pocket, stepped close to the wide wooden door and called, "Who's there?"

"Neola Risling. And my brothers. Open the door."

"Give me one good reason," Ben said.

"We haven't called the police," Neola called. "Not yet."

Ben said, "The police aren't involved in this."

"Not involved with a kidnapping?"

"There's no kidnapper here," Ben said. "Leave us alone. I'd hate to shoot you, but I will if you break in."

"You're there, all five of you. We know you are."

I was trembling. "What can we do?" I whispered to Sophy as I took crying Maria from her. Rhody crouched behind me on the couch, her arms around my neck in a death grip.

"Neola," Ben called. "Send your brothers away. I'll be watching the drive. I want to see them leave. Nobody but you can come in."

I heard low voices outside. Then Neola called: "All right." Ben stood at a front window, watching. "Her brothers are driving away," he told us. Gun in hand, he unlocked the door.

Neola stood there alone. She was dressed in black, as I was. We were two widows staring at each other.

Neola's eyes went over my dress, the diamonds, the children, Ben's tuxedo, but she didn't snarl: *So this is where he keeps you. You poor little Nebraska bastard. Gunther's hidden you away. You're his whore.*

Not this time. She stepped into the room, Ben locked the door behind her, and she said, "I've found you."

I looked up at her from the couch, Maria in my lap, Rhody crouched behind me. "Yes," I said. "You've chased us and chased us, you and the reporters and photographers. Chased and chased."

"I'm not going to chase you—"

"Why not? You've chased us from Chicago to Kissimmee to Plattsburg to Belmont, and out of the country!"

"I've come to you for Gunther's sake. That's all. You must have loved him once."

"I thought I did." I looked her in the eye. "But that was because I thought I knew him. We had a wedding. We had a honeymoon. I actually believed he was my husband—can you imagine that?"

"You married Gunther?" Neola looked bewildered. "When?"

"Before he married you. May twenty-first. Wedding ring… wedding gown…how stupid I was. A fake wedding."

"He did that?"

"Oh, yes," I said. "I was Mrs. Gunther Risling. I had a husband. I even had a baby by the time you came and called me a bastard and a whore."

For a handsome young man in a tuxedo, Ben was amazingly invisible: Neola and I didn't give him a glance. We stared at each other. "Gunther could make you believe anything, couldn't he?" Neola said softly. "Make you love him." Her dark eyes filled with tears.

"I don't remember," I said. "I only remember his lies."

"He told me all his dreams, all his plans," Neola said in a choked voice. "*I need you*, he said. *You can't imagine how I depend on my Neola. I can't do what I want to do—not ever in this world—without you.*"

"He said those identical words to me," I said. "Except that the name was Mary. Just before our wedding. On a beach not far from here." That afternoon on Puerto Marques Bay came back so clearly to me: every hiss of the surf, every sand grain Gunther sifted between my breasts.

I didn't cry. I sat up straight and looked into Neola's tear-filled eyes. "And he was a liar. That's why you could come to my home and call me his 'little side dish.' And say Maria was a bastard."

"I'm sorry for that. I'm truly sorry," Neola said.

"Oh, but you were right," I said. "You did me a favor. I called Gunther. He admitted what he'd done: I *was* his little side dish. Maria *was* a bastard. So I ran away, and I've been running ever since, running with my baby. First I ran from Gunther. Now I'm running from you."

"But think of me for a minute," Neola said. "Just for a minute. Gunther asked me to marry him long ago—long before he knew you existed. He loved me and I loved him. We had such plans! We went house hunting, and found a home we both wanted, with room for the family we wanted..." her voice broke. She swallowed and went on. "He was working so hard at the lab, but we planned a wedding—"

"While I spent weeks in bed trying not to lose the baby I thought was Gunther's," I said. "Gunther made sure nobody saw me. I didn't have any family to find out what he was doing. He told me he'd been working at his lab when he came home late, but he was with you! Planning his real wedding!"

"Yes," Neola said. "And our wedding was lovely. I had my new husband and our new house—I was so happy. And then I found out about you. A friend saw Gunther going into your apartment house."

"So you had him followed?"

"What would you have done? Closed your eyes? Pretended nothing was wrong?"

"No," I said.

"No," Neola said. "So I found you, with Gunther's baby. I wanted to kill you, and her! I suppose you can't understand that."

"Oh, yes. I can."

"Then you ran away! Gunther hated me then, and I lost everything I cared about. I'd never dreamed your baby was the clone he'd worked so hard for. I couldn't explain to my family, and my brothers were furious that Gunther had another woman."

"So your brothers chased Gunther? Killed him in a car wreck?"

"No! They weren't there! But I'll always believe it was their fault. When my brothers went after Gunther for having a mistress, he had to tell them that he had produced the first human clone in the world. They were fools—they bragged to reporters. So reporters were chasing Gunther when he..." She was crying now.

"And you were as bad as they were," I said. "I tried to see Gunther when he was dying. You set reporters on me like a pack of dogs."

"Gunther was going to be the *first!*" Neola cried. "The first in the whole world to clone! And he was! He did!" She came to bend over Maria; her long dark hair fell toward the baby. Maria stared up at her.

"The clone," Neola said softly, and put out a hand, but she never touched Maria. "Get away!" Rhody yelled, and lunged from behind me to slap at Neola's red nails and shining rings. "You're bad! Don't you touch her!"

Neola stepped back. "So you're Rhoda Durfy?"

"No!" Rhody yelled. "I'm not! I'm Peter Pan!"

"You certainly are," Neola said. "You flew away. Your two sisters are worried about you."

"You're a liar!" Rhody's dark eyes glowed under her short, spiky hair. "My sisters are *gone*. Nobody knows where they went. They don't care about me and they never did, and I hate them! They took everything in our house—even my bed—and left me with nothing to eat. I'm never going back! I'm with Mary!"

Neola looked at us for a few moments. Then she looked at Sophy. "You're Sophia Saul, I suppose," she said. "You've been running and hiding with Mary. But do you know what it's like when you can't hide, and you have to stand and face everybody? My father nearly lost his position as dean—the university administrators wanted to know how the 'Sorcerer's Apprentice'—a single crazy graduate assistant—had managed to make a fool of his whole department. His whole university! My mother stayed home like a hermit and wouldn't see any of her friends. My brothers were insulted at work and hounded by the media. And do I need to tell you how the media treated the wife of the Sorcerer's Apprentice?"

"Then why can't you let us disappear?" I said. "Do you want

the circus to start all over again?"

"Gunther's dead!" Neola cried. "Don't you care at all?" She turned to Ben. "You've helped them run away! You hide them! You let everyone think you can't prove what Gunther did! That's why you're laughed at by the whole world!"

"I pity you," I said to her. "The French clone and her mother—haven't you seen them? They've lost everything. They're a peep-show. Animals in a cage. What kind of money or fame could ever be worth that kind of hell? Gunther's dead, but Maria's alive! Doesn't she deserve a normal life? Don't I? No one who cared for us would do anything but help us run and hide."

I gave Maria to Rhody, and got up in my clinging black dress to face Neola. "You've just said that Ben is laughed at by the whole world. Do you know why?" I put my hand on Ben's shoulder. "Because he'll never ask me to do anything but hide. He won't make Maria and me into a side-show." I looked into Ben's serious eyes. "He'll never say to me: *Show yourself with Maria. Prove that Gunther and I created the first human clone. Take away the shame and insults I've had to bear. Give me back my honor.*"

For a moment my words seemed to echo in the big room. Then Neola went to the door and opened it. "I'll give you a day to decide," she said. "You can't escape: we're watching. If you show Maria and prove she's the clone, we'll say the kidnapping was a mistake."

"I'm not kidnapped!" Rhody yelled from the couch. "You're a liar! I'm not!"

Neola didn't answer Rhody; she stood with her hand on the doorknob, her eyes on me. "You're the one I'm sorry for," she said. "I'm here because I loved Gunther. But what man have you ever loved? You love yourself. Ben Carlos gave up everything for you—you've just said so. You can prove he hasn't lied, and give him back that honor you talk about. But you won't." She went out and shut the door behind her.

Ben didn't look at me. He locked, bolted and chained the door.

I took the diamond earrings off and looked for a moment at the cascades of gems.

"What's going to happen?" Rhody wailed. "What'll we do?" When no one answered, she began to sob.

Sophy took her up to bed, trying to comfort her.

"I'll stay down here," Ben said to me. "The Rands want you and Maria. Their coming here to talk might be a trick."

When I went upstairs, my black dress trailing behind me, I looked back at Ben sitting alone in the dark living room. *What man have you ever loved?* Neola's words seemed to hang in the air yet. *Ben Carlos gave up everything for you!*

24

I hardly slept that night, and woke before dawn. Rhody's arm and leg pinned me to the bed, and her breath was hot on my neck. Slowly, gently I eased myself away from her and stood beside the crib. Maria's thumb was in her mouth; she sucked it now and then in her dreams.

Wrapped in a robe, I crept downstairs. Ben lay on a living-room couch, his long, tuxedo-clad legs stretched over the couch arm. The gun was beside him on a table. His tie was gone, his shirt was unbuttoned, and his sleeping face seemed tranquil and young.

I looked out a window. A car was parked in the drive, and a bald man drooped over the steering wheel.

When I went back to Ben, his brown eyes opened, and seemed to deepen when I leaned over him. My long braid fell heavily between us as I took his hand.

He closed his eyes for a moment, then put his other hand over mine. "You couldn't do anything but what you've done," he said. "For Maria's sake. For Rhody's."

"Not for yours," I said.

His eyes didn't waver, looking up at me. "I was caught in my own trap," he said. "You had absolutely nothing to do with it."

"We can't run for it, can we?" I said. They'll certainly have police at the airport waiting for us. They'll arrest us for kidnapping Rhody, and then the media will close in."

"Yes," he said.

"Well," I said, "there's one happy thing. You'll be given your honors and prizes at last."

"Oh, yes," he said, matching my false-hearty tone. "My honors and prizes." He sat up and ran his fingers through his black hair.

"And we'd better rehearse. Think of the television shows," I said. "Think of the reporters twenty-deep, pounding on the door. We have to be ready."

"Breakfast," he said. He stood up and brushed at his wrinkled tuxedo.

"You'd better shave," I said. "Whiskers aren't photogenic." We were trying to make a joke of our defeat.

"But beautiful women…" He lifted my long braid. "Beautiful women are the camera's darlings."

So we had decided what choices we had to make, with hardly a word. And we would try to laugh about it; we had decided that, too.

When Rhody came downstairs, she clung to me or to Ben. We pretended not to notice. How cheerful we were. Poor, confused Rhody: what was she to think when she listened to our banter at the breakfast table? There had been shouts and threats and guns. Now there were smiles and jokes.

"You might have to go on television, Rhody," I said to her. "Again. But this time we'll all be there. The news about us will be in newspapers and magazines. People will come crawling into our lives like ants crawled into our house in Plattsburg—remember? They're a bother, but they don't usually bite."

"They ask questions," Ben said.

"All the time," I said.

"So," Ben said to Rhody, "we have to decide what we're going to tell them. Eat your breakfast. You can't be a television star on an empty stomach."

"The police are coming?" Rhody's sullen eyes said that she didn't trust our smiles, or us.

"No," Ben told her. "No police, and nobody's going to take you away from us. If we let them put us on television and take our pictures and ask us questions, we can all stay together."

"Maria and I were running away from all that," I said. "We ran and ran, but we've been caught."

"I don't understand anything," Rhody said in disgust. She scowled at Sophy. "Even Grandma's never told me anything."

I looked at Ben and sighed.

"Well," Ben said. "It's like this…"

How I admired the story he told her. It was simple, it was clear. Rhody's eyes never left his face.

"Well, of *course*," Rhody said when Ben was through. "Maria looks *exactly* like Mary. I always knew that." Three pairs of eyes looked pensively at me, then at Maria in my arms.

"Look at Maria and Mary," Ben said to Rhody. "Can you think of anybody you'd rather have a pair of—than Mary?"

"No, but I'd like two of Grandma Sophy," she said. "And two of you."

"And I'd like two little girls like *you*," Ben said. I thought that he suddenly looked embarrassed.

"Really?" Rhody said.

"Really," Ben said. "At least two."

We spent the day with questions and answers. Sophy joined in. After a while Rhody began to smile a little; we pretended it was a game. Ben put on glasses and held a comb under his nose. "I'm a reporter with a mustache," he said, "and I want to know whether you came to Mexico willingly, or did you cry and say you didn't want to go."

"I cried," Rhody said, "but it was because I wanted to go with Mary, and I had to go with grandma."

"Did you cry when Mary took you away from Plattsburg?"

"Of course not!"

"You like Mary?"

"Oh, yes! She's my real mother."

"Oops," I said. "Wait just a minute there."

"She's not your mother, so you can't say that, or people will think Mary did something bad," Ben said. "You had a real mother, Mrs. Durfy."

"Say I *seemed* like your real mother," I said.

"Mary *seemed* like my real mother, but of course she wasn't," Rhody said.

"What a clever child," Ben said to me. "Listen to how smart she is."

We practiced with Rhody. By bedtime, she seemed to feel that the only danger was cameras and questions. She fell asleep almost at once.

Sophy and Ben and I sat on the patio, as far as we could get from the car parked on the drive. The beautiful house had been a safe place for a little while; now a man watched our door.

"Our last night," I said. "They'll knock on the door before long. Either I'll be accused of kidnapping, or everybody in the world will watch Maria and me being chased and penned up." Sophy came to sit beside me and put her arm around me.

"We may have one chance," Ben said. His face looked tired and drawn in the light of the patio lanterns. "I've thought about it all day. It's bad enough to have you and Maria exposed like that, but the media are sure to find out that Gunther faked a marriage and lived with you as your 'husband.'"

"Of course!" I cried. "We can't stop them. Maria will be illegitimate, like me, and I'll be a stupid bimbo from Nebraska who believed everything the Sorcerer's Apprentice told her."

"But maybe there's a way out," Ben said to Sophy and me. "See what you think. *Mary* doesn't want the world to know that Gunther gave her a fake wedding and lived with her, but how about the Rand family? They're very well known in Chicago. He's a dean at the University. Will Rand and his family want the world to find out that Neola's husband had a secret "wife," kept in a secret apartment as 'Mrs. Gunther Risling'?"

"Oh, my!" Sophy said. "Couldn't they hush it up?"

"I think they have enough influence to do it. But not if *we* let the facts get out."

"One kind of blackmail for another," I said.

"Yes. It might work," Ben said. "If we're willing to prove that Gunther and I produced the first clone, they will have to drop the kidnapping accusation *and* protect Mary (and Gunther) from charges of a...fake marriage."

"Or they'll have a scandal on their hands," Sophy said.

Knocking on Ben's door echoed through the house an hour later. Ben let Neola and her brothers in, and they sat on a couch in a black-clad row.

"You've decided?" the bearded man asked.

"We intend to prove that Maria is Mary's clone, and that the cloning was done weeks before that of the French clone," Ben said.

"That's smart," Neola said.

"Smart for me, perhaps," Ben said. "But it may not be smart for you."

"You're trying to scare us?" one of the brothers said, and laughed.

"And it isn't very smart, I'm sorry to say, for Gunther's memory," Ben said. "If you care for such things. I do."

"What are you talking about?" Neola said.

"You *are* going to let the media know about this, I suppose," Ben said. "Right away."

"Of course," Neola said. "Gunther deserves every honor—"

"Honor," Ben said in a thoughtful tone. "I think you'd better ask what you mean by that word."

"Why, all the honors for what he did," Neola said. "With your help, I suppose we'll have to admit."

"But the reporters and the newspapers will do their research, won't they, when Mary appears?" Ben asked.

"What's he talking about?" one brother asked the other.

"When they know who Mary is, how will you keep them from discovering the facts?" Ben asked. "I think you might be able to stop them, if we help you. Otherwise…"

"What facts?" Neola said. It seemed to me that she looked, for the first time, frightened.

"There was a doctor present at Maria Risling's birth," Ben said. "There was a Chicago hospital to record that the baby's mother was named 'Mary Risling,' the wife of Gunther Risling. Those documents are available. There was a joint bank account in Gunther and Mary Risling's names. 'Gunther and Mary Risling' rented their apartment."

"So?" one of the brothers said.

"But Gunther Risling married Noela Rand on May thirty-first last year," Ben said. "Ten days *after* Gunther Risling married Mary Bryant in Acapulco."

"He just didn't tell Neola, that's all," the bearded man said.

"But do you want everyone who reads a paper or watches television to know that the Sorcerer's Apprentice seduced a young woman, pretended to marry her, put his name on Maria's birth certificate as the father of her baby, and lived with Mary at the same time he married Neola?"

"Blackmail," said the bald brother.

"Just how much money are you after?" the bearded man said.

"He wants all the credit for the clone," Neola said. "He wants Gunther left with nothing."

"I could never do that," Ben said.

"Then what *are* you after?" Neola asked.

"Protection from publicity for Mary," Ben said.

The bald brother said, "You're not going to blackmail—"

"Don't!" Neola cried. "Don't!"

"Shut up," the bearded man said.

"Let's understand each other," Ben said. "You say that if Mary and Maria aren't proved to be the mother and the clone, you'll charge us with kidnapping a child. Right?"

"Right," the bald brother said.

"And then the whole story of Gunther's secret life will come out, of course."

The bald brother shouted, "That's your blackmail! It won't work! Who cares? Gunther found some..." He stopped and looked at me. "Some female to carry the clone, and he staged a fake wedding—"

"Wait!" Neola said.

"What if Gunther and Mary didn't have a secret wedding?" Ben said. "There were only two witnesses at that wedding. I'm ashamed to say I was one, and the other can be made to keep silent."

"They don't care," I said in a hopeless voice.

"I care!" Neola cried. "He was my husband!" She glared at her brothers. "He died! You killed him when you blabbed about the clone!"

"What do we all want?" Ben asked. "Mary and Maria want a private life, and the Rand family wants Gunther to have the honors he deserves, without any scandal."

"So none of us lose?" The bald brother gave a scornful laugh.

"Here's what we're proposing to you," Ben said. "Neola's father has a good deal of influence in Chicago. I imagine Maria's birth certificate can be found to be merely an attempt to shield the *surrogate mother* of the clone from embarrassment—yes? And the bank account, and the rented apartment? We think that Dean Rand can easily state—officially—that Gunther used a *paid surrogate mother* for the cloning, and hid her in the apartment to protect her privacy."

"Keep Mary out of it?" Neola said.

"I think you can approve of that," Ben said. "The media know Mary's name, but they have no pictures of her as an adult, and your father can make sure they don't get any. A *paid surrogate mother* is guaranteed privacy in such scientific work."

"But who gets the credit for the clone?" the bald brother asked.

"Him!" the bearded man snarled. "That's what he's leading up to."

Ben said, "Obviously, the University of Chicago will receive the credit, first of all, and Dr. Rand as dean. And I've never claimed anything more than half the credit for the cloning. Gunther was my friend; I want his name to be honored. He had the idea, and knew the method that could be used, and he found the surrogate mother. But I did the actual cloning. He had to use the only man who could, and would, do such an illegal procedure for him."

Neola and her brothers sat a while without speaking. Then Neola said: "I need to call my father." She spoke to us as if her brothers weren't there. "I'll let you know what we decide." She left the house then, not even looking back to see if her brothers were following.

25

Ben was gone until dark the next day. Sophy and I played games with Rhody, and helped her pick bouquets for every room in the house. We carried Maria with us wherever we went. She was three months old now, and I could see myself in her eyes, her face, her hair that was already curling and blonde…my dear baby…my sister…yet I was her mother. At breakfast I asked Sophy: "Won't Maria and I be closer friends than any other women on earth? How could we be anything else?" Sophy smiled and said Yes, and Maria gurgled and waved her arms, as if to say Yes, Yes, Yes.

We wandered Ben's big house that we would leave soon; it would be emptied and sold. I wondered who would sleep in my scarlet bed where Ben had slept, or read the books he had read there. The children of strangers would play on the patio, or splash in the pool.

The thought of Neola haunted us all day. Ben had not come home when Sophy and I ate supper with Rhody, and put the children to bed. We talked with Mrs. Alvarez in the kitchen for a while, until I walked away through the lamp-lit rooms to the gardens. The sky was overcast, and trees tossed in a restless wind.

The chapel door stood open. When I stepped inside, the light of a garden lantern glowed through stained glass to the stone floor. I sat there for a long time, listening to the rising wind and praying for us all. The image of a bride and groom rose from my memory to stand at the altar. I shivered. I would never be in this place again.

Suddenly I held my breath to listen. Ben had come home: I heard his voice, then Sophy's. They were walking along a path nearby.

"I've had enough," Ben said. "I'm just a man who raped her and lied to her. She can never forgive that."

"Spain will give you a new start," Sophy said. As they walked away, their voices faded, but I heard Sophy say, "Tell Mary everything. Before it's too late."

They were gone, and I was alone in the dim chapel. Garden trees creaked in the pouring air. *Tell Mary everything*. What was there to tell?

Thunder rattled the chapel windows, then rain fell in wind-blown sheets. I ran through the gardens, but the downpour soaked me to the skin before I reached the patio. I shivered, dripping on the tile floor.

Thunder cracked. Lightning bleached the room as I went in. I heard Sophy call: "I think she's in the gardens somewhere."

Ben came downstairs and saw me. "I was afraid you were outside," he said. "Here's a blanket. Slip your caftan off under it, and you'll soon be dry."

I turned my back and did as he said. The big blanket warmed me; Ben hung my dripping caftan on a hook in the hall. "Sit down and have some brandy," he said, bringing a glass from the bar. "You're shivering."

My hair dripped down my back. I undid it from its heavy braid and spread it over my shoulders to dry. The brandy warmed me and my shivering stopped. Ben stood looking into his brandy glass. "We won't hear from Neola and her brothers for a few days. They called me just before you ran through the rain to me."

"Then I'll say goodnight," I said. "Thanks for saving me from drowning." I stood up with the blanket wrapped around me.

"No," Ben said. "Don't go to bed yet." He lifted a heavy handful of my hair just as lightning through a window turned everything in the room to silver. "Put on that blue robe of yours, and come down again, will you?"

I found the blue robe and put it on. In a few moments I came downstairs to sit on a couch, push my hair away from my face, and wait for him to begin.

"Let me tell you about the first days you spent here in Acapulco," he said. "Tell you what Gunther and I—"

"No!" I jumped up. "I don't want to have to imagine the two of you! I can't bear to see it in my mind the rest of my life!" I ran toward the stairs, covering my ears, but Ben blocked my way so that I ran into him.

He pulled my hands from my ears. "Listen to me."

"No! Let me go!" I struggled, tight in his grip.

"Mary!" He held me tighter than ever. "Listen. I'll never be able to tell you this again. Will you listen, if you care for me at all?"

He held my hands against his chest; all I could do was to turn my face away.

"When Gunther phoned and said he'd found a surrogate mother, I was amazed," Ben said. "Where had he found the money? And was he really crazy enough to try cloning? I'd never thought he was serious. He said he was bringing this woman to Acapulco. I told him I wouldn't do it. He said he'd never forgive me if I didn't."

Ben was big and strong. I struggled to get free.

"I came to the airport, and there you were with Gunther: the most beautiful woman I'd ever seen. And Gunther threw his arms around me and whispered, 'Don't say a word about a surrogate mother or a clone. She thinks we're going to be married.'"

"Let me go! I don't want to—"

"Listen." Ben's voice was stern. He shook me a little. "It's hard for you to listen, and it's hard for me to tell it."

I tried to wriggle out of his grasp. I couldn't. It was humiliating. I stopped fighting and stood in his arms like a stone.

"You showed us your wedding dress," Ben said. I was so close against him I could feel the deep breath he drew. "Your wedding dress! And remember how Gunther and I argued in Spanish after our dinner that first night? Gunther had already given you drugs—I watched you slip into unconsciousness as we talked." Ben held me with one arm and touched my hair with his other hand—I pushed his fingers away.

"We examined you, waited until your cycle was exactly right, then carried you to my lab. We could shout at each other all night there. No one would hear. I said he was crazy—he couldn't do that to an unsuspecting woman. He said he could. He said you trusted him. He'd pretend to marry you, take you home and hide you away, and have the first human clone ever born in the world."

216

I stood rigid in his arms, trapped.

"And you lay there unconscious," he said. "Beautiful and young…"

"So you helped Gunther, not me. You did what he wanted."

"He'd begun the treatment in spite of me. We fought at the lab—fought when it came to impregnating you. He said we had to do it—it was that one particular night or never, and he was right, but…" Ben's voice was low and ashamed. "I don't know if you can imagine it: a beautiful woman unconscious. *Of course* I was looking at your naked body. I know that's part of your outrage. I wanted you, and I'd never have you. I'm not proud of it, but I can't lie. There we were: two men crazy with love for one woman—so in love with her that they'd kill any man who touched her."

Wind howled around a corner of the house. Rain thudded on the windows, pounded on the roof.

"Gunther wanted to be the only one to lay a hand on you, but he wasn't a doctor. He couldn't do what had to be done." Ben's voice sounded as if he were wringing his words out of his throat, one by one. "It was raw. One of us was willing, but couldn't do it. The other one could do it, but wouldn't. I think we were both half out of our minds and there you were between us…"

"And you fought?"

"Like wild men. It scared me to find out how much I loved you—I couldn't believe how much—it's a wonder I didn't kill him. He wasn't going to have you, he wasn't going to touch you!"

Thunder growled in the gardens, another wild voice.

"Gunther knew we had to impregnate you before it was too late. And I fought because I couldn't bear to do it. I'd done hundreds of in vitro impregnations. I wasn't going to do that one. I told him to call off his marriage to Neola. I told him to take you back to Chicago untouched."

"But you did it."

Ben wouldn't look at me. He said, "Gunther yelled at me: 'Your father was a Mexican! Why would a woman like Mary ever love a Mexican?' He laughed in my face and shouted: 'But you're crazy for her, so I win! Because if you don't impregnate her, I'll kill her!'"

"*Kill me?*" I flattened my hands against Ben's chest, pushing away from him, trying to look into his eyes.

217

"Gunther had a gun. He stood there, a gun in his hand, and laughed."

"Why?"

"Because he knew me, right to the bottom of my most secret ambitions." Lightning through a nearby window lit Ben's black hair and high cheekbones and was, for a second, a silver fringe on his lashes. "He knew me," Ben said in a voice I could hardly hear. "My best friend."

The man holding me was trembling slightly, as if the storm were playing on him. "My God," Ben said. "An *excuse*. He knew all I needed was an excuse. So there he stood with the gun on me, smiling, and said that you didn't have any family. No one in Chicago would miss you. He'd dump you in the bay. You might wash up on some shore—what was left of you—and nobody would know who you were. Or care. Then he laughed. 'Except Ben Carlos, of course,' he said. He picked you up and carried you to the door, your long hair trailing..."

"So you raped me in order to save my life?" I leaned back in his arms to look him in the eye.

He let me go. "I wish I could say Yes. How I wish I could! I wish I could say I believed he'd kill you! Can't I tell you that?"

We stood together in silence for a moment or two, except for the pounding of the rain.

Then Ben said, "I never believed he'd hurt you. That's what I have to tell you, and I'll live with that truth the rest of my life." He sounded as if he were talking to himself, not me. "I saw Gunther was playing with me. I saw he didn't care about me, or you. But he knew me so well. I needed to have an excuse to do what he wanted. That's all." He gave a bitter laugh.

"An excuse?"

"An excuse for me to listen to my demons, and stop caring about you. Wasn't I ambitious? Didn't I want to be the first in the world to clone—be the famous man, the rich man, winner of the biggest prize going? I did! I did! And he knew it. So he gave me an excuse to *pretend* I was saving your life, while I did what I *really* wanted to do!"

Suddenly Ben took my face in his hands. I saw tears in his eyes. "And do you want to know the final reason I did it?" he said in a low, tortured voice. "The truest reason? The worst one of all? I

He said he'd kill you. He carried you to the door, your
long hair trailing.

knew Gunther was right. I told myself: *What do you have to lose? Mary will never love you.*"

We stood for a moment in silence. The storm was over; rain dripped from the roof to the tiles of the patio. I left him, went up to my room and sat on my bed.

The room was dark, but I didn't need any light; I could see my first hours in Acapulco: Ben, handsome and sullen and silent, and Gunther throwing himself backward in his chair, then sitting up to yell at Ben.

Gunther had drugged me that first night. For days and days I was unconscious, until Gunther told me lies: "You've had food poisoning."

Ben and Gunther had fought—more than once. I'd seen Gunther's bruised face when he said, "Some men down on the Zocalo jumped us. They got most of my money." I remembered two men far away on the beach, their bodies as rigid as if they meant to fight, their bodies half buried in the tide coming in.

Ben had watched Gunther's hands moving over me in the sunshine, in the sound of the waves. Gunther had yelled at Ben: "I'll make my mark!"

"It's so dangerous," I'd said, watching the divers and their torches leap from the cliff to the black sea. *They learn young to take chances*, Gunther had said. The torchlight of a diver had glittered in his eyes.

S ophy wasn't asleep yet: her bedroom light showed at the bottom of her closed door. I tapped and she said, "Come in."

"Sophy," I said, sitting beside her on her bed, "Did Ben tell you what happened before I 'married' Gunther?"

Sophy hesitated. "It was a matter of making him tell me. I said I knew him too well now; I was sure he couldn't have been willing to make you pregnant and give you a fake wedding." She gave me a sad look. "I didn't know how cruel I was: I said Gunther must have made him do it."

"And you believe Ben?" I said. "Believe that Gunther taunted him, driving him to choose the fame and the prizes? Told Ben I'd never marry a Mexican? Pretended he was going to kill me so that Gunther could pretend he was saving my life?"

"Yes," Sophy said. "I believe him."

"Why?"

"Because Ben had everything to gain by not telling anyone what really happened."

"Because we would have thought he saved my life?"

"Yes."

"If he'd said that, he would have cleared himself," I said. "He would have put the whole blame on Gunther."

"But he wouldn't do that," Sophia said. "He wouldn't lie."

"No," I said. "Not Ben." I kissed Sophy and said goodnight.

Rhody and Maria were fast asleep when I went back to my room. I tried to sleep, and at last I did, but I dreamed a long, clear, wild dream. I thought that I threw off my nightgown, pulled on my red bikini, and ran downstairs and through the dim house to the patio.

Was Ben asleep in bed? No. I dreamed I saw a ripple raveling across the surface of the pool in the dark: Ben swam there with long, even strokes.

Ben, I dreamed I was saying. *Ben.* I slid into the black water, and as he made his turn, I was there. Before he could speak, I kissed him. I felt his lips for the first time.

Startled, he cupped my head and my floating hair in his hands to keep my mouth on his, holding me in that kiss.

26

I woke at sunrise, dreaming of a man in my arms, but it was only Rhody holding me down, her sleeping face on my shoulder.

The sky was a deep, washed blue after the rain. I woke Rhody, and diapered and dressed Maria. Rhody jumped from step to step as we went downstairs, and ran ahead of us to the kitchen and her breakfast with Mrs. Alvarez and the kittens.

Ben and Sophy were already at the breakfast table on the patio. "Good morning," they said. My dream was so real to me yet that I couldn't look at Ben. "I've finished eating, so I'll feed Maria for you," Sophy said.

Sophy took Maria and her bottle. I ate, hardly tasting the food because a man watched me, there in the morning sunshine, and I thought how his lips would feel as we kissed, and remembered the strength of his grip, holding me.

His sun-tanned hand poured my coffee. "We should hear from the Rands in a few days," he said.

Rhody came from the house, and heard him. "Can we go swimming then?"

"I'm a club member where there's a private beach." Ben smiled at me. "Did you bring that red bikini?"

"She did! And I've got my swimsuit!" Rhody cried, and ran upstairs to put it on.

I couldn't shake off my dream as I rummaged in a drawer for the red bikini: I yanked it on and found myself posing in a mirror, until I whispered to myself: "Stop it," grabbed a robe and towel and went downstairs.

The day was blue and gold from sand to sky as we waded into the surf on the private beach. Rhody ran along the water's edge; Ben and Sophy and I left the surf to spread blankets on the white sand. For a little while I could bask beside Ben with my eyes shut, remembering what he had said: *It scared me to find out how much I loved you.*

The constant rush of the waves...warm sun on my skin and hair... "You'll burn," Ben said to me, raising himself on an elbow. "You need some sunblock."

Gunther had found that sunblock excuse to stroke me all over—I almost snatched the bottle from Ben. But when I'd covered all of me that I could reach, Ben said, "Now your back," and took the sunblock from me. Stroking my hot skin, he was so close that I could have touched the hair on his chest, his lean face—

"Thanks," I said. I looked at him, and he laughed. "Now mine," he said.

I stroked the smooth, hard muscles of his back, and his neck under his curling black hair, then covered his lower back all the way to his low-slung trunks, and started on his arms—

What was I doing? I backed away from Ben, called Rhody and smoothed the sunblock on her wriggling body; she didn't like it. Then I rolled over to lie on my stomach and hide my face. Rhody and Sophy walked off in the frothing surf that surged in, ebbed back.

"Do you know another poem about the sea?" Ben's voice was close to my ear.

I knew he was remembering Gunther. I sat up and looked across the water at yachts and fishing boats that would find their harbor that night. "I told you once that I don't know any happy poems about the sea," I said.

Ben smiled. "Then tell me another unhappy one, like the one you gave us before: *"Behind my back, seas pull the rug out, pull the past out, pull my footprints out. I walk the crumbling floor..."*

"You're remembering Gunther," I said, looking into his dark eyes. "And there's a poem about the ocean that reminds me how much I loved and trusted Gunther once. But now I stop myself and say: 'No. Not now. Never again.'"

224

I catch myself drifting
toward you yet.
When I am tired, hours seem to be lifting
me into an old harbor. I forget
the tide is out now, foam breaking
on reefs; on black water, the hissing shelf
of the last wave shoreward, waking,
I catch myself.

Salt air from the bay moved over us. Suddenly my eyes filled with tears. "I can't forgive Gunther!" I cried, my face in my hands as tears ran through my fingers and dripped on the red bikini.

Ben didn't touch me, close as I was. "I should be able to," I said with a sob.

"Why shouldn't you hate both of us?" Ben said. "Two liars."

"But at least you lied for one good reason: you owed Gunther's father so much," I said. "And last night you didn't lie: you told me the truth when you didn't have to...when you could have pretended you saved my life." I rubbed away the tears on my face. "Neola's right. You've lost everything you ever wanted—money, prizes, reputation, your laboratory, your house, your practice—all to pay for one mistake."

Rhody came running along the shore with two handfuls of shells. "We can't find any shells that aren't broken!" she said.

"Let's wade out a little," Ben said, getting up to take her hand. "Sometimes the best ones don't flood all the way in."

They made a charming picture: a man and child in glittering surf. Slender and strong, Ben crouched on the shore. Rhody clung to him as she bent to grab shells, trusting him to keep her from waves that were trying to knock her down and carry her into deep water.

We showered and dressed in a little beach house and drove home, drowsy with hot sun. Rhody and Ben had found enough shells to weigh down a big bath towel. Rhody carried them to the house triumphantly, but we all halted just inside Ben's front door. Two lovers were entangled on a couch, kissing with such single-mindedness that they only stopped when Ben shut the heavy door behind us, and Rhody trotted close to them to have a better look.

Mrs. Alvarez appeared. "Carmela and Joseph will stay with me for a little, if that is all right?" she said. "Their house is not ready." She beamed at the newly-weds, who were now on their feet and holding hands.

Joseph was a beautiful boy like Michelangelo's "David," with hair as black as Ben's, and hands and feet that would not be too big in a year or two. Ben's cousin Carmela was small and pink-cheeked, with a curvy plumpness that kept Joseph's hands on her whenever he thought no one was looking.

But we were looking, of course, with laughing eyes and rueful smiles. We could see how invisible we were to those lovers—invisible as the marble fireplaces or the gleaming floors. It was funny, of course, but I couldn't laugh, for I was aware of hardly anything but Ben.

We gathered for a late lunch in the garden: Mrs. Alvarez's *antojitos*, then turkey with her *mole* (a sauce which, unbelievably, had bittersweet chocolate in it), and her *chiles rellenos*: plump poblano peppers filled with sausage and cheese. Sun and sea air had made us hungry, and the scent of sausage made us ravenous—we emptied every bowl and plate.

When all of us had had enough, Carmela and Joseph lay on a blanket in the blue-green shade of late afternoon. Carmela's small, deft hands plunged into the very tight back pocket of Joseph's very tight jeans. And the kisses, hidden from us by a back or a shoulder...Ben walked off.

I sat by Sophia. She was arranging Rhody's beach treasures on the blanket as she talked to Mrs. Alvarez: a row of pebbles, then a row of small white shells. After a while, I curled up on the blanket at Sophy's broad back. The vivid patches of sun hurt my eyes, but the most wounding sight was the couple entwined in the quivering shade.

I closed my eyes, tired after a night of dreams and a morning by the sea. I must have slept, for when I woke the shadows were long, and soon the twilight would come. Rhody was far away among the flowerbeds, Sophy was gone with Maria, and Ben was nowhere in sight. I crawled off the blanket in the cool breeze and took the garden path past the chapel, farther than I had gone before. I saw Ben. He sat on a wall that was half crumbled away, his elbows on his knees and his chin in his hands.

226

The tide is out now, foam breaking
on reefs; on black water, the hissing shelf
of the last wave shoreward, waking,
I catch myself.

How quiet it was, there above the bay in the last light. A forest of gnarled trees stood behind Ben; they breathed out a scent of damp earth and sea air. Now and then Ben tossed a stone or twig down the steep hillside.

He didn't know I was there. That morning Sophia had said to me: "The newspapers report that no one but Ben will be given the Nobel, and stand before the world just as Robert Edwards did in 2010 when he received the prize for 'the development of in vitro fertilization.' Ben has taken that 'development' much farther indeed! Can you imagine? Ben! They say he'll be given the gold medal and more than a million dollars."

But this afternoon Ben was only a shadowed shape against the far shore: a silhouette, like a face on a medal.

These were our last days together.

Ben, I murmured.

He must have sensed that he was being watched: he turned, but he only glanced at me as I sat down by him on the old wall. Neither of us spoke while my wild mind hunted for words.

"You can find all kinds of things in Sophy's attic," I said at last. "Books, books, books. I brought down armfuls when I first stayed with her. One of them was by Sigrid Undset, who won the Nobel Prize. The book was just an old, yellowed paperback with half the pages loose or fallen out, but on the cover was a drawing of a woman spinning. She wore her hair in a long braid like mine, so I read it: Sigrid Undset's *Gunnar's Daughter.*"

Ben said nothing. He tossed a twig down the hill.

"It's medieval Norway, and Gunnar's daughter will soon marry a man," I said. "But he rapes her, and this is unforgivable. She's been shamed and dishonored; it's worse than death. So she won't marry him, though they're promised to each other, and she raises her son. When the son is a man, she sends him to revenge her, and he does—he kills his father, cuts off his father's head, and puts the head in his mother's lap."

The grisly story hung between us in the silence.

"But that isn't the end—" I stopped. Someone was shouting. It was Rhody, racing toward us. "Come quick!" she yelled. "Pictures! Pictures of all of us!"

The shout and her wide eyes made us hurry to follow her. When we came through the gardens, Mrs. Alvarez stood at the table by the wall, her face horrified, her mouth open. Sophy was spreading newspapers on the table.

We bent over the papers. There, on the front page, was a picture of our breakfast that morning in Ben's garden! Rhody's arms were around my neck; Sophy was feeding Maria. Our faces were so clear, so horribly clear.

Another page showed a handsome Ben on a beach. He knelt close to a woman in a red bikini who held her long hair out of the way as he stroked her back.

"This caption says that Mary Bryant is the mother of the first human clone," Ben said. "It says that Gunther and I told the truth. That the clone is here."

"Who took those pictures?" I cried.

"Someone who was well paid, I suppose," Sophy said.

"Paid by the Rands?" I asked.

"It is on the television too," Mrs. Alvarez said. We hurried to the patio. On the TV screen was Ben's house, his laboratory and clinic.

Fernando stood in the doorway. Ben asked him questions in Spanish, his voice cold. Fernando answered in a nervous flood of words, jerking his body and waving his arms.

"Lilia has a lover," Ben translated for us. "She talked about us to this man, Fernando thinks. This lover works for an Acapulco newspaper, and he took shots of us this morning, evidently. He said he needed the money to marry Lilia."

I couldn't stop watching the television screen: we were exposed in a life we had thought was hidden. The pictures of our relaxed bodies sprawled on the beach showed how safe we had felt that very morning.

"Will they ask me all those questions?" Rhody wailed.

Now the television showed the French clone and her mother behind a steel fence. Crowds yelled, pressed against the wire.

Rosa came to us, chattering in Spanish, her eyes wide. Ben answered her, and turned to us. "She says her sister Lilia is gone, and the driveway and road to town are filling up with trucks and cars. Come inside."

Ben locked doors behind us as we left the patio. Knocking and doorbells rang through the house. We hurried to pull heavy draperies over windows until the rooms were dark.

I looked through a gap between curtains: people were filling the road, the drive, the gardens. Rhody grabbed my shirttail and followed me from window to window.

Maria would have to be fed soon. As I went upstairs with Rhody I heard my baby crying—doorbells and pounding fists had frightened her. "Never mind," I crooned, bending over her; she was hot and red-faced. I lifted her from her crib—

Photographers! They balanced on the wide windowsill above the pool, peering into my bedroom! I slammed the blinds shut, but they had already caught us. Rhody grabbed me, shrieking. The next morning Maria and I would be on front pages: a woman with a baby, and Rhody clinging to her, terrified.

I hurried downstairs with the children, and told Ben the photographers had climbed to take pictures of Maria, Rhody and me. "I've asked my aunt and Carmela and Joseph to tell reporters: *No comment. Go away*," Ben said.

As we sat in the kitchen while I fed Maria, we could hear the shouting outside. I asked, "What now?"

"I think we should stay here," Ben said. "The Rands can come and tell us what they've decided, but there's no way we can escape the media."

When he turned on a television set, a large man was brandishing his fist. "The president of Mexico. He's says that Mexico will want to claim the cloning and keep us here," Ben said. "The U.S. is claiming it, too." And there was the White House and the president in his rose garden, speaking to the press.

Men and women on the screen talked in excited voices. "They're calling you the surrogate mother," Ben said. "And so far no one has mentioned kidnapping."

Now familiar pictures appeared: Gunther looking wild and trapped at Epcot. I had been only a blurred figure in newspaper pictures, but now my face was clear in the Florida sun: I was the scared-looking blonde behind him. They showed Gunther as a school boy, then dancing with a girl, then shaking his father's hand, then saying: *Dr. Girard of France is not the first man in the world to clone a human being.*

"He never mentioned you," I said to Ben. "He never meant to."

Now Gunther's car filled the screen: a wreck smashed against a wall. Neola ducked her head under a sign that read: "Emergency Entrance." Then pictures appeared I had never seen: Ben as a teenager with his tall, sour-looking mother. Ben with his high school friends, Ben at the door of his clinic…

"Oh! Look at me!" Rhody cried. The camera had caught her in Ben's garden, one of her kittens on her shoulder. A picture of Neola and her brothers followed. Then there were scenes showing Ben and me on the day before, sprawled on a beach blanket like lovers asleep after love.

Fernando came to the kitchen door. "We have talked to them," he said. "They won't leave. Even more are coming."

"There's a path downhill from the back gardens," Ben said. "We could get away in the dark, perhaps, but it's dangerous. It's steep. And what good would it do?"

Rhody said in a small, frightened voice: "We can't get out with all those people in the way."

"They won't hurt us," Ben told her. "They'll just yell at us and take pictures."

Night came, but no one yelled at us. The pictures on television the next morning showed the long road to Ben's house after midnight. Policemen worked to crowd trucks, cars and a silent crowd to one side of the narrow way so that an ambulance could pass.

27

I remember Maria's shriek. It ripped through my bedroom in the dark night. Rhody and Ben and Sophy and I leaped from our beds, hardly awake.

Ben picked the baby up, but she still shrieked. He put her down, unbuttoned her little shirt, and felt her all over, then ran to the phone and spoke in Spanish. I hung over the baby, afraid to touch her. She shrieked and shrieked, white-faced and writhing; her eyes—my eyes—stared at me in terror.

"Get dressed," Ben said to us. "Mary will have to drive behind the ambulance—take my car." He found the keys in his coat pocket.

We dressed. Maria screamed. She screamed as police cleared the road while Ben hurried out with the ambulance men and Maria. When the ambulance pulled away, I drove after it with Sophy and Rhody. We picked up speed, rushing down a forest road along a line of cars and trucks, photographers' cameras flashing along the way.

The streets of Acapulco were almost deserted as we passed, trailed by the media, car after truck after car. Now and then a driver swerved to the curb to let us pass. Red light, green lights, we never stopped until the ambulance pulled into an emergency entrance. I parked Ben's car nearby in a dark lot, and the three of us ran for the hospital, followed by a crowd.

"Do you speak English?" I asked a nurse at a desk. "My baby has just been brought to emergency."

"Yes," she said. "You may go to the intensive care waiting room on the third floor. Take the elevator."

Nurses stopped the crowd that followed us to the elevator, turning them back. When Sophy and I sat on a couch in the empty waiting room, Rhody climbed on my lap. "What's the matter with Maria?" she wailed. "Is she going to die?"

"This hospital has so many good doctors," I told her. "They can make her well if anyone can, and they're trying now. Ben will come and tell us how she is." I lifted Rhody off my lap and took her to the couch next to mine. "I'll be right here beside you," I said. "Lie down and see if you can sleep a little." She lay down and I put my jacket over her, hiding her eyes, for the waiting room lights were glaring. Windows, black with night, reflected two silent women.

Maria was fighting for her life somewhere in the hospital.

"Oh, Sophy," I whispered, sitting beside her when I saw Rhody was asleep. "I didn't want to have Maria. Even when I thought that I was married and safe, I didn't want her. How could she have been healthy, growing inside me when she wasn't wanted, wasn't loved?"

Sophy put her arms around me.

"I let her live, but she was a freak!" I whispered. "She wasn't my baby. She wasn't my sister. Her father was my father, and I don't even know who he was, or if he's still alive. Her mother was my mother, and all I know about her is her name." My eyes filled with tears. "Even my baby's face didn't belong to her, or her body. Or her soul?"

I prayed for Maria with Sophy's arms around me. Rhody slept, and the slow hours passed. How many prayers had been said in that waiting room? The black windows turned gray.

The door opened, startling me. Neola's bald brother came across the room to us. At the sound of his clicking shoes Rhody woke, took one look at him, and climbed in my lap again.

The bald man looked uneasy. "I'm sorry," he said. "We're sorry. We hope the baby's not seriously ill."

I opened my mouth, then shut it. Rhody's obvious fear of him said more than words could. I turned my face away, picked up a magazine from a table and held it open before Rhody like a paper wall. The bald man left.

Rhody hid her face in my shoulder. I held her close and rocked her a little, humming the tune I had heard her sing as she hid in an empty shack in the dark. In a minute or two she began to hum, too. The first sunlight slid a narrow shaft through a window.

Then Ben opened the door and came to me. I set Rhody on her feet and ran to him. One look in his face was enough. I pressed my hands to my mouth. Tears spurted from my eyes. He put his arms around me. Neither of us had said a word.

Finally Ben whispered, "We couldn't save her. She's left us."

The shock made me push him away. "You made her, but you knew she wouldn't live!"

"We had no—"

"She was your guinea pig! She never had a chance!"

Ben shut his eyes as if he couldn't bear to look at me. "We couldn't save her."

I heard the door open and shut again, and looked over Ben's shoulder to see three in a row: Neola and her brothers.

"They've told us that the baby's…gone," Neola said. "We're so sorry."

The bald brother said, "But we have to know—"

"Not now!" Neola said to him. "Don't talk about it now. We'll wait in the lobby." She pushed her brothers out the door. Their voices diminished down the hall. We were alone.

Sophy came with Rhody. They put their arms around Ben and me.

Ben picked up Rhody and pressed her head to his shoulder. "We tried to save your Maria. We tried and tried."

"Oh," Rhody moaned, and began to sob, her arms around Ben's neck. "Can't we see her?"

Ben looked at me. "I know the staff here. I think they'll let us in."

Nurses at a desk watched as the four of us went by. Cold white halls. Cold shining floors. The last door shut behind us without a sound, and there was Maria.

She lay on a blanket on a long table…such a small child, so perfect. Her white nightgown stopped at her ankles; the little feet curled against each other as if to show that she would never take a first step. Her hands had been fists when I saw them last, jerking and flailing; now they lay open, each finger with its dimples. When I touched her fine hair, it was still damp with her agony.

235

I lifted her to cradle her in my arms. She seemed to be only a dreaming child, too fast asleep to stir. In a minute her eyes that were my eyes would open, and her mouth that was mine would smile.

"Maria," I whispered to her. "Maria."

Her body still fitted against me. One of her hands almost seemed to cling to my sleeve. But when I put my cheek on hers, I felt the chill that had come over her already. She had left her strange body behind her. She was gone.

Sophy was crying. She took Maria for a moment, and kissed her small face.

"Let me," Rhody whispered, and Sophy gave the baby to her. "Isn't she just sleeping?" Rhody said with a sob, cradling her. "Can't we wake her up?"

"No," Ben said. "She's gone away, but she knows you're here with her. I'm sure she knows."

"She's safe," I said, and put my arms around Rhody and Maria, ducking my head so my tears wouldn't fall on the two small faces. "She won't have to run and hide her whole life long."

Ben lifted the baby gently from Rhody's arms. "Kiss her goodbye," he said, and Rhody kissed her and cried. So did I, and Sophy. So did Ben.

We had to leave her there. Ben said there would be tests. There were regulations.

When I looked back, a baby was lying alone, a small body on a table, watched by the blank faces of machines.

The four of us took the elevator to the lobby like sleepwalkers, too wrapped in a bad dream to notice that another day had begun. Neola and her brothers were waiting for us, but when they saw our faces they left us alone.

Sunlight poured through hospital doors as we stepped into morning air. For the moment the light was only the sun. Then it was sun after flashing sun: cameras. Shouts seemed like stones thrown at us. A crowd covered the hospital steps, the sidewalk, the street, opening before us when we pushed, closing behind us and following us.

Ben caught Rhody up in his arms as cameras were shoved in our faces or clicked overhead. People jumped hedges and trampled a flowerbed and flowed around cars in the parking lot. Ben found his car and held the back door open against the crowd, shielding Rhody, Sophy and me, then fought his way to the driver's side and his seat behind the wheel. Photographers lay on the car's hood; their flashes lit us as the car inched forward. At last they let us leave the parking lot, the crowd still trailing after us.

I looked back. We were driving through Acapulco like a hearse leading a funeral procession. "What can we do?" I asked Ben.

"Nothing," he said as he drove. "We can only hope the Rands have told them the kidnapping was a mistake."

"I'll tell them!" Rhody cried. She crowded close to me, tense and white-faced.

"You've been through all this before," I said to Ben.

"Yes. We'll get to the house and lock the doors; that's all we can do."

It was all we could do. Reporters leaped from their cars before we could climb from ours; they followed us across the driveway, shouting questions. Fernando opened the door. "I came as soon as I heard," he told us. "I am so sorry, so sorry."

Ben thanked him, shut the door and locked it. "Sit down here with Rhody and Sophy," he said to me. "Fernando and I have something to do." They went upstairs.

I sat on a couch. Rhody clung to me. Loud voices surrounded the house, and a car horn brayed.

In a little while the men came downstairs. "My aunt has breakfast ready for us," Ben said.

Mrs. Alvarez and Rosa hugged me, but I couldn't eat; I sat at the table until Ben said, "Why don't the three of you try to take a nap? There's nothing to be done now."

Sophy put her arm around me, and we went upstairs with Rhody. At the door of my bedroom, hideous sorrow struck at me: Maria's crib would be in that room—her pink crib where I had put her to sleep hardly a dozen hours before...

Maria's crib was gone. Rhody's bed was there, and Rhody's clothes and toys. But Maria's playthings, the pile of diapers, the shirts and bibs were gone. Nothing in the bedroom or the bathroom belonged to a baby.

Ben came to the door. I turned to him. "You didn't need to see those things any more," he said.

I thanked him. I lay down with Rhody and tried to rest, but I couldn't. After an hour, I went downstairs and turned on a TV set. There we were on the screen: a six-year-old, a tall, black-haired man, an older lady with flyaway white hair, and a blonde woman: four tired, rumpled, cowering people at a hospital door.

Ben joined me, and translated what was said, phrase by phrase: "Dr. Benjamin Carlos, formerly a gynecologist at the Gardia Associates Clinic...leaves the hospital with Mary Bryant and Mary's young step-sister...Bryant is said to be the surrogate mother of the first human clone...born weeks before the French clone...Bryant's baby girl, the three-month-old clone, died early this morning at an Acapulco hospital."

The picture showed the crowd on the hospital steps surging around us as we pushed our way to the walk. Ben lifted Rhody in his arms, and her frightened face stared over his shoulder. He fought the crowd to get us in the car; we drove away with a procession of cars behind us. Ben shut his house door in the face of the cameramen.

"They never mention kidnapping," Ben said.

A Rand brother appeared next on the television screen to tell how his family had hunted me, and how Gunther had been injured. "Gunther Risling died without receiving the credit he deserves. His widow and her family want him to be given that honor. Tests will prove that he told the truth."

"He never mentions you," I told Ben.

A sober-faced man appeared, speaking Spanish. "What does he say?" I asked Ben.

"He's a doctor I worked with," Ben said. "He's trying to explain what might have been wrong with Maria. And he says the cloning was done in Mexico, so Mexico deserves the honor, and he wants the final tests to be done here."

The doctor on the screen was still talking. "He's saying much more than that, isn't he?" I asked.

Ben hesitated, then said, "He's just saying what he thinks."

"What is he saying?"

"He doubts that Gunther could have done the cloning, because he couldn't have known enough—he was only a graduate assistant—he had no experience with in vitro fertilization." Ben was watching the screen intently; suddenly he came to his feet.

"They've found my lab records—all my data!" A frightened Fernando appeared on the screen. "I gave the cloning records to Fernando to hide, but they must have threatened him!"

I knew I should care about tests and prizes and honors and secret records. They were only a blur in my mind. The television played and replayed pictures of us. I didn't care.

The wall of not-caring grew higher and higher all day long. Soon it was so high and thick that even Rhody's hugs and kisses couldn't break through. She was on the other side of it, and so were Ben and Sophy, the constant television pictures, the shouts at our door. I was with Maria. She was so little, so perfect in her white gown that showed her feet curled against each other. Her fine, light hair was still damp. Her fists had opened. My baby lay alone on a table, watched by machines.

Nothing mattered.
   I didn't care.

Rhody's eyes were worried. She talked to me as if I were a child.

Sophia told me that something or other was important. It was important, she said, to take a shower, to wash my hair, to let her comb and braid it, to put on this or that.

I answered her. I did what she told me to do. It didn't matter.

I remember Ben's patient voice. The clone born in France was very sick. Would I allow a detailed autopsy of Maria so that we could, perhaps, save another baby's life? I said Yes, and signed the papers. Why should another woman lose her Maria? I turned my head away from Ben's sad face and crawled into bed.

As time went on, part of my mind listened to Ben. We planned what I should say, and I understood, but I didn't care.

A group of quiet, serious men and women waited for us in a large room. One by one they examined me. Their voices were gentle, and they thanked me.

I sat beside Ben under a television studio's hot lights and said that Yes, I had been a surrogate mother because I needed money to attend the University of Chicago.

Sometimes I stared at interviewers, trying to think why every detail mattered. A man asked me how much I had been paid to carry the clone. Ben had told me what to say, I said it. Yes, the impregnation had been done in Acapulco by Dr. Benjamin Carlos...

That was one of the few times I broke through the wall of my grief. I remembered how important it seemed to tell the truth about Ben, and yet how astonished I was that anything could be that important in a world where nothing mattered. "Gunther Risling brought me to Acapulco," I said over and over to a parade of questioners. "That was all he was able to do. Dr. Carlos was responsible for the first cloning of a human being, and I was the baby's surrogate mother."

Then the wall rose around me again, and my answers were mechanical. Yes, Gunther Risling had hidden me away in a Chicago apartment for nine months. Yes, I had given birth to Maria—

I broke down then, and cried.

I saw that interview weeks later on television. A woman wept there under the bright lights. Her blonde hair fell down her back to her waist, her face was hidden in her hands, and tears dripped to the front of her dress.

"They're leaving Rhody out of it," Ben told me. His voice was tender, as if he were trying to comfort me. "The Rands say they regret the mistake: Rhody was never kidnapped."

I nodded. I didn't care.

My sorrow for my lost child was seen around the world. Perhaps it kept the media away: Ben insisted on it. He was the one who was interviewed. Every detail of his past was told over and over in magazines and papers and television shows. He answered the same questions again and again.

I couldn't bear to see pictures of the French clone, tethered to machines. Seeing her, I felt the warmth of Maria in my arms... smelled the scent of her hair and skin. I spent hours before a mirror, trying to believe it was Maria who looked back...

"Mary," Rhody would say, pulling me away from the mirror. "Come and eat. Don't. Don't cry."

I didn't care. I had so little feeling. Days went by, and I didn't notice. But one morning Ben drove Rhody and Sophy and me to the hospital. A nurse took us to a big table covered with fresh flowers, except for a little white casket—so small—hardly larger than the dresser drawers my baby had once slept in.

"They follow me, pesky as flies, with their television trucks and big black lenses and questions, questions, questions. Let them shout at my windows and pound on my door. I'll never tell them anything."

Maria lay in the box lined with white satin, holding her favorite teddy bear. Her ruffled pink dress was trimmed with lace. She was a pale, sleeping child.

Somehow a photographer managed to take a picture of her in her casket. I might open a magazine or a book and see her, or meet her image mounted on a wall, or find her on my television screen. Without warning, I saw how death had made Maria's face even more like mine: the same cheekbones, the same eyelids. Her hair was like mine, and so were her hands holding the teddy bear: the straight thumbs, the long fingers.

My daughter. My sister. Myself. She was only asleep in her ruffles and lace. Surely her small eyelids would lift. Mary would look at Mary.

28

Crowds waited the afternoon we left Ben's home to fly from Acapulco to Boston. A woman put a small bouquet in my hand; her sad eyes looked into mine. "She says she's lost a baby, too," Ben told me. Women caught at my sleeve or touched my arm, offering pictures of a baby, or a rose, or a note.

Reporters and camera crews waited for us at the Acapulco airport, and travelers stopped to watch. When I sat beside Sophy on the plane, I felt the eyes of other passengers on us, and heard the whispers, but what did it matter? Rhody was excited by another airplane trip, and pressed her face to the window, or crawled on Ben's lap to talk.

No baby in my arms. As the slow hours passed, I sat beside Sophy with hardly a word. Sometimes I pretended to sleep. Ben played games with Rhody, or read to her.

The media met us in the Chicago airport. Ben was angry. "Leave her alone!" he told them.

"But she's so beautiful!" a photographer said, running beside us.

Ben had told me there would be more examinations in Boston. I didn't care. But I had a faint feeling of home when we flew to Boston and drove to Sophy's house.

Reporters and photographers were there, of course. Sophy and Ben shut them out; Sophy's big front door closed on their eager faces and yells.

Rhody dragged Ben by the hand to show him every room of

Sophy's house. Maria's crib and clothes and toys were gone from my room. As I stood in the downstairs hall, Sophy hurried past me, shouting: the front-porch window was full of faces and cameras. "Pests!" she cried, and closed the clattering shutters. "Pests!"

"You can have the whole top floor to yourself," Sophy told Ben.

"Ben's going to live with us!" Rhody shouted in delight, and I felt a vague pleasure that Rhody was proud of "her house."

I know now that the French doctor was fighting his way through the courts, battling to make human cloning legal. The Rand family endowed a chair at the University of Chicago in honor of Gunther Risling. Debates on the glory—or sin—of human cloning poured from pulpits, the halls of Congress, and commentators in many languages.

One afternoon Ben came to me. "We need to have a gravestone for Maria," he said. "They're sending her home to us. Would you like a white stone, perhaps? With some symbol carved on it?

"A rosebud," I said. My voice sounded dull and lifeless, even to me.

"And call her 'The daughter of Mary Bryant'?"

"She was mine," I said. "You told me her father was my father, but I don't know who my father was. I used my mother's name when I ran away from the Durfys."

"But should there be more on the stone?" Ben said in a gentle voice. "To say that she gave her life for knowledge—for us?"

"Yes. Something like that," I said, and turned away.

I know now that pictures of Maria in her casket were on the front pages of American newspapers and the covers of magazines: *America's First Clone Dead In Mexico...The Sorcerer's Apprentice Told the Truth...Honor of First Human Clone Shared by U.S. and Mexico.*

Sophy's television was seldom on, but one day I saw a mother grieving in her fancy house, and the French clone-child in her small casket. Sophia found me, led me into the kitchen, put an apron on me, and handed me potatoes to peel.

One morning we drove to a cemetery. The green lawns were shady with summer trees in full leaf. Reporters and camera crews and hundreds of people stood at a distance, cordoned off with another crowd that made no noise: the cemetery's weeping angels, grieving marble maidens, stone sphinxes, winged skulls.

245

A little white casket in a bed of flowers lay in the shade. A minister's words were scattered over us like leaf shadow. When the words stopped, and the small box disappeared, Ben and Sophy and Rhody walked with me down a winding path to our car.

I dreaded the thought that I would watch that scene again through the years, when I least suspected it—our slow walk to the little casket, and away...the sad faces of Ben and Rhody and Sophy, and my face, too, half-hidden by the shining curtain of hair that had been mine when I was young.

Nothing mattered. I hardly cared that Ben was in his study upstairs fighting battles, one by one. No—he said over and over—No. There would not be china or plastic figurines of Maria, or postcards, or candy confections of a sleeping baby. A film of her story was out of the question. I would give no interviews. He would explain what he had done, and not done, to the proper authorities and qualified medical persons. That was all.

He couldn't speak for the Rands, Ben said. If they did not mind constantly hearing or seeing the Sorcerer's Apprentice scenes of Disney's *Fantasia*, he had no comment. If stores were allowed to sell figurines of Mickey Mouse wearing Gunther's face and waving a wand, that was their affair. But he saw to it that the song, "Little Clone Baby" was not sold, or aired. When a Madonna-like doll with my face and my blonde braid was advertised, complete with a baby Maria in her coffin, Ben threatened to sue, and that tourist item was never offered.

I remember so little. I think I noticed that Rhody was losing her frightened, hunted look. She had found a nest for herself: a white-haired grandmother, a fatherly man who loved her, and a woman named Mary who was not quite a sister, or a mother, or even much more than a sleepwalker wandering at the edges of her life.

After breakfast one morning Ben said, "The newspapers and magazines and television are getting tired of us. We're old news at last."

"*You* aren't," Sophy said. "So you'll get the Nobel?"

"That's what they say."

They looked at me. I was clearing the breakfast table.

"And every university in the world, nearly, is offering you honorary degrees and chairs," Sophy said.

"I've decided it will be Harvard," Ben said. "If I can stay with you for a while, and escape the last of the media?"

"Belmont's a dormitory for Harvard folk," Sophy said. "You'll feel at home."

Ben said, "There's something I'd like to show the three of you. Come for a drive."

Rhody, Sophy and I climbed into his car, and he took us to the cemetery. It was beautiful in its late June sun and shade, but nothing prepared us for the carpet of color where Ben parked our car.

We walked to the edge of a slope smothered in flowers: bouquet after bouquet. Little American flags and hundreds of notes and cards were scattered among them.

Rhody knelt to gather the notes and hand them to Ben and Sophy. "*Bless the Amrican clone baby and her mother Mary,*" Sophy read aloud. "*Dear Mary: our family grieves with you for Maria... To Maria Bryant and her mother Mary Bryant...*" So many notes. Rhody got up with grass-stained knees. "There's hundreds!' she said.

The flowers and flags and notes surrounded a polished white gravestone; I shaded my eyes to see the rosebud carved there, the dates, and the lines below:

Maria Bryant,
Daughter of Mary Bryant.
Never Before Was There Such a Child.
She Gave Her Life, the First In a New Age.

"Is the stone all right?" Ben asked.

"Yes," I said. "Exactly right. Thank you."

Rhody was on her knees again, collecting more notes and cards to save. Ben began bringing them to her, and helped her put the top layers of flowers aside to find the messages beneath.

Sophy and I sat on a bench to watch Ben and Rhody. "He loves that child," Sophy said. "He hates to leave her."

"Leave her?" I said. "But he's going to live with us, teach at Harvard—"

"No," Sophy said. "He isn't. He's going back to Mexico."

I was too shocked to speak. Sophia took handfuls of notes and cards from Ben and Rhody and piled them on the bench. Suddenly the sight of those three people together made tears come to my eyes, the first tears for a long time. I would lose Ben, one of the few who loved me.

Ben knelt again in the sunshine. The world would offer him gifts for years: he had created the first human clone. Maria lay nearby in her grave. The world wanted him and waited for him, but he was on his knees near her burial stone, hunting among heaps of wilting flowers.

T he next day brought a week of summer storms. I wandered through Sophy's house, listening to rain drumming all day on roof and windows. Rain was falling on a small grave.

Sometimes I saw a mother drive past the house, her baby in the car seat beside her. Sometimes the voices of small children came from the home next door. I often woke in the night, thinking I heard Maria cry.

One of those shadows of grief fell over me on a late evening after Rhody was asleep in bed. Sophy and Ben were watching a comedy on television.

I couldn't bear the television's canned laughter. I went upstairs, wiping my eyes on my shirttail. When I thought of Maria, my breasts hurt, as though they were full of milk.

Boxes lined the upstairs hall. When I stepped into Ben's dark bedroom, faint light from the stairs showed me more boxes along the wall, and drawers standing open and empty. I heard steps on the stairs, and Ben stood in the doorway in the faint light.

"You're packing," I said. My throat ached as I spoke.

"Yes."

"Will you come back often?"

"No."

I ran a finger around the edge of an empty drawer. Rain pounded on the roof above us. "It's raining on her grave."

"It won't touch her," Ben said. "She's safely tucked away."

Safely tucked away. "You loved her, too," I said. "You dressed her for her funeral, didn't you? Found the little white casket, and the pink dress? Put her teddy bear in her hands?"

"Yes."

"I should never have had her!" I cried. "If I'd had an abortion, I would have saved her all that pain!" I was beside myself, and I asked a question I had been too numb to ask before: "What killed her? Didn't you suspect something was wrong?"

Ben's voice was sad. "Her mental development was slow. The French clone died of the same brain abnormality. I suspected there might be that sort of trouble, and Maria would never have a normal life."

"And you never told me!"

"Why would I?" Ben said. "Why hurt you more than you were hurt already? Worry you?"

"Gunther wouldn't let me have an abortion—he wanted the baby so much." My voice was full of scorn. "I thought it was because he loved me and wanted our child."

"He phoned to tell me that you were talking of an abortion. He was frantic."

"The two of you might have lost your clone," I said in a bitter voice.

"I don't know how *he* felt. I knew I didn't want you to ever take that risk."

The two men had talked about me behind my back—decided behind my back! Fury made me tremble. "Look what a clone has done for you!" I said. "She's dead. You knew she would die. But you're a celebrity!"

Before I could take those words back, Ben was gone. I ran for the stairs. He was almost to the bottom already. "Come back," I called softly. "Please. Come back."

Ben mounted the stairs slowly.

"I'm so sorry!" I said when he stood in the doorway. "I should never have said that! Never! To Gunther, maybe, but never to you. For more than a year you've put Maria and me first, and Rhody, and Sophy. We spent your money and ran to you for help. And I *know*...I *know* you loved Maria." Tears ran down my face. I didn't wipe them away. "And what have I done? When you told me Maria was gone, I blamed you, and then I shut myself away from everybody. Selfish! Selfish! As if none of you ever loved Maria too, or missed her."

Rain hammered on the windows, as it had when Ben said: *I told myself, What do you have to lose? Mary will never love you.*

"I didn't tell you the end of the book *Gunner's Daughter*," I said.

"A man's chopped-off head laid in his lover's lap would about finish a story, I think," Ben said. I couldn't see his face in the dim room.

"No." I took a deep breath. "Gunnar's daughter couldn't forgive the man who took her by force, so she ruined her life. She looks at that man's head in her lap and tells her son: 'I would rather have loved him than any man.'"

Thunder cracked overhead. Before Ben could touch me, I threw myself into his arms, using the language of two bodies pressed tight from breast to knee to say everything he had to know. He kissed me until neither of us had any breath, there in the dark and the sound of the rain.

We murmured and laughed at nothing more sensible than our own happiness. Ben locked the door, "When did you come to this?" he whispered. I heard him catch his breath as he felt me slide out of my clothes. "I'd given up. I was leaving."

"Listen," I whispered against his mouth as we lay on his bed. "I want to say something I've never said to any other man."

Ben's kisses hardly left me breath to speak. "Give me *your* child," I whispered. "That's everything I want—*our* baby." I was shaking with desire, but I wanted to show him he must be happy, must be truly sure of me.

Ben was happy and sure of me, Oh, yes. He did his best to give me what I'd asked for—over and over that rainy night. "I can't leave you alone," he whispered once. "An hour without you is a long day, and I've spent too many of them to count."

I must have slept at last. First light woke me. Someone's arms were wrapped around me—Rhody's? No. Ben was there at last, smiling beside me, kissing me, shaking my hair out of its braids.

Finally I managed to say, "You've made me a new woman, haven't you—in the world's eyes. I'm not Mary Dirty. I'm not Mary Risling. I'm not The Surrogate Mother. How did you do it? I feel brand new."

"With love," Ben murmured. "But how did you ever come to forgive me? You hated me. You ran away—"

"Because of your one mistake. *One mistake.* And you did it for your friend. I wouldn't believe how loving you were, how sorry you were. If I forgive you, will you forgive me?"

Yes–Yes–Yes, we said, and kissed, and just then the first ray of morning sun fell on our bed from rain-streaked windows.

"Newlyweds!" Ben said. "I had to watch Carmela and Joseph—"

"Torture!"

We laughed together. "I asked you to marry me once upon a time," Ben said. "Are you saying Yes?"

"Yes," I said. "Truthfully."

At last I had his warm, tanned face in my hands in the sunlight. I smoothed his feathery eyebrows and ran my fingers through his hair and thought, *How handsome he is, and mine!*

"I seem to remember that you are dead set against having the man without the matrimony," he said, his face in my tumbled hair.

"I am," I said. "Dead set. Once was enough. But what am I saying? Isn't it a little late—"

Someone rattled the knob on Ben's locked bedroom door, then pounded on it—bang, bang, bang.

"Mary!" Rhody cried from the hall. "Mary!" She was frantic—I wasn't in my bed, or anywhere. I was gone.

"I'm here!" I called.

"Don't worry!" Ben called. "She's with me!"

"Rhody?" Sophy called from the stairs.

"Mary's in there with Ben, and the door's locked!" Rhody cried. "She wasn't in bed! I couldn't find her at all! What are they doing?"

"Come away!" Sophy said. "Let's go and make breakfast for them. Whatever they're doing in there, it's about time." Ben and I laughed together like guilty, hidden lovers.

"Sophia means 'wisdom,'" Ben said. "Will she come to live with us in Acapulco? Be our mother and grandmother?"

"I think she will," I said. "She hasn't anyone in the world but us."

Ben climbed from bed and took a wrapped gift from a bureau drawer. "For you," he said. "A going-away present—but I'm not going away. Not now. It's from Colette and Jack Jordan."

I took off the ribbons and wrappings and gasped—there was my only picture of my mother and me that I'd ever had! I'd told Ben I'd lost it, running and hiding, leaving almost everything behind in Kissimmee.

But the snapshot wasn't worn and dog-eared any longer. The Jordans had enlarged it and tinted it with soft colors: a large, framed portrait. Every strand of my mother's bright hair was distinct, blowing against her forehead, almost touching the baby in her lap. And how clear the little girl's face was—

"Oh!" I cried. "I thought I'd never see this again! Isn't Maria such a pretty—"

"Not Maria," Ben said.

I stared at my mother sitting on a battered chair, a slim woman in a sleeveless red dress, holding… "But it is!" I cried. "It's Maria!"

Maria smiled, her small hands raised as if in greeting, her short blonde curls catching the light—my baby in my mother's arms.

They smiled at me from their frame, together in the sunlight of a summer day.

THE END

Critics praise Nancy Price's novels:

A NATURAL DEATH
Who is Nancy Price? Not since Mary Boykin Chestnut has there been such a biting voice, such an accurate eye. *—Charlotte Observer, N.C.*
A rich first novel...quite remarkable.*—Kirkus*   Vividly-recalled times past.
Persuasive and saddening.*—N.Y. Times Book Review*   —Chicago Tribune
BEAUTIFUL, TERRIBLE, HEART-BREAKING—A POWERFUL EVOCATION
OF WHAT IT MEANT TO BE BLACK AND A SLAVE.
—PUBLISHERS WEEKLY
My God, what a film it would make. It's not just fiction: it's Literature. *—Mary Carter*

AN ACCOMPLISHED WOMAN
Seductive...I found myself racing...excited by all its elements. *—Chicago Tribune*
Moving, even terrifying... a rare richness, subtlety and depth.*—Publishers Weekly*
Elegant detail.—The New Yorker   Heady and powerful. *—Booklist*
INNOCENTLY PASSIONATE AND ACHINGLY EROTIC. *—DETROIT NEWS*
Strangely haunting story.   **Finely written.**   Read this book. It will change
—Cleveland Plain Dealer   *—Kirkus*   your *heart.* *— Sacramento Bee*
**Compelling and poignant...More than just an accomplished novel;
it is a work of art.***—Houston Chronicle*

SLEEPING WITH THE ENEMY (filmed by 20th Century Fox starring Julia Roberts)
**Rich characterizations, an ability to move the reader emotionally, and
a lovely sense of atmosphere...right on the money.** *—San Francisco Chronicle.*
A tense, tightly woven novel...so vivid that one is troubled, longs to know
what becomes of these people. *— Louise Erdrich, Minneapolis Star and Tribune.*
Every woman's nightmare...you won't be   **Powerful, moving.**
able to put it down. *—Houston Chronicle*   *—Publishers Weekly*
ABSORBING...SENSUAL...THE READER ROOTS FOR SARA/LAURA
ALL THE WAY. *—WEST COAST REVIEW OF BOOKS*
Terror grips like the coils of an anaconda. *—London Observer*

NIGHT WOMAN
Brilliantly disturbing...Price is masterful in her characterizations. *— Houston Chronicle*
**Well-written and engaging...gritty, wry characterization, chilling
images...will keep readers flipping pages.** *—Publishers Weekly*
THE TENSION RISES ALMOST UNBEARABLY.   Highly recommended.
—EXPRESS NEWS (SAN ANTONIO)   *—Library Journal*
NIGHT WOMAN is so well-written that it raises the psychological thriller
to another level. *—Orlando Sentinel*
Fine...moving...highly   *Gripping...a nail-biter of a climax*
recommended.*—Chicago Tribune*   *...engrossing. —Kansas City Star*
A terrific suspenser...Don't even wait for the movie.   *—Kirkus*

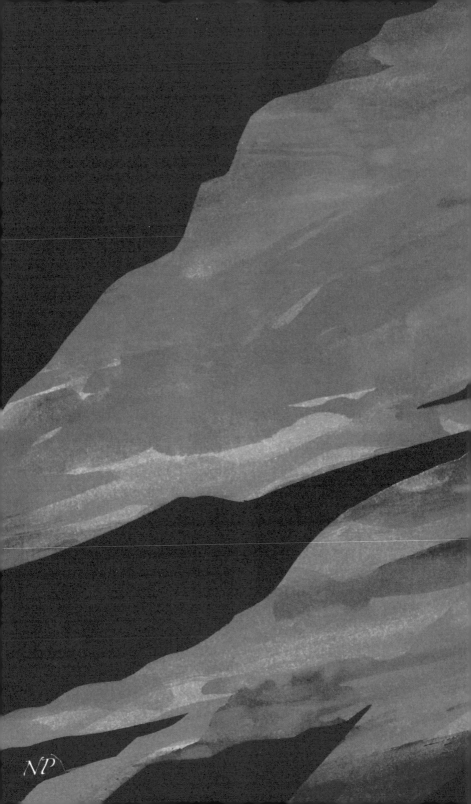